# Emrysia

*Endurance*

Volume Three of the Three Sisters Trilogy

C.A. Morgan

*Endurance*

Copyright© 2016 by C.A. Morgan

Artwork and cover design by C.A. Morgan

ISBN 978-0-692-66388-2

Fireweed Press
Lyndonville, VT

## Dedication

*For everyone who has a dream, in the hope that they will make it their reality.*

C. A. Morgan

# Contents

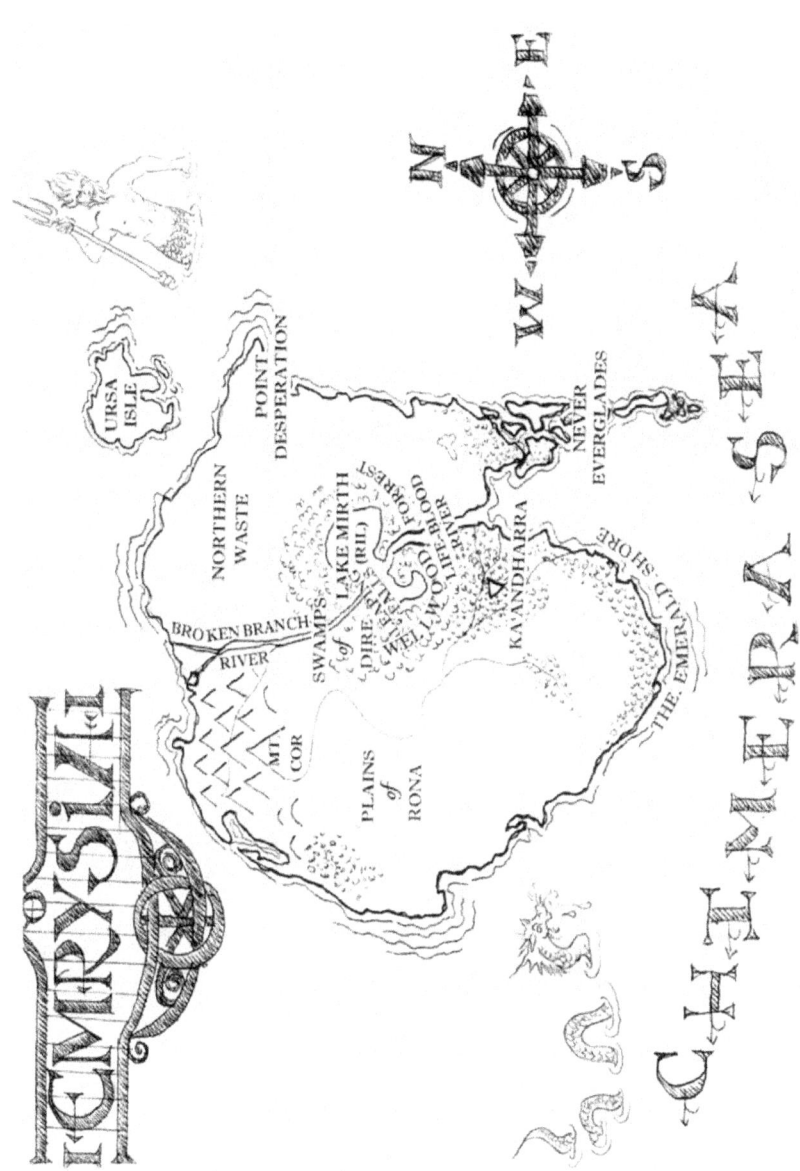

EMRYSIA

N
E
W
S

URSA
ISLE

NORTHERN
WASTE

POINT
DESPERATION

NEVER
EVERGLADES

MT
COR

BROKEN BRANCH
RIVER

SWAMPS
of
DIRE SMIRTH
LAKE MIRTH
(RIL)

WELLWOOD FOREST
BLOOD FOREST
LIFE RIVER

KAVANDHARRA

PLAINS
of
RONA

THE EMERALD SHORE

CHIMERA SEA

# Synopsis

Sent their separate ways by the Lydian muse, Mandelbrot to prepare for their role as "Chosen", each of the Three Sisters finds herself in treacherous and unexpected circumstances from which there is no easy return.

# From
## *Emrysia: Awakening*

Defying her father's wishes, Aryelle - luminarie maiden and heir to the Seat of Ka'Andharra - heals a wounded messenger bearing portentous tidings. In response, Elazaryn sends Aryelle on a two-fold journey of self discovery, charging her with the care of her younger cousin, Karril. They are joined in ancient Wellwood Forest by Lureli of the Mer and her four mute slaves. Together, they seek to overcome the *Reign of Shadow* by attending a Summit meant to unite the varied races of Emrysia. Overwhelming obstacles challenge the trio along the way, including a run-in with three ancient, cannibalistic hags, keepers of the Swamps of Dire. These "Omniscients" unwillingly offer the key to conquering the present darkness. With the help of Eleanor and her foster father Nodd, fauen of the Aurrac clanherds, the youngsters finally ascend Mt. Cor only to find that the Summit is a sham. Borrac, Aurracan Head Chieftain shows that his true colors are as black as his beard. The luminaries, their new companions, and a handful of others escape with their lives - if not spirits - intact. At least one of their number is not to be trusted as they begin their perilous journey homeward.

From
# *Emrysia: Lament*

Barely into the homeward journey, disaster strikes as Lureli's servants vanish and her precious transformation potion is lost. Tensions rise and the group splits up, reaching Rona's warren separately. But before they can query the Stone of Seeing or even witness the birth of Rona's pups, they are swallowed in a timeless void. Traveling through what they come to know as the Connectedness Locus, they encounter Lydian shape shifters, an angry Dezrot, and Lureli's evil former mentor, Japhra. Alone, but now certain they *are* the Chosen who must save Emrysia from the Reign of Shadow, Aryelle, Lureli and Eleanor go their separate ways until fate calls them together once again.

*Indulging in any pleasure too often reduces it to vice, enslaving the free.*
- Aridhina the Wise

*What evil intends for destruction and death, love- if it endures - restores to good and life.*
- Mandelbrot, Lydian Muse

*What goes around comes around.*
- The definition of Karma, origin unknown

## Chapter 1 – Home Sweet Home

Eleanor's knife arm swung in a deadly arc as rocky cave walls coalesced out of the void, and the ground solidified beneath her hooves. Whoever waited in ambush would soon feel its sting! Her blade, alas, made no contact. She kept it drawn while her vision cleared, her body a coiled spring, tensed and ready for action. Every fiber, every nerve bristled with the all too familiar sensation of controlled fear.

Quickly, she sized up her situation. The cave was familiar, as well-known to her as the fleece of her thigh, even though years had passed since she had last visited it. She scanned the interior a second time, more thoroughly now, having confirmed that she was indeed alone. Whoever Mandelbrot had thought would be waiting for her must have already moved on.

She stepped cautiously toward the cave's opening, still hung with a mottled gray fleece, a windbreak translucent enough to let in some light but, as she knew from experience, practically indiscernible from the rocky slope outside. She recalled watching Nodd hang it - "to keep out the cold" he had said, though she knew better. Little clouds of her own expelled breath told her that it was winter here, too. She stood listening for movement outside the cave, and finally, sheathed her blade. Shivering, she made her way toward the back of the old, familiar hideout, relieved to find a stockpile of warm blankets still there, right where she remembered them. She wrapped one around her bare shoulders. Her simple chamois halter provided scant warmth, but as a fauen of the Aurrac clan-herds - half human, half mountain goat - she required no covering on her lower half save her own soft wool.

As she began to warm up, Eleanor turned and inspected her surroundings yet again, but for memories this time, not foes. Hollowed into the northern face of Mt. Cor, this isolated chamber, and the smaller one that led off of it, had always been crowded when she and the rest of the lower village children camped out here following each harvest season. When she was younger, one of the village elders – usually a ram, though a ewe was less apt to be missed by the patrol - had hidden with them. Later on, Eleanor herself had taken on sole responsibly for the other youngsters. Older than Jode and the nearest foundling by several seasons, and the only so called "normal" one among them, she had always been their protector. Distorted features and missing limbs had never lessened her love for any of them. If anything, it had grown fiercer, especially when she considered the poor ewes of the Upper Village who entrusted their blemished offspring to the thaw-swollen rapids rather than subject them to their chieftain's wrath. She had felt that wrath and barely survived it, wouldn't have, in fact, except for a chance encounter with an empath. And not just any empath as it turned out, but a fairy - a Ka'Andharra luminarie - Aryelle's uncle, Erildhil. Not that she remembered him. She was barely weaned when he saved her life in the aftermath of Borrac's butchery in the lower village. Saved it just as Aryelle had, with the help of her cousin Karril and the Naturra, only days ago after the bloody, yearly games held as entertainment by the same depraved chieftain. She shuddered at the thought.

Squatting by the fire pit near the cave's blanketed entrance, she poked the ashes with a stick she found lying there, confirming that the fire was long dead. She dropped the stick and stroked her long braid, thinking. She still owed them for that, though she was loathe to admit it. It was a debt she couldn't wait to pay off.

When she and Nodd had set off to escort the fairies and mermaid – er, luminaries and Lureli – safely home, it was barely autumn. As a precaution when they left, all of the lower villagers, not just the children, were to have hidden here. The plan was that they would return home as snows fell. Hopefully, everything had gone according to plan. Eleanor paused, her hand hovering mid-stroke. What if Mandelbrot had sent her to another

19

time altogether? It was already midwinter back at Rona's warren, but was it the same one?

She and her companions had literally stumbled upon the Connectedness Locus - a pathway connecting all places and times. Traveling along it was almost effortless as long as one of them was holding the key. Lureli had mistakenly assumed the crystal key was only a vial to contain one of her nasty remedies – how pathetic! As it turned out, the hollowed crystal was really part of the Stone of Seeing, key to the Maze of Ages and the Connectedness Locus. But key or no key, the Lydian, Mandelbrot, could send them where and whenever at will. After finding them back at the warren, he had relieved them of the key and sent each of the "Chosen" - Aryelle, Lureli and herself – home, supposedly to prepare and say their goodbyes. When the time was right they were to reunite to save Emrysia. Bah! Three young women, two of them practically helpless, were somehow going to put an end to the Reign of Shadow - who'd dreamt up such an insane scheme? The Omniscients' riddle, Accora's prophesy, and even her own tattoo offered unmistakable evidence that they were, indeed, chosen for the task, but who had chosen them? And why not three more suited for it? If only Nodd could come along, at least then she'd have some real help!

Where was her foster father now, she wondered? Had Mandelbrot sent him and Accora home like he said he would, or were they still in an enchanted sleep on some isle off the Emerald Shore, right where the mermaid left them? She had decided to believe Lureli's far-fetched tale despite her misgivings. After all, hadn't she risked her own neck returning for them after her little side jaunt? Still, she couldn't quite believe the gesture was totally unselfish. That would be too far out of character.

For the time being at least, Eleanor was alone. What a relief! She liked it better this way. No whining mermaid, no blind fairy, no chattering praircat. No responsibility for anyone other than herself. There was firewood stacked along the far wall, near the narrow passage that led to the second chamber, and she still remembered where the cache of grain and roots were stored, *if* the villagers hadn't finished them off. No matter. She was used to fending for herself. In no time at all she could have a roaring fire going. Tomorrow would be soon enough to hunt a nice fat hare or ptarmigan, or maybe something bigger. She could be snug here all winter if she needed to be.

She let her mind wander. The last time she suffered the confines of these rock walls she had delegated responsibility to Jode and Silene - next oldest and first of all the floating babies - to watch the younger children while she got some fresh air. Really, she had just wanted to escape the noise and demands for her attention. Taking her knife and bow, she had set off for higher ground thinking she might spot some game. Instead, she was spotted by the returning patrol when her hoof slipped on some loose scree. Determined to lead them away from the cave's hidden entrance, she made a break for it, heading into the morning sun's glare. When they finally caught her, she put up a worthy fight;

though outnumbered five to one, only four patrol rams lived to bring her to their chieftain. Nodd had taught her well. She fought for her life in the arena next. Borrac's idea of blood sport was kill or be killed. She had gutted several of his best rams before he called a halt to it. She could still picture his greasy smile – imagine eating while watching such carnage! – as he offered her his congratulations and her freedom, after a fashion. Since then she'd been in the chieftain's service, ironically, as part of his patrol. As such, she enjoyed privileges that usually only rams knew, including being able to escape the walled Upper Village to patrol the plains, and to clandestinely visit Nodd and Althea in the lower village.

There would be no returning to the summit now that Borrac knew where her true loyalties lay, and no telling what he would do if he found her again on his mountain. When she agreed to be his bride, fending off his amorous overtures by using every coquettish trick she could think of, she had had to disguise her true motive – revenge! His pawing had repulsed her, not only because he was old enough to be her sire, *he was her sire!* He hadn't recognized her for who she was. But once the truth was revealed, it hadn't deterred him in the least. In fact, it seemed to excite him further! Since he actually believed that he was a god, and she a goddess, he dreamt of siring a race of gods through her. Not only was he perverted, he was delusional! Thank Cor for narrow escapes! And the other Chosen, she supposed.

Eleanor grew weary of her own rambling thoughts. She took a quick inventory of the limited stores at her disposal, and then made a fire. She knew the cave was well hidden from all but those who knew of its existence. As tired as she was, with winter snows piled high, she was confident she would sleep undisturbed.

\*\*\*\*\*\*

Lureli was afraid to open her eyes. She was dry, which meant she still had legs and not a tailfin. But if she was back inside that horrid cave on the Mer shore she would just die! She wrinkled up her nose and took a tentative whiff. It didn't smell like the cave. And now that she thought about it, she couldn't hear the pounding of the surf either. Cautiously, she pried one eye open. Her heart lurched. Same rocky walls, same muddy beach, and same subterranean lake - wait! That wasn't a lake at all, and this wasn't mud underfoot, but wet sand. Behind her, and beyond her wildest hopes, was an expanse of blue sea. She was home!

Not giving it a second thought, she hefted the skirt of her gown and ran toward the water - only to crash headlong into an invisible barrier. She bounced awkwardly off the clear, hard surface, staggering backward and rubbing her forehead. She stood there, perplexed.

Of course...she was in the Asylum! It was where she had planned to come herself, though certainly not as an exhibit. It made sense now why she still had legs.

But, how fortunate she was that this was where Mandelbrot decided to send her! Overhead, she could now see the bubble that held back the watery depths of the Chimera Sea. Looking around inside the glass enclosure, she saw that she was surrounded by a replica of the cavern that Japhra had said was to be her new home.

Well, at least it wasn't the real thing! She was back in the undersea realm, that's what mattered. She could beg her father's forgiveness and everything would return to normal. She had learned her lesson the hard way, and was swearing off men and libations for good!

She wondered how long it would take them to find her. As a child she had visited the Asylum almost daily, though rarely in recent years. But back then, the collection of enclosed land habitats and the fascinating creatures they housed had held her rapt for hours on end, a veritable bubble wonderland. The Mer awaiting transformations were her favorites, so much like the Glisseon they would eventually become - once taken to the shape-changers - but for those strange lower appendages that allowed them to move about on land. Oh, how she had longed to be able to walk on shore amongst them!

And, now that she had, she wanted nothing more than to bid land good riddance! She didn't give a fin-flip about Aurrac prophesy and being Chosen. She was back, and she wasn't leaving ever again! Aryelle and Eleanor would do just fine without her, and if not, well, Mandelbrot would just have to find them a replacement. She got up and paced the confined space, littering the sand with layered footprints. Time to get out of here and get her tailfin back!

She could see only one other bubble enclosure nearby, and it appeared empty. She saw nothing of the lush coral city she had grown up in. The spires of Orpheas' palace *should* be visible from here; she'd always navigated her way home by them before. It was almost as if she was alone beneath the sea, not even a shoal of tuna or stray jelly passing by. Nothing but the endless blue she was unable to touch, or, turning the other way, a dismal cavern. Except, what was this? She spied her bundle of odd mementos beside a large rock; had she brought it with her? She didn't think so. A stone knife, a chipped horn cup, a charred bone, a ruined silk net and a praircat's tail: What good were they to her now? And where was her valise? That she had use for. She was beginning to feel parched again. Oh, when would someone come for her?

\*\*\*\*\*\*

A songbird's trill...the rustle of a light breeze...the forest sweet-smelling with newly unfurled foliage and a blanket of winter-pressed leaves underfoot...dappled sunlight warming her skin. Aryelle needed no vision, T'sura or otherwise, to know that it was spring. She could recognize the scents and sounds of the reborn New Forest in her sleep. Mandelbrot had kept his word and sent her home. She wondered how the other two had fared, and how long they would have until they must be reunited.

She was glad to be back in familiar territory, though she was, of course, still not safely inside the treeborn city of Ka'Andharra. And, she supposed, he had not sent her to exactly *when* she expected to return either. If it was already springtime here, then she and Karril would have been missing for several candles time. Whether or not Kayanna had made it back ahead of them, her father would be frantic with worry. Worse, he might already have assumed them dead.

She employed T'sura, the othersight that, among other things, enabled her to navigate since losing her vision. Her perception intensified. All around her the trees and undergrowth blushed with auras as varied in hue and concentration as the growing things themselves, auras that she could feel in every fiber of her being. But no valleo were among them. The immense grove must be nearby; the unmistakable perfume of the flowering nut trees that meant home tantalized her nose with the very next breeze. She turned into it, trying to get her bearings. Sensing no pathway, she began to grope her way along, hands outstretched. Hopefully, she could hold steady in one direction without tripping over any roots or fallen trees.

After a short while Aryelle sat down to rest. Traversing the open landscape of the Plains of Being was one thing. The going here was much harder than she had imagined it would be. Without anyone to guide her even T'sura was little help. How had Elazaryn managed for so long? Of course, he never left Ka'Andharra anymore - no one did. And the familiar corridors of the El'Kandhar's residence held no surprises, just smoothly polished wood. Every door boasted a uniquely carved façade, each wing or swinging walkway a crew of dedicated stewards to make certain nothing was ever out of place. The crystal domed rooms she knew and loved intensified the natural sunlight so much that, even on overcast days, the furthest corners were awash with light. She was sure that she would have no trouble finding her way around once she found her way there. But, first things first; she had to get out of these makeshift wing bindings! At Nodd's bidding, Accora had fashioned them from his own wool, since Eleanor had so thoughtlessly ruined her silk bindings from home. Though waterproof, these were heavier than she was accustomed to, and very, very scratchy. How could the Aurrac stand their own wool?

A spectra owl hooted off to her left. Aryelle cocked her head to listen, and a katydid twirred behind her. The surrounding forest was burgeoning with sound, but both seemed somehow out of place. A tingle ran up her spine. She had only managed to free one wing so far, but suddenly, the need to move was overwhelming. She rose and felt her way onward, face pointed into the breeze. A growing sense of unease followed her.

Stumbling, she caught herself against the rough bark of a maple. One tentative step later, the owl hooted a second time.

Of course, that was it! Owls hunted only at night, and it was the wrong season for katydids. She was being trailed! Since she had yet to reach Ka'Andharra, it could only mean one thing...

-*Come out, cousins. I mean you no harm*- she coaxed, certain that whoever was following could hear her thoughts inside their minds.

There was no response. Turning slowly, hands open at her sides to prove she posed no threat, Aryelle tried to sense where they might be hiding. Hopefully she was right, and it was Naturra. That would mean at least some of her wilderness cousins had escaped the Dru'noch, the Black Death. And that meant there was yet hope for a reunited Empaya. But...if these were Naturra, they were certainly keeping their distance.

She appealed to them in thought-speak a second time, still not trusting her voice, afraid it would reveal her growing apprehension. *–If it is the plague you fear, I am not infected. But I am lost. Would you be kind enough to escort me home to Ka'Andharra?* - She was confident they could understand her, and any Naturra this close to the treeborn city were certain to know the way.

Without warning, something heavy - another Aurrac net? – fell over her, knocking her off her feet and pinning her to the ground. She cried out in surprise. It took only a moment to realize that struggling was futile; with her wings partially unbound as they were, she would only entangle herself further. Forcing herself to remain calm, she waited for her captors to approach.

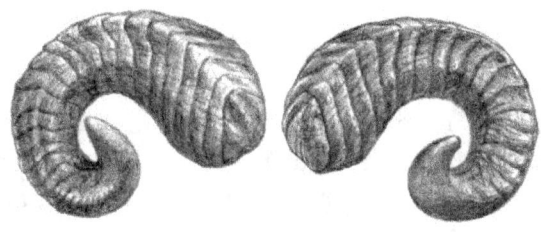

## Chapter 2 – Winter Blooms

The fire died as Eleanor slept on. With no one but herself to look after, she had stoked only a small blaze, and then fallen asleep from sheer exhaustion without bothering to bank it.

She chided herself when she woke up, chilled and teeth chattering, colder, in fact, than she could ever remember being. She pulled her blanket closer. To get a fire burning again, one big enough to warm up the entire cave, would take more effort than she could muster. But, there was nothing for it; she would have to try.

Still wrapped up in her blanket, she shuffled over to the pile of woolens and draped another about her head and shoulders like a mantle. She dragged a third back toward the fire pit, then decided to rest a bit before hauling over more wood. Folding her legs beneath her and tucking the extra blanket around herself, she closed her eyes and began to drift. The last thing she remembered was feeling a draft.

Sometime later, Eleanor struggled awake again, her head throbbing like a hammered stake. She reached up to touch the back of her aching skull, gingerly fingering the tender lump she found there. She winced, and tried to pry open her eyelids, only to find them crusted shut.

"Sorry about the noggin, but I thought you were patrol."

The voice sounded a long way off. She made an effort to lift her head toward it. Her bones ached beneath the weight of a pile of heavy blankets. She tried to throw them off and found she hadn't the strength. Her throat was afire, and her foggy brain registered that she must be very sick. Otherwise, no one would have taken her by surprise. If the voice belonged to Mandelbrot and he'd come to fetch her back, he could just forget it.

"Take it easy, Sunshine; you're not going anywhere - at least, not for a while. Now that you're finally awake, let's try to get a little something into you, shall we?"

A large hand cupped her face, guiding her mouth to a horn of bitter smelling brew. At least she could still smell. She wrapped her cracked lips around the rim of the horn as best she could, and sucked greedily. The steaming liquid burned all the way down, searing her tongue and throat, yet soothing it at the same time.

When she was finished, the hand gently guided her head back to the rolled up blanket serving as a pillow. "Now, let's see about clearing that crud out of your eyes."

She was too weak to protest as a warm, wet cloth fell across them. She must have dozed off then, because the next thing she knew, the compress was cold and water had trickled down to fill her ears. She felt it being lifted from her face, and resisted the urge to bite the hand that carefully dabbed away the loosened matter from her lashes. Once the job was done and she managed to pry them open, it took a few moments for the cave to come into focus. The face staring down at her between curved, oversized horns was agonizingly familiar.

"Wanna spar?" Eleanor croaked, smiling weakly.

"Only if you promise not to cry when I beat you," Gord teased. His warm brown eyes crinkled at the corners, and when he smiled, his face creased with the deepest dimples she had ever seen. And his teeth – so white and even!

Eleanor couldn't tell if she flushed more from fever or embarrassment. She remembered that smile, had thought of it often since their first match in the arena. It lit the face of the most ruggedly handsome ram she had ever met. Only now, one of his cheeks sported a scar from where she had nicked him with the tip of her blade. She had admired his skill then, and his integrity even more, and hoped she'd run into him again someday. And now, here he was her nursemaid! She started to laugh, and ended up coughing instead. The fit lasted several minutes, until tears streamed from her eyes as Gord pounded her firmly on the back.

"Hey, I thought I told you not to cry!" he joked.

She would have retorted, but her mouth was full of phlegm, and for the first time in her life she felt bashful about expelling it.

"I hope you're not going to swallow that," he said grimacing.

Looking up at him through feverish eyes, Eleanor saw that he was serious. He held the empty horn back to her lips and, self-consciously, she spat into it. As he pulled the horn away, a long string of spittle swung back onto her chin. He wiped it away using a clean corner of the compress. Eleanor closed her eyes to hide her embarrassment and fell back into her blankets, exhausted.

"Go ahead and rest some more, Lazybones."

"How long have I been asleep?" she managed.

"Two days. Bet you're hungry. I'll whip up my specialty."

A ram who could cook? While she mulled that over, he moved around the cave as if it was home, pulling out ingredients from the food cache and adding them to a pot that hung over the fire. He had moved her and the pile of blankets further away from the fire pit, against the wall of the cave. Eleanor followed him with her eyes as he stoked the embers into a roaring blaze. Already too warm, she struggled to free her legs. Gord heard her thrashing and came over to help. As he tossed the covers aside, his hand brushed briefly against the wool of her thigh. Tingles shot up her spine.

"I'm not a total invalid," she gasped, flustered. She tugged the last blanket from his grasp, and held it modestly over her heaving chest.

"It's no crime to need a little help," he countered turning back to the fire.

"I wouldn't need any if someone hadn't knocked me senseless!"

*Hoof-in-mouth disease - that's what I've got,* thought Eleanor, wishing she could take that back. The last thing she wanted to do was offend him, but somehow she couldn't help herself.

He cocked a crooked eyebrow at her. "Well, it was easier than trying to knock some sense into you." That smile again.

So, he was as adept at witty banter as he was at swordplay. Eleanor found herself stuck for a comeback. She leaned back against the wall and closed her eyes.

"Come on, you're not giving up that easily, are you? I'm just getting warmed up."

"Later," she promised and pretended to be resting. Soon, she really did fall asleep again.

The cave was filled with a mouthwatering aroma when next she woke. Her empty stomach growled noisily and she sat up, clamping her arms around her middle and willing it to quiet. Gord glanced over, and she lowered her eyes, not meeting his gaze. She was uncomfortably aware of how awful she must look. Eventually, he approached carrying a steaming pot, and she shrank back against the wall even further, wishing she was invisible. No such luck. He stopped just in front of her. Squatting, he began dishing the steaming concoction into bowls, and held one out to her. Eleanor tucked her hair behind her ears and took the bowl in her hands. They shook. She glanced up at him, and couldn't help but smile as he reached up and produced a bone spoon from behind one of his massive horns.

"We'll have to share," he said apologetically. "I could only find the one – but, you first."

She took the spoon and slowly scooped up a mouthful of steaming brown mush, eyeing it critically. Hopefully it tasted as good as it smelled, not as bad as it looked. She took a tentative nibble, and then cautiously put the entire mouthful between her lips. Warm and savory, the stewed rabbit melted over her tongue. He had seasoned it with herbs and just a hint of sweetness from the same ground root that Althea used. Her mother had a bit more finesse of course, and didn't cook her meat and vegetables till they were unrecognizable. Still, she was impressed that he had managed at all. She took a second bite. Then hunger took over and she gobbled the rest greedily, handing him the spoon when she had finished, and licking the bowl when she thought he wasn't looking. Noticing his smile out of the corner of her eye, she realized he was more observant than she had hoped. But, now that she had a little food in her, her spunk was returning, and she met his gaze unapologetically. Gord dished up a little more before enjoying his own meal, eyes laughing at her over the rim of his bowl. And then, when he was done, he too licked his bowl clean.

"There's more if you'd like," he said, wiping his mouth against the shoulders of his raw fleece vest. Below it he wore a simple, long sleeved jersey of spun wool. Its soft brown contrasted nicely against his own lighter brown wool. Despite the layers, Eleanor noted that his exceptional physique was unchanged since last they'd sparred. If anything, he looked stronger.

"Thanks," she said, "that was perfect." *You're perfect,* she thought, blushing, and leaned back to watch him clean up.

What was wrong with her? It must be the fever making her feel all flush and giddy. That, or something he put in the stew. Her eyes followed every movement as he went about tidying the cave, stoking the fire again, and sitting down beside it to sharpen his knives. The flames grew too warm, and he stripped off his shirt and vest, muscles rippling as he worked by firelight. He looked up at her and winked.

Had to go and spoil it, she thought, rolling her eyes.

The handsome ones were always so cocksure, and the plain ones such sheep! Finding a ram to suit was an impossible task. Eleanor willed herself to think of Nashor, the only ram she knew who was a little of both. If only she could make herself be interested! But he was too pliable for her tastes.

For all she knew, Gord had a harem waiting back on whatever mountain he hailed from. She couldn't deny the attraction, and she couldn't blame it all on her fever either. From the moment he bested her in hand-to-hoof combat in the arena, she had felt irresistibly drawn to him. Finally, here was a ram worthy of her attention! And then, to top it off, rather than take unfair advantage, he had instead opened the holding cells, fortuitously freeing the luminaries so they could heal her. She realized, belatedly, that she owed him her life. So, why did his flirting irritate her now?

"You must be feeling better," he interrupted her thoughts, "since you're scowling again."

"I'm not scowling," she retorted.

"Yes you are, but don't worry. It becomes you, which is more than I can say for your matted hair."

"Those are fighting words!" she said only partially feigning offense. His lopsided grin as he rose and walked toward her was infuriating.

"Just stating the facts. But, lucky for you, *I* know how to braid."

Eleanor slumped into shocked silence. She had never heard of such a thing! But when he nudged her forward and sat down behind her, leaning against the cave wall and drawing her back toward him, she realized he was serious. Her eyes shifted nervously as she felt his hands upon her hair, but still she held her tongue. Let him enjoy playing nursemaid and beautician if he wanted to, but he wouldn't fool her with his smooth moves. She sat still as stone while he loosened the still-woven sections of her hair, running his fingers through her pale, sun-bleached tangles to straighten them. She closed her eyes trying to calm her jangled nerves, and found herself relaxing almost against her will. And when his strong fingers began to massage her aching scalp, she sighed with pleasure.

"Where did you learn how to do this?" she asked. His thumbs were moving in widening circles along the base of her skull.

"My granddam taught me. I helped her take care of my mother and grandsire when they were dying. They both said it was the only thing that helped."

"Oh? And what did they die of?" Eleanor asked indelicately.

"Brain worms, is my guess. Gran called it scrapie. Not a pretty sight, or an easy way to go."

Eleanor bolted upright, throwing blankets aside. Her head swam. Swaying on her unsteady hooves, she glared down at him. "How long ago?" she demanded.

"Relax, Little One, it's been years! I didn't catch it from them then, and you won't catch it from me now."

She allowed herself to breathe again. Scrapie was indeed a horrible way to die. First the worms ate your nerves, causing you to itch so badly that you scraped the wool from your own hide, and then they ate your brain. It was highly contagious, though it randomly skipped some of those who came into closest contact with it. If Gord was one of those few, then he was lucky.

"Sit back down" he said, "before you fall down, you silly ewe!"

Little one? Silly ewe? At any other time those words might have earned him a knife in the gut, or at least a good tongue lashing. Inexplicably, Eleanor felt herself sinking back to the cave floor between his knees so that he could continue his tender ministrations. The last time anyone had taken care of her like this she was but a wee lamb. She had forgotten how good it felt, almost worth feeling so sick and miserable.

"Bet you're wondering how I came to be here," he said changing the subject.

She nodded, and so he began to tell her. After wandering the slopes just below the Upper Village, he had started out for home, but never made it off the mountain. Instead, he had stopped in at Nodd's village and, finding it empty, holed up there awaiting the villagers' return. No one ever came. Maybe, like him, they were out making the most of the extended good weather. He had never known the snows to hold off so long.

Had he hoped she would be with them? -she wondered sleepily, but only to herself.

He had spent most of his time there replenishing the villager's limited stores. Then one day while he was out hunting, a traveling pack of Wulfen had driven him up the northernmost escarpment. He eventually eluded them, scrambling up a steep cliff and hiding in a deep crevasse. That night it finally snowed. He waited a day or two to make sure they were gone, then, on the way back down, found this cave. It had recently been vacated; he wasn't sure who had been making use of it, or for how long, but it didn't appear they were planning on returning this season. There were still some grains in the food cache, and he had just made a fresh kill, so he made himself at home just as the first heavy snows fell. That was weeks ago. He had not seen another living soul until, by some miracle, she showed up while he was out hunting for the day. And, he admitted, despite all the trouble she was, he was happy to have her company.

Gord waited for her sassy comeback, but it never came. Instead, she had fallen asleep in his arms.

C. A. Morgan

## *Chapter 3 – Fish in a Dish*

The sea in all of its tantalizing beauty - if only she could get to it! It felt like hours that she had been waiting and still nobody had shown up to set her free. Lureli smacked her palm against the glass and pouted. Turning her back on the unreachable blue depths, she slouched against the wall of the bubble enclosure and sighed. Sooner or later someone had to come along. Maybe she shouldn't appear too eager. What was the saying? A watched whale never blows.

Instead of just sitting here, she supposed she should be working up an apology. She was almost certain Orpheas would welcome her home, except for one small part of her that worried he would still be angry. He had never been known for his even temper, even when her mother was still alive. Vivianne, however, had always managed to soothe him, but how? There was another saying Lureli remembered then, about calm, not wind, deflating full sails. That one must have come from the Mer, who always seemed so anchored amidst life's waves. Tranquil, that's what they were. Maybe it had something to do with their enchantment.

Tranquility…hmm...being tranquil - nope; not her. Vivianne had been especially good at being tranquil, even in the face of the sea king's tirades, but all Lureli ever seemed capable of was brewing up bigger storms.

At least, the old Lureli had. But her old self hadn't cared a fin-flip what anyone else, especially her father, felt either. Watching Rona, the praircat, whom she'd come to regard as a friend try to be both mother and father to his pups, had finally opened her eyes to how hard it must have been for Orpheas after Vivianne was gone. There was a reason it took both a mother and father; they complemented each other, filling in the gaps where the other was lacking. For all her sweet and loving attention, Vivianne had been impulsive and more than a little flighty, whereas Orpheas was solid as a rock, though sometimes just as hardheaded. Tempering, that's what it was called, this balancing out of each other's natural temperament. Lureli knew her own fell somewhere in between the two, but she would try to make an effort to be more like her mother, at least as far as diplomacy was concerned. Maybe that would help her relationship with her father, *if* she ever got out of this blasted bubble!

Growing bored, she sank her fingers into the sand, scooping out a damp handful and plopping it aside. She scooped out another, and then another, stacking them like shells. Soon the mindless activity took over and she was scooping and piling, sculpting and decorating with bits of shell and seaweed, until she created a reasonable facsimile of the undersea palace she used to call home. So close, yet still so far away - *arrrgh!* The Asylum should have been swimming with visitors long before now. Whatever kept everyone away was keeping her stranded, and she didn't like it, not one bit! How could she have ever imagined imprisoning her father here? What kind of monster was she? Thankfully, she'd come to her senses before she and Japhra actually followed through with their plan. Well, Japhra's plan really - to depose Orpheas and keep him captive. How could she have ever thought that was merciful? Anyone would go crazy trapped like this, their heart's desire only a finger width away, never to be grasped.

Bobbling barnacles! Where was everyone?

The sun had to be nearing the horizon, she guessed. Light still filtered down from the surface, but it was warmer hued, and westerly. In another hour or so it would be too dark to see. If no one had found her by then she would be stuck until morning. Though surrounded by the vast open sea, inside the bubble there was no water to speak of; she had checked. If necessary, she supposed she could partially bury herself in damp sand so that her skin could at least soak up a little moisture, but that wouldn't slake her thirst. Or her hunger, she thought as her belly rumbled. She looked around the enclosure and for just a moment wished it actually was the cave it so resembled. At least there

C. A. Morgan

she'd had food and water. No! She gasped, squelching the thought. Never again! She shuddered and closed her eyes, willing herself to be calm. It will be alright...it will be alright...everything is going to be alright.

She didn't remember falling asleep, but when Lureli's eyelids fluttered open again it was morning, and she was no longer alone. In fact, she was totally surrounded, the sea silvered with a shoal of blue fin tuna so dense as to appear solid. They shifted, a pewter wave folding back upon itself, flickering steely gray and silver again as tuna by the thousands flowed around her prison like sea water. Occasionally one would bump into the glass; she could feel the vibration against the side of her face no matter where it struck. A sense of panic rose within her as the shoal shifted, heading toward the surface, burying her in a silvery cascade. With the side of her face still pressed against the glass, her eyes rolled upward with them. And then, they were all above her, even the stragglers. She yearned after them as they swam out of sight.

Slowly she lifted her head off the glass. She had been sitting the whole time, sideways against it, her bare arm and shoulder glued to it despite the dryness of her skin. She peeled them free, flopping in the opposite direction, and smashed a section of the castle she had so carefully erected. Drool like a snail's trail still clung to her chin. Lying on her back amid the ruined structure, she stared straight up as if she'd forgotten how to blink. Her eyes felt dry and gritty, and burned though no tears came to soothe them. Slowly she closed them, willing herself to become as still as stone. Her breathing became shallower, and she cleared her mind of everything but the physical sensations she was experiencing: the grit of the sand; the smell of rotting kelp; the rawness of her throat and bitter tasting, pasty-tongued mouth; the itch of a scratch that was healing on her left knee; the tender lump that was still receding on the back of her head from when Eleanor had knocked her senseless; the hollowness of her belly and the rumble it was making; a rhythmic, distant pinging -

Lureli's eyes flew open and she bolted upright. Her gaze swept the enclosure, but there was no change, and there was no one immediately outside looking in. Then her eyes fell upon the second enclosure; it was no longer empty. She rubbed them, and strained to see past a monstrous barracuda that chose that exact moment to swim lazily between the two enclosures.

"Move, you blasted codfish!" she croaked, impatiently waving it forward.

It seemed almost to grin, the track along its sleek side flashing like a strobe. Then, with a flick of its powerful tailfin, it swam away. Lureli pressed her nose against the glass and peered toward the other enclosure. There, with the rock he had tapped with to get her attention still clasped in his webbed-fingered and now fully developed hand, stood Tad. No matter that he had changed, she would recognize this particular Anuran anywhere. Though only a tadpole when she found him in Lake Mirth, he had grown up with lightning speed. When last she saw him he was still more frog than man,

C. A. Morgan

but in his newly adult form he was as tall and leggy as Mandelbrot had been, with that same shock of straw-colored hair hanging limply over his bulging yellow eyes. He had tied the fronds of a palm (how come he got a tree?) into a makeshift loincloth which hung between his meaty, green-skinned thighs, but was otherwise unclothed. The paleness of his surprisingly full chest contrasted with the darker, mottled green of his back, shoulders, and legs, which sported a pattern that was his alone. A huge smile split his face as he dropped the rock and plastered his palms and forehead against the glass.

He was the most beautiful sight she'd ever seen.

## Chapter 4 – A Matter of Time

*"Dhella tru! Aben'zu dhe krado chadhin zur p'sone!"*
*"Anazu Ka'Andharra dher dhin, n'et kradhinbo an*
*surpa! Ro'da wyllo wydthe..."*
*"Et adhil n'et lith dhinzu aya empa'quo, dhe'ja."*
*"Ana T'sura du surpanet, aben kanzu ana ala dhe?*
*Surpa'zu ana risil."*
*"Ja, ana leanno kradhe! Ana erriss dhenm, zu t'surde?*
*Aben ana tortissil."*
*"Dhe na! Ana Tri arilnor, da druy'dharka valleo!"*
*"Lumin'dhe kra valleo flytes jata arilnor azu Tri!"**

(\*translation follows)


"Well thrown! But you nearly snagged me in your
net!"

"She claims she is from Ka'Andharra, but just look at her skin! Red as a willow withy..."

"Those bindings were not made in the city; that I guarantee."

"She seems to be blind, but do you think she can hear us? See how still she lies."

"Of course, she can hear us! She mind-spoke, remember? But she could be slow."

"I know! She fell out of her tree, and cracked her nut!"

"I guess some nuts do fall far from the tree!"

Aryelle waited patiently while her captors circled closer, cackling over their feeble witticisms. Speaking perfect Empayan, the voices belonged to two youngsters - a boy and a girl possibly close to her own age – and she could tell by their accents that they were Naturra, as she had guessed. They sounded just like Jonazat, whom she had met while held prisoner in the Upper Village on Mt. Cor. With his help, she and her cousin had healed several of the other captives, of various races, helping them to escape. She and Karril were recaptured and forced into the arena, but not Jonazat. And to their grateful amazement, he had returned for them. Because of it, they were able to bring Eleanor back from the brink of death, and eventually escape along with the rest of their friends. Only this time, Jonazat did not escape with them. He had kept his promise…and paid for it with his life. And now, the only way she would ever be able to repay him was to mend the rift between their people.

*"Ana surpan zu mi'kra-"* said the boy, *"-aben dharzun."* She looks a bit like you, but older. The girl switched to Commonspeak, thinking perhaps that Aryelle would not understand; by the sound of it, she was holding her nose. "Stay back! This nut was too ripe for falling – she stinks!"

"Very funny, but I only fell because of your net," replied Aryelle trying to remain calm.

"You speak Common?" the girl snorted back a laugh in wary surprise. "I thought the Kandharra were above that."

Aryelle took her time answering. It was such a relief to learn the Dru'noch had not wiped out all of the Naturra, that she felt an instant, overwhelming fondness for them. However, she also sensed that diplomacy would be necessary in dealing with these wary youngsters. She didn't want to scare them off with too many questions. Though she didn't care much for the girl's tone, or her tactics, she also didn't want to offend her young captors - especially since she was at such a disadvantage. Perhaps they knew what had become of Kayanna, maybe even Karril. Before the silence grew uncomfortable, she finally spoke.

"Yes, I do speak Common, almost exclusively, but I can tell that you do not." She didn't wait for her to reply, dispensing with stuffy formalities. "My name is Aryelle. As you can see, *I* cannot... and I have lost my way. If you would remove your net and help me find my way home, I would be happy to pay you for your services. Perhaps we could even get a little better acquainted along the way, since you seem to know as little about the Kandharra as I do about you."

"Why should we want to know more about you? You city dwellers, with your heads in the clouds - you treat Naturra like mud on your slippers! Our fathers and mothers slave away at the work you think you are too good to do, leaving us children to fend for ourselves. And where does it get you? Too smart for your own good, I say."

"Me too," chimed the boy.

"What do you mean?" asked Aryelle, cocking her head toward the girl's bitter recriminations. From the sound of it she had pushed the boy behind her, putting herself between them. Whatever the girl felt for her, it was not fondness.

"If we stop helping you, your kind will die out eventually. You no longer know as much as you think you do, not of what is truly important - how to love, how to feed or clothe yourselves. You think you are enlightened, but you live in crystal halls, easily shattered. One day the Naturra will be all that is left!"

Her words came as a jolt. In their own way, they echoed Aryelle's thoughts exactly. Had she not recently shared with Karril her fears that their people would soon die out? Turning the tables, he had surprised her with his own insightfulness. "How old are you?" she asked now.

"Why do you want to know?" the girl countered.

"Because you remind me of my cousin. He too is a deep thinker."

The girl smiled despite herself; though Aryelle couldn't see it, she could hear it in her voice when next she spoke. "I am fourteen revolutions," she announced. "My brother is ten, and...and...and we have other siblings at home that we must feed," she said in rush, as if just remembering their duty. "We are done wasting time with you!"

She tugged angrily on the net. Aryelle felt it being lifted as the girl's brother moved around to the other side.

"My name is Lorian," he offered, brushing past her.

"Hush, Lorian! Do not give this one power over you," cautioned his sister.

"*Dhanka'zu*, Lorian," Aryelle thanked him softly as the net cleared her body. "You must be very strong. Could you help me with my bindings next?"

"Do not answer her! Fly home, Lorian – now!"

"Wait!" cried Aryelle hearing his wings snap open in flight. "I need your help!" she added. She struggled to rise, but he had already flown away.

"Your people are coming," the girl said in a hushed whisper. "I hear them - I must go!" Quickly, she gathered the net and stuffed it behind a tree, knowing it would be too heavy to carry while flying.

"But, I believe what you said. I want to help you, too," said Aryelle.

"Pah! Empty promises!"

"I will tell them your words. I will warn them of their pride."

"You do that!" she said, spreading her wings. "You tell them that without us there is no Empa'aya. You tell them that with only one wing, no one flies!"

Aryelle reached out blindly, grabbing hold of her hand, and a current ran between them like a miniature lightning bolt. Both of them gasped. Then the girl shook her hand free, and waiting not a moment longer, took wing.

"Tell me your name," Aryelle called into the sky after her.

"My name is my own..."

Aryelle sat wrapped in coarse silk, sipping a restorative concoction which tasted faintly of juniper and wintergreen. Its bittersweet vapors reminded her of the ground floor room she was taken to at first, little more than a laundry full of sweet, hot steam, and perspiring Naturra workers who refused to speak to her. They had been told, in reluctant Empayan, to "make her presentable" by the Kandharran Elders who had found, but not recognized her as heir to the Seat of Ka'Andharra. Funny, she'd thought, traipsing the short distance to the treeborn city with them. Perhaps they were common Kandharra, and had never seen Elazaryn's heir up close. They had bid her hold onto one end of a staff, leading her that way as if afraid of contamination. They did not even offer to help her free her other wing! She realized that her journey had changed her in more ways than she could account for, but did she really look so different? Or did she smell like the girl had said? She would have guessed that, coming upon any lost, young woman in the forest, they would have been more concerned with how she felt, than how she looked or smelled. More importantly, they would have asked who she was. But, besides noting her blindness and wondering amongst themselves what she was doing out there, they had spoken very little, and she had been too lost in thought to offer much in the way of explanation. They seemed only too glad to pass responsibility for her on to someone else, dashing off as soon as they reached the ancient grove, and before she could even thank them. Only after she was cleaned up and taken to a waiting chamber did anyone consider offering her food or drink. And still she kept her tongue. If this was how her people treated foundlings of their own kind, no wonder they treated andhruypa so carelessly! She couldn't wait to tell her father, the El'Kandhar, just what she thought of his policies. And then she remembered; she was showing up without Karril and Kayanna. He would be happy to see her, no doubt, but devastated that she was returning alone.

A door to the chamber opened. "Come" said yet another unfamiliar voice. Aryelle stood and waited for the hand that would guide her, but none was offered. Instead, groping blindly after the receding footfalls, she was led in silence through one twisting hallway to another, up several flytes of elevated walkways using T'sura to sense her guide until, finally, a door opened into the El'Kandhar's audience chamber. It's familiar, hollow resonance gave it away. The door closed behind her, and she was left to make her way across the vast, vaulted hall all on her own. She took a deep breath and stepped nervously forward, keeping her arms by her sides. Though her wings trembled, she was determined to appear as calm as possible. Inwardly she cringed as the patter of her bare feet echoed off the pillars and walls; they had forgotten to give her slippers. She could hear the El'Kandhar drumming his fingers at the opposite end of the hall as a page ran up the steps to whisper into his ear. Someone nearby cleared his throat. The sound of rustling wings and shifting bodies told her there were a great many people gathered around the throne. She could feel them around her, though no one touched her as she neared the exalted Seat of Ka'Andharra. Sensing when to stop, she bowed deeply at the waist, and rising, spoke one word.

"Da'dher."

The crowd gasped, and Aryelle fidgeted uncomfortably. She had breached etiquette, true, by speaking before being spoken to. But the El'Kandhar was her father, after all. She took another step forward...and felt herself crushed in the grip of powerful arms. They came at her from behind, and the embrace was *not* a friendly one. Instead, it stole her breath away.

"Release the child!" boomed a voice that could only belong to the reigning monarch. Immediately, the arms that held her fell away. She felt wingtips brush her as the guard made a bow of acquiescence behind her. Aryelle swayed in place. The voice that had spoken was not Elazaryn's.

"Why do you call me thus? I am known as 'Father of Many', tis true, but of no Naturra that I know of."

There were appreciative chuckles from the crowd. "Speak child – or are you now dumb as well as blind?" His stern tone belied an underlying compassion, and his voice was tinged with good humor.

"My lord, Azadhar-" a woman's voice addressed him from her left.

Aryelle's center of gravity shifted. A hole opened in her mind, and she fell dizzily through it, crumpling to the floor. The twitter of voices around her was like so many birds.

"Give her air!" The El'Kandhar flew down off his perch and gently lifted her to her feet, careful not to tread on her wings. A current ran through her at his touch, this time a healing one, and she felt immediately better, though her mind was not comforted. She stared blindly up at him, knowing now beyond a shadow of a doubt, that this was not her father. This was not her time.

"Does she require a more thorough assumption, my love?" asked the same woman.

"I think not, Jacharra. She has just had a shock."

"Silly creature - thinking you were her father! Let someone take her to lie down. When she is rested, she can fly home."

Aryelle clutched the El'Kandhar's sleeve, begging him. "No, please! I am not...I- I have nowhere else to go! You say you are Azadhar, Father of Many. But in time, people will come to know you as Azadhar, Father of All."

"How say you, m'yana?" he asked, perplexed. "Are you fey?"

Her head still swam as truthfully, she answered him. "I know not, sire, only that I know. Please, believe me!"

It must have been the urgency in her voice that caused him to relent. "Come. We will speak of this further in private." He wrapped a supportive arm around her and, turning his back on Jacharra and the rest, led her out a side door of the chamber. Their murmurs and grumblings followed them from the hall.

Almost too numb for words, Aryelle allowed herself be led. After all, one did not argue with one's great, great, great grandsire.

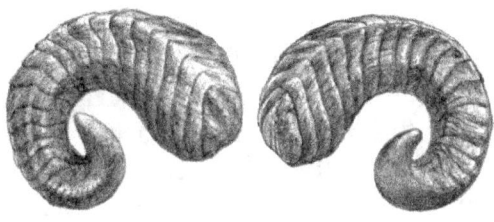

## Chapter 5 – Fever With Chills

"-and it took twelve rams to hold him down long enough to be shorn!" Gord slapped his thigh, laughing so hard he had to wipe his eyes.

"How did they all fit around him?" challenged Eleanor, though it felt like swallowing knives to speak. Her voice was so raspy he had to lean in to hear her.

"Why, they were ten feet away!" he guffawed, and seeing her confusion added, "You see, they had pinned him to the ground with yay-long pikes! And who could blame them? The stink on him was so bad the whole village reeked for weeks! It was a good thing ol' Wornack had a cold and couldn't smell; it was him they made do the sheering. You can bet Big Gord, and everyone else, stayed away from that particular trail after that. But no honey badger was ever seen on the mountain again."

Eleanor gazed up at him from where she lay. Gord's tale about the uncle for whom he was named sounded pretty incredible, though she had to admit, it was entertaining. "Who knew life on Mt. Hope was so dangerous?" she teased, and then grimaced.

"Awww...you're just jealous that my mountain is more fun than this one," he teased back. Then confiding in her he whispered, "I'd been feeding that honey badger for months, and had it almost tamed. I was kinda sad to see him go. I think Big Gord scared off most of the wildlife with his caterwauling; the hunting has been lousy ever since!"

"He sounds like a real hoot," she said, stifling a yawn.

"And you sound like you're tired," he said, tucking the blankets in around her. He stood and bent over to plant a kiss on her hot forehead. Eleanor felt herself grow even hotter.

"That's some fever you've got raging there, little sister. What do you say we get rid of a couple of these blankets?"

"No thanks," she whispered, closing her eyes and pulling them protectively up to her chin. *Little sister...*

He started to walk away, but then thought of something else. "Is there anything you might want?"

She shook her head, and he turned and walked away to busy himself on the other side of the cave. Tucking her chin down under the covers she mouthed - "Just you."

Her fever broke just after dawn, and a good thing, too, for she had fallen into another stupor Gord couldn't wake her from. Having just about exhausted his knowledge of herbal remedies, he was at wits end. When even packing her hooves in snow didn't bring her fever down, unable to do more, he had drifted off, sitting up and holding her hand so that he would know when she woke up...or passed away in her sleep. He opened his eyes with the muted morning sunlight to find her staring at him as if he was a riddle she had yet to figure out. He sighed, and Eleanor, instead of lowering her eyes with embarrassment, continued to stare him full in the face. He wasn't discomfited - on the contrary, something passed between them, something that had no words, only current. He squeezed her hand lightly. Her palm felt cool and dry, and when she returned the pressure, he knew the unthinkable had happened.

He had tamed the fiercest Aurracan warrior of all, Eleanor of Cor.


The next few days passed in a blur. Eleanor found herself more and more at home with the handsome bighorn. From her sickbed when she wasn't sleeping, she shared part of her incredible story. Some were events leading up to their meeting in the arena, and a few guarded snippets of her adventures with the other two "Chosen". Gord hung on every raspy word. Then, as her strength and appetite returned, it seemed he spent all of his time either hunting or cooking to please her, pausing only to share an occasional yarn, and to ask or answer some question. She enjoyed being waited upon so much that she almost wished she could stay sick forever. But, she had always had a strong constitution, and soon she was dying of boredom, feeling the need to move. When Gord came back from a hunt with only an ermine to show for it, Eleanor decided it was time for action. She jumped up and reached for her knife.

"Well, it's about time!" exclaimed Gord smiling. "I'm getting pretty tired of my own cooking. Here – you can skin and clean him, too."

"You would get tired of my cooking even sooner," quipped Eleanor. She took the ermine from his outstretched hand, stroking its silky, white fur. "There's not enough meat on this fellow to bother with - all ermine are good for is wearing!"

"Wait a second! That'll make a fine stew!" he said snatching it back.

"Then you make it! I'm going hunting for something I can chew!" For the first time in over a week she headed outside.

Gord laughed and tossed the ermine beside the firepit. "Even better!' he said. "I'll join you!"

Stepping out onto the snowy mountainside, Eleanor filled her lungs – *ahhh!* The crisp mountain air had never smelled so fresh! No matter how long she was stuck inside that cave, it was always too long! A fresh, heavy snow had just fallen, blanketing the incline in white. It took a few moments for her eyes to adjust, even though the sun was low in the western sky, lower than was reasonable to set out on a hunt. But even if they came back empty handed, it would be worth it just to be out in the open again. She scooped up a big handful of snow and took a bite of it, letting it melt down her throat as she peered around for tracks. This boulder-strewn slope was generally good hunting ground in the fall of the year. She assumed it would be now, too. The patrol never ventured down the mountain during the winter, so they need not worry about being caught. She spotted some fresh rabbit tracks and let out a whoop, tossing the snow in Gord's direction as she took off after them. He batted it away, scooping up his own handful. A moment later, his snowball exploded against her wooly backside. She turned in shocked surprise. Then her lips curled into a wicked grin. All thoughts of hunting evaporated as she reached down and packed a hard ball of snow. Soon it was all out war.

"Truce! Truce!" cried Gord a while later, laughing and holding up his hands in surrender. The boulder he had ducked behind barely covered his broad shoulders. Her last projectile, like most of them before it, had found its target. His face was plastered with wet snow. He stood up, wiping it away.

Eleanor considered the perfectly packed snowball in her hand and couldn't resist. It smacked against his thick chest with a thud.

"Why, you little-" In a shot he was after her.

Unfortunately, Eleanor's convalescence had cost her some of her coordination. Instead of leaping nimbly out of reach, she tripped on a snow-covered outcrop of rock and went rolling down the slope. She didn't fall far, coming to rest on a wide ledge. Gord was upon her in an instant, making sure she was alright.

"Never better," she assured him, looking up into his concerned eyes.

"Good!" he said…then rubbed her face with a fistful of snow.

She sputtered, laughing. "Okay, I deserved that – truce!"

He reached down to help her up…and she pulled him into the snow beside her. She noticed, however, that he fell a little *too* easily. "Hey! You let me do that!" she complained, sitting up. She poked him in the chest.

"Who, me? Never!" He grinned, leaning back on his elbows to survey the view. The rosy glow to the west had bathed the mountains in a soft pink wash that was breathtaking – like her, thought Gord. "Why would I let you win when I came all this way just to beat you?" he said casually.

"What's that supposed to mean?" she asked. When he looked at her like that, she could feel her cheeks burn with a fever that had nothing to do with her recent illness.

"Well, a strapping, young fellow like me couldn't resist such a challenge. You were making a name for yourself in that arena, but you had yet to face the best." He smirked.

So there it was again, that overbearing cockiness. She should have known he was too good to be true. "I didn't know my reputation had spread so far," she countered, not bothering to hide the disdain in her voice.

"Oh yeah, you're quite the legend on our mountain. My village elders were plenty interested to hear that a feisty little ewe had come into her own on Mt. Cor. Especially my granddam."

"Your granddam?"

He nodded. "Yep, she's an elder on our village council. Took my grandsire's place, and not a single ram stamped a hoof in protest. She had been working alongside Paps for years, and he made it clear before he died that she was the only one fit for the job." Gord enjoyed watching her absorb that little bit of information.

"But...your chieftain? What did he have to say about it?" asked Eleanor, hardly daring to believe him. He was such a contradiction.

"Paps *was* the chieftain." He said looking smug.

Well, well, well! "But, wouldn't-"

"- some other first-sired ram have stepped in?" he finished for her. "Mmm-hmmm, normally, but there were none on our council, and since Paps had only sired ewes, I guess he came to appreciate them for more than just their cooking. They are equally respected on Mt. Hope." His warm, brown eyes twinkled.

"But there was a chieftain from your mountain at the games with Borrac." She remembered every detail before the final blood sport. All thirteen chieftains had been present.

"An imposter" insisted Gord. "We didn't send a chieftain, since Gram never claimed the title for herself. Instead, she makes sure each of the elders has a fair say in the way things are run. Most have figured out that they kind of like it that way. Besides, I was there to represent us, and to bring back any news."

"So who was that other ram?" she argued, half-heartedly now.

"No idea. He was probably hired to make Borrac look good. There are a lot of Aurrac disgruntled with their Head Chieftain; I'll bet he wasn't the only one paid to be there. Borrac might not even have known the difference, that's how little he knows them."

Eleanor wasn't sure what to think. Except...she knew she wanted to believe him. Was it possible Borrac wouldn't have recognized some of his lesser chieftains? They rarely gathered; years and leadership might pass without the head chieftain hearing of it, she supposed. But what a way of working things, both ewes and rams making all the important decisions together - it was unheard of! Talk about too good to be true! However, if it was...

"Maybe he came from that other mountain - you know, Mt. Hope*less*," she offered tentatively.

Gord's grin grew even wider. "Sounds about right," he said. "We've always been more the other sort."

If he was telling the truth, well then, his sort was exactly what Eleanor had been waiting for. "So...you're the best, huh?" she asked, lying back against the snow.

"So they say," Gord said leaning over her and leering, "But, why don't you tell me?" His eyes closed as he moved in for a kiss, and Eleanor rolled neatly out of the way. Gord's face planted into the snow as she clambered to her hooves.

"Better get tracking before there's no light left," she said standing over him trying to hide her disappointment. Rams were so clumsy! He had purposefully misunderstood and ruined everything.

He wiped his snowy face yet again and looked up at her, perplexed. "I already caught what I wanted," he said, reaching for her hand. "Let's say we just stay here and enjoy the sunset."

"I, um...well..." she stammered, fumbling for an excuse as she wormed her hand free. Her brain felt like mush when he looked at her that way, and her heart was hammering away in her chest. What was the matter with her? She wasn't some soppy, silly ewe just waiting to fall at his hooves! He should have known she wasn't interested in being just another notch in his game belt. So why was he suddenly acting like every other boorish lout she had ever met? She had so hoped he was different, but apparently there was just one mold. The thought made her fume. "I'm still hungry!" she managed finally, barely concealing her frustration.

"That makes two of us." His eyes were deep wells, so deep she longed to fall into them. Almost.

"Go eat your stringy ermine then; I'm getting my own dinner!" Before he could move, she disappeared around a boulder and was gone, leaving him scratching his head.

C. A. Morgan

## *Chapter 6 – An Undersea Welcome*

If that ridiculous Anuran didn't stop staring, Lureli thought she would scream!

Not that it would do her any good. Sound like that, no matter how loud, couldn't escape the bubble she was in. There was no one else to hear her anyway. It was a good thing she couldn't reach him, otherwise she might twist that big 'ol head of his around in the other direction by his topknot! That, or pull out her own hair.

At first, she was happy to see him, ecstatic even. He had survived! Besides the fact that her conscience was now clear, it was comforting to know that she wasn't alone. And, she had to admit, the Anuran was sort of attractive in his own strange – and green – way. But after a whole day of his dopey face plastered against the glass, the attraction was wearing thin. As the sun began to set in the west on the second day of her captivity, and waters grew dark, his constant, disconcerting devotion shone out through those huge, glowing orbs that passed for eyeballs. It was like something from a nightmare! Lureli rolled her own eyes – properly sized - and turned her back on him, returning to the task at hand. Luckily, there was still enough light filtering down through the water that she was able to see. She was digging herself a hole, and she had never worked so hard at anything in her life. Outside the enclosure the sand on the sea floor was light and easily stirred up; in here the surface was hard-packed. Handful by damp handful, she was getting out of this blasted bubble before another night went by! Turning her back on the barnacle next door, she leaned further into the hole and grabbed another scoop. The texture was finally changing from heavy, damp sand to soupy. Seawater was filtering in, and it felt spectacular! She drizzled wet sand up and down the length of her arm watching it form into little stalagmites of coolness. Ahhhh! She did the other arm the same favor. Sheer bliss! Before she dug much deeper she would be able to climb in and settle into all that soothing wetness – but carefully, so the hole didn't cave in.

Unfortunately, a short while later it did just that.

Flat on her belly and leaning over the side, she was just reaching for one final handful - by then the hole was nearly as deep as her extended arm and as big around as a sea turtle – when her fingers grasped something stringy at the bottom. It felt like frayed fabric, or the pulp of rotting driftwood; by moonlight she couldn't see far enough down to tell. She tugged, but whatever it was remained rooted firmly in place. Maybe it was a log buried in the sand. If she could dig around it and pull the whole thing out she would be that much further ahead. She scooped wet sand to the side, and more stringy fibers emerged. In no time she exposed a bowl-sized portion of whatever lay buried. She tugged on a handful of the fibers again, and though they gave a little, still she could not pull them up. Reaching down with both hands, she decided that she would push off with one while she pulled with the other and...oh! The object below the sand moved! And not through her efforts either!

Was it a giant clam, or maybe a massive crab tangled in seaweed? Her mouth almost watered; she was as famished as she was parched. Eagerly, but still being careful so as not to get pinched in crushing claws, she scooped more wet sand from around the edges of the hole. If she could just get under it and flip it out onto its back, there would be fresh seafood for supper! Too bad she didn't have a stick. Poking her fingers cautiously along one side she felt for the edge of its shell, but it was bigger and rounder than expected. She leaned further in, tossing out more wet handfuls. The thing shifted again, and suddenly it began rising up out of the sand and seawater slurry. Startled, she drew back in alarm. Her elbow caught the side of the hole, driving into it hard, and the whole thing gave way. Tumbling headlong, Lureli fell directly atop the squirming creature, and now she really did scream! Two spindly appendages with wiggling tentacles poked through the wet sand

C. A. Morgan

and wrapped themselves around her, and she screamed even harder! Flailing wildly, she beat at the creature, struggling in its grasp. Wet sand flew in every direction. But no matter how hard she fought, the creature never released its grip.

Eventually she tired herself out.

*Let it eat me then*, she thought, exhausted beyond caring - *at least one of us won't starve to death!* She gave up the struggle and willed her body to go limp. But, just out of curiosity, with her final act she would open her eyes and see whom she was feeding.

Two huge, yellow eyes bulged out at her, and a mouth - wide and enormously pleased with itself - croaked "Tad's ba-aaack!"

## Chapter 7 – Renamed

Aryelle didn't have much time to collect her thoughts. The room Azadhar led her to lay just off his main audience chamber. She recalled sneaking into this very room with Karril when they were younger to listen in on formal proceedings to which they had not been invited. Then, the door had always remained open a crack, but now Azadhar closed it with ominous finality. A moment later a cushioned chair was pushed under her legs, and she fell into it as if stone, while, by the sound of things, the monarch settled in opposite her.

"So... first things first. You know my name, but I am afraid I do not know yours!"

He sounded robust, almost cheery, as if this were a pleasant game. But how to answer him? Aryelle was named, as were all luminaries, by combining her parents or near ancestors' names; that meant those she was named for would not even have been born yet!

"My name is... A...um...Ary..." she stammered.

"Ari? That is a very short name! I did not realize the Naturra had become so nonchalant about naming their numerous offspring. Hmmm..." he mused, "I will call you aught more common... Aridhina! - for your sky blue eyes. They were not always so though, were they? But they are very beautiful, and show you much, I can tell. How long have you had the T'sura?"

She cleared her throat. "Only a short while," she managed.

"Why so timid? You spoke your mind a moment ago. Am I so frightening now?"

"No, sire, it is just... I mean... I am..." she trailed off.

"What?"

"I must warn you!" she blurted.

Azadhar was taken aback. "Warn me of what? Are the Naturra planning another revolt? Come now, tell me what you know," he coaxed.

"I am not Naturra-" Aryelle cringed. How could she explain? Then, thinking of the Naturra girl she had met, her old familiar confidence flooded her being, and she knew what she must say. "I am *Empayan*. We - both the Kandharra and Naturra - we are *all* Empayan! We must remember what the Book of Illumination says-"

"What do you know of the Book of Illumination?" he asked, somewhat vexed.

"It contains the collective wisdom of our fore-bears."

"But only the reigning El'Kandhar has access to it!"

"Or those he deems worthy."

"It is in the ancient tongue-" he argued.

"You are having it translated from Empa'ayan into Common, are you not?"

"Translation of it has only just begun..."

"And translation will continue, as will our understanding of it." Aryelle could sense his discomfort, but she could think of no other way to explain.

"Surely the Naturra do not read! How do you know all of this?" he repeated in growing agitation. "What magic do you possess?"

"None, sire" she answered, recognizing too late that she might have flown too swiftly ahead. If only she could approach it from a different angle.

"T'sura is telling you this?"

"In part," she admitted. "But my heart is telling me what is truly important; that Azadhar, Father of Many, is setting in motion the healing of the Empaya."

The room was silent, the two of them facing each other, even their breathing suspended in this moment. Aryelle could feel his eyes searching hers, puzzling, yet acknowledging what she claimed was his chosen path. Had she overstepped hers? When he finally spoke, his words flooded her soul with fear.

"My eldest son, Elazar, has of late come to the same conclusion. You two should meet, O' Wise Aridhina. You are practically soul mates."

C. A. Morgan

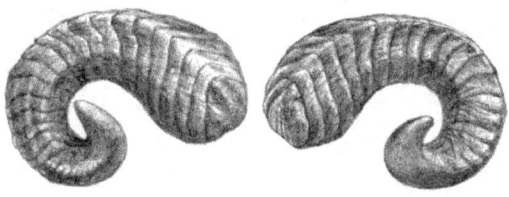

## *Chapter 8 – Kiss & Tell*

The cave felt decidedly chillier when Eleanor returned, empty handed just as she had predicted. Not only had the fire gone out, but Gord was nowhere to be seen. What's more, the ermine still lay where he had tossed it, which meant he had never come back. Maybe, she thought, he never would.

Regret smacked her right between the eyes - what had she done? After all he had done for her: nursing her back to health, keeping her fed and warm, making her laugh, treating her for the most part like an equal. Cor's horns! How could she be so obtuse? He was a dominant ram - of course he was going to act the part occasionally! She didn't have to like it, *or* playact herself to please him, but she could have at least not stomped off in an ungrateful huff. Her blasted temper again! Emphasizing the point, she aimed a well-placed kick, and the ermine went sailing into the air. Instantly she regretted that too. It bounced off the cave wall, landing in some dark recess. Sheep dip on a biscuit! Nodd had warned her more times than she could count about letting her anger run unchecked, but she just couldn't seem to rein it in. It was as much a part of her as her wool and hooves, an unfortunate gift from her sire. She had long since wished the more self-controlled Nodd was her flesh and blood sire, not just the father of her heart. If only he was, maybe things wouldn't have taken such a sour turn.

She wandered half-heartedly toward the back of the cave in search of the missing ermine. Now she must decide if she should track Gord down, apologize and ask him to come back, or just take one on the chin. She had never understood this kind of game, barely knew how to be a ewe at all, at least not the kind of ewe that was acceptable in these parts. But, by Cor, she was darned if she would pretend to be something she wasn't, or share her ram with any other ewe, for that matter. She doubted she would ever get the chance to make that clear to him now.

Tripping over the ermine, she picked it up and tossed it next to the fire pit, making her miss Gord even more. Too bad just thinking about someone couldn't make them reappear. "I just wish I could've told him…" she muttered.

"Told me what?" asked Gord ducking through the windbreak, and Eleanor's head snapped around so fast her neck cracked. Her jaw went slack. He and a strangely familiar old ram stood framed in the mouth of the cave, one holding another ermine, and the other a lantern and peddler's pack. When no answer was forthcoming, Gord stepped back allowing his visitor to hobble further inside.

"I thought you'd have a fire and supper going by now" he said, handing her the ermine before lifting the pack from the older ram's shoulders. He leaned it against the wall of the cave. "Hope you don't mind, but I brought company. Eleanor, this Dornub."

"Gord, are you crazy!?" she cried.

"Well, hullo agin to you too, missy. Fancy finding you 'ere!" said their visitor, tipping a horn.

"No offence, old-timer, but-" she hissed the rest toward Gord, "-no one else was supposed to know about this cave!"

"Oooh...I loves me a good secret!" said the old ram rubbing his hands together. "Is this yer love den then?"

Eleanor bristled. "You can't st-"

"Excuse us," interrupted Gord, pulling her aside. Eleanor tensed, uncomfortably aware of the pressure of his hand on her arm, and his warm breath on her ear as he whispered, "What has gotten into you?"

"What were *you* thinking bringing him here? I told you this was the lower villager's hideout!" she snapped under her breath. Anger, the beast, was raising its ugly head again.

"Don'tcha worry none, missy; these 'ol lips are tighter than a drum!" called Dornub, squatting down next to the fire pit.

C. A. Morgan

"Stop calling me missy, you old coot!" she snarled from around Gord's shoulder.

"Eleanor!" Gord growled back, and forced her out into the cold night air. She pulled away as they cleared the cave's mouth, and he let her go without a struggle, shaking his head. "You're starting to make me regret coming back. In fact, I might not have if not for him! He's been three long weeks hiking down off that summit! Those passes are treacherous now, and he's practically lame, but do you care? I offered him a little hospitality. The least you could do is not embarrass yourself."

"Embarrass myself? Who gave you leave to go inviting an upper villager into my hideout?"

"Your hideout, is it? Who was here first? I found it easily enough on my own, and you didn't kick me out! He would have found it, too, if I hadn't found him first; we left tracks enough to lead a whole army to it!"

That cooled her down more than a face-full of snow. While the patrol might not be stupid enough to venture down the high passes in wintertime, there was no telling who else might be wandering around the lower half of the mountain. They had littered the slope with hoof prints without giving it a second thought. Where was her head?

"Besides," Gord was saying, "-he might have news from the Upper Village. Wouldn't you like to know what Borrac is up to?"

"Oh, yeah, and what if he trots right back up the mountain and tells Borrac where we are?"

"'Ol' Dornub wouldn't do that. He wouldn't even scratch an itch if he thought he might hurt it. He's been wandering these mountains longer than anyone can remember. I've talked to him before, and he even recognized you. He's probably passed through your village many times over the years."

Eleanor wasn't sure where she had seen him before, and supposed it might have been in the lower village, or in the Upper, more like. "You still should have asked me first," she said, unwilling to concede.

"And if you weren't so pig-headed, I might have been able to. I'm not the one who stormed off without an explanation now, am I?"

"Maybe you didn't deserve one," she said, though part of her wanted nothing more than to explain. "And, I am not pig-headed!"

Gord caught up her hand in one of his own ham-sized fists. She struggled in vain to pull it free, as with his other hand he turned her chin, forcing her to look at him. He didn't have to say a word, she just stared at herself reflected in his eyes.

Her heart gave a little flip.

"Okay, so I am pig-headed," she admitted reluctantly, "but it's just becau-"

His lips covered hers, cutting her off mid sentence, bruising them with the fierceness of his kiss. At first she tried to bite him, and then all such thoughts evaporated. Her eyes fluttered shut, and other instincts took over. She felt her free hand reach up unbidden and curl into his thick brown hair. The fingers of her other hand twined with his. As his body pressed closer, every single fiber of her being tingled with desire.

When at last they came up for air, his lips trailed over the skin of her neck, and Eleanor fairly whimpered with delight. Slowly, she opened her eyes. His smug face smiled down at her.

"So…who's the best?" he asked softly, running a finger along the curve of her ear. He twirled a loose strand of her hair and rested his hand lightly upon her collarbone.

His arrogance no longer baffled her, though it took a moment before she could speak. "I wouldn't know," she answered truthfully, and added with just a hint of admonition, "since I don't kiss and tell."

"You've never been kissed like that before, have you?" he guessed.

"Only once" she replied, remembering, "-and I nearly gutted him on the spot." Borrac was the last person she wanted in her head right now. But, think of him she had, and it was sobering. "I let you kiss me though – remember that. And you're right. I suppose we should ask the old peddler what's happening up top."

If surprised at her sudden change of heart Gord didn't show it, but the mood was broken. He nodded in agreement. Without another word, but still holding onto her hand, he led the way back inside.

The cave was filled with the aroma of roasting meat. Their visitor had started a small fire, and having spitted both ermine whole, was turning them over the open flame. He rose stiffly as they entered.

"T'was the durndest thing 'ow that weasel just up and multiplied, almost like you two was expecting company. There's nothing I like better'n spit weasel!" he grinned. When neither one of them commented he continued awkwardly, "But, if my being 'ere is causing you two to lock horns, well then... I can just skedaddle! There'll be other nooks and crannies fer me to hole up in." He started toward his pack. "Not much in the way of company though..."

Eleanor was more than a little bothered, and still ravenous. There wouldn't be more than a mouthful to go around now, but through gritted teeth she invited him to stay.

"Kind of you, miss-, um...well, I was 'oping you'd say that! Pull up a rock and sit back – I'll cook supper tonight." Dornub winked at Gord and squatted back down by the fire. "I can see yer lit'l spat ended well 'nuff."

Eleanor was surprised to feel herself blushing as she sat down, her lips still aching with the memory of Gord's kiss. "How do I know you?" she blurted indelicately. Gord's eyes sparkled in warning as he settled in beside her.

"We've met a time or two, don'tcha remember? That weddin' dress I delivered was the last time," he prompted, and then acknowledged with a nod when she suddenly did remember. "I saw that you made an armband outta it, even if I didn't stick 'round for the rest o' Borrac's festivities. The Games 'ave gotten a lit'l too mean fer me taste, wot wit' blood sport n' all. I'm guessing that'cha never married the Chieftain then?

Good! This chap looks like a better choice fer ya any'ow."

"So you're not in league with Borrac?"

"Cor, no! Can't say as he and I is on speakin' terms, or any terms, more like." Dornub got up and began rummaging through his pack. "Care for a pull?" he asked producing a short bottle. When both of them shook their heads he slowly slid it back where he got it from. "Me neither then, I s'pose." He licked his dry lips and wandered back over to the fire.

"Any news from the Upper Village?" asked Gord.

"Well now, that depends on wot a ram calls news, dunnit? Word has it there's a bit o' trouble brewin' wit' Borrac's own patrol. Seems they're not too keen on the new policy they're being made to enforce."

"And what policy is that? We haven't been in the Upper Village since the Games," said Gord.

"Oh, you don't 'ave to tell me," he smirked. "Lots of folk decided to up and leave rather than 'bide by it. A real 'ardship, that's wot it is. He – Borrac, that is – has decided no one else can mate till he gets his virgin bride back."

"What?!" exclaimed Eleanor, leaping to her hooves.

Gord laid a restraining hand on her arm, and reluctantly she sank back down beside him. "And just how does he expect to enforce that?" he asked as if it was only polite conversation.

"That's the trick, innit? At first they was bustin' down doors and such, coming into folk's 'ouses an' pulling 'em apart-"

"Spare us the details," said Eleanor, her face growing beet red.

"Sorry, miss," said Dornub, "but then, you two know-"

"No, we don't," Gord admitted, so she wouldn't have to. "The lady and I aren't even promised to each other, so I'll thank you to keep your snoot clean."

"Beggin' yer pardon, I dint mean to wet yer wool. But, if you'd like a right proper ceremony first, I'm the chap wot could 'elp you out. I've tied the knot a fair share fer folk when there weren't nobody else around."

"Just get back to your story," Eleanor choked, more embarrassed than ever and hoping Gord wouldn't notice.

"Right, well...where was I? Oh, yeah. Next he sends 'em out to round up all the ewes and wot lambs still needs their mothers. Keeps 'em all 'idden away in his complex up top. He tells the rams he'll take good care of 'em, an' that they can 'ave 'em back once they finds *you* for 'im, missy. And now, things is gettin' really out'a control! I sees it all since I was still allowed to peddle me wares up top. Oh, but I were watched like a hawk when I were wif 'em; they gots patrol hauntin' 'em day an' night. Only, when they're wif themselves not as close, I thinks. Guess they don't figger ewes be much of a threat to one another. Now, some of them ewes is holdin' up jest fine and dandy, but others, well, they be actin' right strange. No offense, but some is even taking up arms, actin' like they got 'orns! There's fightin' 'mungst 'em. Same wit' the rams, only they gots a bit more rage behind 'em, bein' born wit' 'orns 'n all. Beggin' yer pardon agin, miss, but it's a right mess. It's throwin' off the natural order, it is. The 'aves an' 'ave nots fightin' agin each other - it weren't civil, I tell ya! Time fer ol' Dornub to take his leave. Was late at it any'ow, what wit' winter holdin' off fer so long. That were strange, weren't it? But now the passes is snowed shut behind me, and it'll be bloody murder up top wit' the lot. There'll be no new lambs come spring, that's the worst of it. Borrac's slittin' his own throat, messin' wit' things he don't unnerstand."

Eleanor's color had faded from crimson to pale as Dornub rambled on. Though she had no great love for the Upper Villagers, she wasn't heartless either. That she could be the cause of so much trouble was more than she could take in. Why hadn't she just finished off Borrac when she had the chance?

As she sat there, speechless, Gord summed up what she was feeling. "He's gotta be stopped," he said squeezing her hand, and then asked the question that was bothering him most after this news.

"Has anyone come further down looking for Eleanor?"

"Course they 'ave! Wouldn't you? Only, most of 'em come back when it looked like snows would fly. They's so used t' havin' their lit'l comforts they can't do without, even for somethin' so important."

Eleanor heaved a sigh of relief. That meant the lower villagers had most likely escaped notice. Gord had said the cave was recently vacated when he found it. While hiding here they wouldn't have ventured outside, having brought along their own provisions. It would have defeated the purpose. They must have vacated only shortly before Gord arrived. And by now, any reasonable Aurrac were holed up for the winter, including those who might be searching for her.

Her relief was short-lived as Gord spoke up again. "Well, as long as nobody was desperate enough to follow you down that mountain we're alright. Otherwise, you've led them right to us."

C. A. Morgan

## Chapter 9 – Déjà Vu

How had she not seen this coming? How could she have been so blind? Aryelle choked on the irony, a laugh that was also a sob shaking her slender shoulders. She stood suddenly and began pacing. She had memorized the room's dimensions to avoid stubbing her toes, though the Naturra woman who cleaned for her each day seemed to delight in moving the furniture around. Her foot connected with a piece of it now, and painfully! She clenched her teeth, rubbing her toe briskly as she sank down onto the cushioned seat.

What was she going to do?!

She had been living this lie for two candles' time now, not knowing how to get herself out of it, or where to turn for help. Every day grew more uncomfortable than the last, knowing but not knowing what was coming next. It was like playing a game without first learning the rules, yet being inexplicably good at it - great fun had she not cared about the outcome or anyone other than herself. But such was an empath's curse. And the greater the healer, the deeper the empathy, so she believed.

As a child, everyone had always said how much she resembled her great, great grandmother, a renowned healer with wisdom beyond her years. Not that any of them had known her personally. Since luminaries rarely lived beyond sixty revolutions, multiple generations seldom overlapped. Aryelle shared her ancestress' giftedness, they said, having heard of it from their parents, who heard of it from their own. That, and her eyes. Green eyes, like the forest, were rare even for Naturra, but totally unheard of among the Kandharra. Yet, Aryelle's eyes were green, or at least they had been before the T'sura. Blindness had turned them the color of pale sky. But originally they were green, like those of her direct ancestor, Aridhina the Wise. A foundling.

When Azadhar first called her thus she had been surprised, and even a little pleased, not yet understanding its full portent. There was no hiding from it now. Everyone currently alive in Ka'Andharra, from Azadhar, the El'Kandhar to the lowest Naturra scullery maid; they all thought she really *was* Aridhina! She was living her great, great grandmother's life, trapped in a net from which there was no escape! It was almost as if, by sending her to this time, Mandelbrot had filled a hole in history. As if there would never have been an Aridhina had not Aryelle gone tumbling through the void. Yet that could not be true for the very fact that her ancestor, with those wise, green eyes of hers, had been Naturra, and she was not.

Had she somehow altered the stream of time?

It was too much to think about right now. She was supposed to be getting ready to meet Elazar, Azadhar's son, who was returning this very evening from his own questanna. The thought of how that might go was too terrifying to consider, so that too she pushed from her mind. Robes had been laid out for her, fine silks crafted by the sun-darkened, hardworking hands of Naturra who would never themselves wear such finery. Considering the lingering tension between the separate factions of Empaya in her own time, it was nothing compared to the open hostility she found here now. It was odd. These Kandharra welcomed all others – Aurrac, Minoans, Silvans, Centauride, Ippotanians, Teledhines, Wulfen – more races than she had dreamed of in all her sheltered life frequented the treeborn city in this age. But of their own wilderness brethren, the Kandharra now living fostered only pained tolerance, accepting their presence as a necessary evil, and an unwelcome reminder of their baser selves. For all of their elegance and enlightenment, they were blind to the evil of their own prejudice. It was no wonder the Naturra resented them so strongly, they who labored without rest to make the city so delightful, only to be thought less of because of it. Over time, as her own travel-worn appearance faded and her fairness returned, most in Azadhar's court no longer found her objectionable. She had wondered at the difference, not being able to see herself, and pried the reason out of her reluctant maid.

It had always been clear to her that she wasn't Naturra. Had the real Aridhina had a much harder time of it, she wondered? The history lessons part of Aryelle's education had mentioned little of her ancestress' day to day life, glossing over what must have been a very trying time. How had the royal family ever come to accept and revere her as one of their own? And yet they had, for she was living proof of it...at least, she hoped she still would be.

A knock on the door dispelled her reverie. "It is time, Aridhina," called a lilting voice from the door's other side.

"A moment, please," replied Aryelle, dipping her hands into the folds of luxurious silk laid out for her. Dress in this age was more elaborate than in her own day, and the quality far surpassed anything she had ever known. These robes were sublime, like wearing air itself, only richly colorful, so she was told. They were to be draped about the body in colorful cascades, but these were so long, she wasn't sure how to begin. "Come in, Ladhelle," she called finally, giving up.

"Oh!" exclaimed Ladhelle, pausing in the doorway. With hair the opposite of Aryelle's chestnut coloring and features just as delicate, she was no less fair, though a tad less confident in bearing and manner. She was barely fifteen revolutions, so perhaps that would come with age. After all, she had grown up knowing that she was the offspring of commoners, not the favored child of an El'Kandhar father. Yet, she seemed more than content with her lot. Even her name, which meant "song-maker", attested to her good nature. She breezed the rest of the way in with a smile. "I see you are in need of my help! Where is your maid servant? You should have been dressed long before now."

"Yes, you should have," agreed a second visitor, pushing into the room at her heels.

"Come in...both of you," said Aryelle, resigned. Elazar's younger half-sister, Jadharra was practically Ladhelle's mirror image, and never far behind. The El'Kandhar and his third wife, Jacharra had enlisted Ladhelle as a companion for their overindulged youngest daughter, and though she had come to mean much more than that to everyone in the household, Jadharra looked upon Ladhelle as her own personal property, rarely letting the girl out of her sight. She never said as much, but Aryelle could tell that she resented her intrusion on their friendship.

"My Natur-...um...the maid was needed at home, so I let her go," Aryelle explained. "I can manage, truly."

Jadharra brushed past clicking her tongue in disapproval. "She should have attended to her duties first. And, I doubt that you could manage all of this" she said taking the length of silk from Aryelle's arms and tossing it carelessly on the bed, "even with wings bound, which I see she did not help with either."

"No matter, I can do it," offered Ladhelle pleasantly, taking up the silks in turn. "No doubt her family needed her more. Come now, Aridhina, turn around and let me drape you."

"Really, Ladhelle, how can Father see you as a fitting wife for Elazar?! How will you ever be able to manage this household? You must try harder else my brother may decide not to marry you!"

"Half-brother - and who says I want to marry him?" she shot back.

"I hope you are not still thinking about Rachazar, the little gnat! He was bad enough before, but since Elazar has been away on his questanna, he has become absolutely insufferable!"

"He has always been charming to me."

"That is because he likes you more than he ought. But we cannot have you settling for second best now, can we? Elazar will rule one day, and you must be by *his* side - that way I will always be in his favor! Why must my other brother always try to take what is not rightfully his? Oh, how I wish you were younger, not older than me – then Rachazar would have to leave you alone!"

"Well, none of us are getting any younger," said Aryelle, growing impatient with their chatter. Ladhelle on her own was fine company, but both of them together made her want to fly the nest, as the saying went. Right now though, she really could use their assistance, and she told them so.

"I will call for my own maid to help you," said Jadharra.

"No need, really," insisted Ladhelle. "I like doing it. Here, Aridhina, turn around and fold your wings in."

Aryelle did as she was bidden. "*Dhanka'zu*, but do I wish you would call me Ari, Ladhelle. I insist."

"*Ho'kay,* Ari... *dhe suip.* Is that right? And, you can call me Dhella."

"*Ho'kay*, Dhella. Yes, *dhe suip* – you will chance it, and the imperative would be *di suip*. Your Empayan is sounding quite good, you know. Before you know it you'll be able to converse with ease. "

Jadharra harrumphed disapprovingly, and then plopped herself into a chair to watch as Ladhelle deftly wrapped the first loop of silk around Aryelle's folded wings to hold them in place. Criss-crossing the lush folds over her shoulders, she draped and wrapped, tucking and folding, turning Aryelle this way and that like a spider cocooning a choice morsel. When she was nearly done, she unwrapped Aryelle's wings, tying off the remaining ends to form a simple bow between them. The result was breathtaking.

Even Jadharra was impressed. "Can you teach me to do that?" she sighed.

"Make sure you-know-who sits next to me at tonight's feast, and I will!" she said tweaking the bow, and then circled Aryelle to view her creation. "Too bad you cannot see yourself, Ari. Elazar will never want to leave Ka'Andharra again once he sees you!"

"I am clothed, am I not? I wish to impress no one, least of all Elazar!"

"Oh-" the little syllable was heavy with Ladhelle's disappointment. "But I thought perhaps if you...well...you see...oh, never mind."

"You thought if Elazar preferred me, you would be free to stop pretending that you do not prefer his younger brother, Rachazar."

The flush on Ladhelle's cheeks spread all the way to her wingtips.

"Why not just get it over with? Tell Azadhar that you do not wish to marry Elazar-"

"Oh, but she must!" insisted Jadharra. "They are practically betrothed; she has no choice! Father would send her away if she tried to go against his wishes."

"There has been no marriage feast yet, Dharra. Who knows? Perhaps Elazar has come back from questanna with a changed heart. Then I might be free to choose..."

"Sometimes I do not understand you at all!" Jadharra pouted.

"-but, of course, I will do as my El'Kandhar wishes. As will you when your time comes."

"Father will not tell me who to marry like he did Adhanna." Her older, half-sister had wed earlier in the season. "I am the youngest. He may well be dead by then."

"How can you say such dreadful things?!" cried Ladhelle.

"What does it matter? It is true. He will be dead, Elazar will become the new El'Kandhar, and everyone will forget that I even exist. My veins run with blood just as pure, but *I* will never sit upon the Seat of Ka'Andharra! So, we must ensure that *you* do!"

"Jadharra! Really!"

"PEACE! You two are worse than Lureli and Eleanor!"

Both girls turned to look at Aryelle. "Who?" they asked in unison.

"No one you know," she answered, still exasperated. Feeling her way to a chair, she sat down. "It does not matter. They are not here - you are, and your chatter is giving me a headache."

"Lu-ril... sea laughter? And what does the last part - "li" - mean? You must at least tell that much!" needled the younger girl, while Ladhelle blushed sheepishly. "Bringer or taker? Or rest? I am learning the old tongue too, you know. But there are too many meanings. Ella...*nor*, did you say? What kind of name is that?"

Aryelle sighed and rubbed her forehead with the tips of her fingers, ignoring Jadharra's questions. Then, without warning, she felt a hand rest lightly on top of her head. A moment later her headache was gone.

She reached to lift the hand from her head and squeezed it gently. "*Dhanka'zu*, Ladhelle – again; but you do not always have to heal me. And, I am sorry. I am just nervous."

"It is really no bother," Ladhelle replied, squeezing back "A child could do it."

"Aridhina, if you do not care what my brother thinks of you, why should you be so nervous?" asked Jadharra, as petulant as ever.

How could Aryelle answer that? She did not want Elazar to like her, but he must. He had fallen in love with the real Aridhina at first sight, and she with him. Hadn't her father, Elazaryn, often compared his own love story with her mother - who was not his intended bride - to theirs? But everything was wrong! She was *not* Aridhina. Her eyes were no longer green. She was older than her ancestress would have been, less wise and more confused than ever. If Elazar married

Ladhelle and not Aridhina, she would never exist! But, she simply could not go through with the ruse to that point! It was too much to ask.

"Your heart is racing, and your cheeks are flushed. Forgive me for being such a poor healer. I will fetch someone else-" Ladhelle started for the door.

"No, I am fine. See?" she said, taking a deep breath and smiling.

"You do not lie well, Aridhina," Jadharra noted.

No, she most certainly did not.

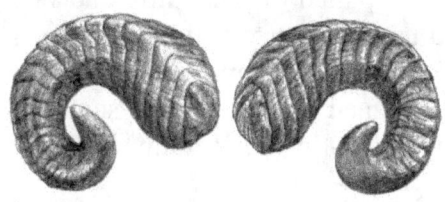

## *Chapter 10 – What's in a Name?*

Dornub licked his fingers, finishing off the last bite of a perfectly satisfying meal. He had told them he never turned up his nose at weasel, even if it was a little burnt. But to watch him devour it you would think he couldn't get enough! Since neither of them had much appetite after receiving his news, Eleanor and Gord sat by as he made the most of his favorite dish, sucking the bones clean.

Both had fallen silent, each lost in their own thoughts as they watched him eat. Not that Dornub seemed to notice. Between (and sometimes during) mouthfuls, he was perfectly capable of carrying on enough conversation for all three of them.

"So, like I tells ya" he said, smacking his lips, "worryin' 'bout it won't change things a tic. I knows wot yer thinkin', but I don't think anyone 'ad their eye

C. A. Morgan

on me when I packed up, an' no one would'a wandered down that 'orrible pass just out o' curiosity. Yer in the clear, so's jest sit tight an' enjoy yo'selfs a lit'l snuggle right 'ere!" He pulled out his knife and began picking his crooked teeth. "Course, I'll still be hoofin' it in the mornin' like I was a plannin', so's I'd draw 'em off any'ow-" he rushed on at Eleanor's scowl, "-only there won't be no need, I'm fair certain. But wot'cha might need helpin' wif is-"

Eleanor shook her head emphatically. "No! We don't need any help. Now that I'm strong enough to travel, I've got to make sure the villagers down below are safe. You can go whenever you want to, but I'm leaving at first light."

"Don't be foolish. We'll all go together," insisted Gord, despite his obvious reluctance to leave their cozy nest; things had just been getting interesting before Dornub showed up. He heaved a resigned sigh and told the old peddler, "It took weeks for you to get this far, and you know these mountains like you know your own wool. The snow surely isn't as deep down below, but it will take at least another week to reach the lower village. On the off chance you were followed..." he hesitated, working it out in his head, "-maybe we should all sit tight for a few more days." Eleanor started to protest and he hurried on. "You could probably use a longer rest, you know, and if anyone did follow you, better to face them right here."

"Better still to let them get ahead of us on the trail..." Eleanor calculated, trying to use her head though she hated the thought of waiting any longer than

98

was necessary. She scrambled to her hooves, standing over the two rams. "Doorknob is right," she agreed to their surprise. "He should go as planned. He hasn't seen anyone, so if they are there, they're keeping well behind him. They will have found shelter for the night, too. If he hikes back to where you found him early enough in the morning, then takes a slightly different route, he'll draw them off. Maybe he could skirt around the lower village altogether-" she saw the peddler frown and quickly amended her plan, "or at least come in from the north foothills instead of veering south at the next pass." Dornub nodded, and she continued. "We'll give him a day's head start – that should be plenty – and come in around them as they reach the lower slopes. That should put us in the village before him and any tail. And if he doesn't show up, we'll know he's in trouble and go out looking from there. But I won't wait around here any longer than that. If Nodd didn't make it back, the villagers will need me to look out for them."

Gord looked up at her in surprise. She hadn't told him Nodd wasn't with the rest of her clan. Come to think of it, there was a lot she hadn't told him about the last few months. If they did as she wanted, they would be filling some of their extra time here with a few more explanations…and hopefully, a little more than kissing. But, for now all he said was, "Alright then, that's the plan - agreed?"

"Right. An' the name's not Doorknob, miss. It's Dor-*nub*, like nubbins, see?" The old peddler had gotten up to rummage in his pack again as she spoke, and Eleanor found herself staring at his nubby little tail.

"What's the story behind it - that?" she asked bluntly.

"Me name?" Turning, he saw where she was pointing. "Cor, no! It's for me horns!" He laughed, patting them. Eleanor realized she had barely noticed them, but then again, Gord's horns made any other rams' look insignificant.

"Not the mountain?" offered Gord, embarrassed for him, and because of her rudeness.

"Isn't Mt. Nubbins the name of the next one over from yours?" Eleanor asked him. Althea had taught her to recite the entire Aurrac range. It was one of the few things she could recall learning from her dam, since she had preferred spending her time shadowing Nodd. "I heard the rams there trim their horns so that they're no bigger than a ewe's."

"Innit, though? Me mum was from Mt. Dorn an' not married to me sire, see. We was shamed off our mountain an' settl'd on Nubbins. The chieftain of the clan wot took us in had me horns cut down even before they growed in right proper. Said if we was goin' to make a home on 'is mountain, we was goin' to 'ave to look the part, an' I oughta 'ave a name t' match! There's some wot would 'ave resented it, but I figger it makes me right special."

Eleanor looked skeptically at him, and he snorted. "How's that fer a story? Might be short, but, everybody's got a tale, get it?"

"Very funny - a tail," said Eleanor, brooding. "What's the real story?"

"Named m'self" he answered simply. Then he gave her a penetrating look. "An' wot's yours?"

She didn't feel like going into details with him either, so she kept it simple. "My stepfather renamed me."

"Awww...an' after yer own sire gave you such a pretty lit'l name, too," Dornub lamented. "Still...it suits ya."

Eleanor was baffled. "How would you know my real name? I don't even remember it."

"Oh, sure 'nuff it was me wot helped yer mum sneak down the mountain t' get away from Borrac. I told ya we'd met a time or two. I jest 'appened t' be 'round these parts then, an' I bumps into her, see. Course, you wouldn't remember. You was only a wee lamb then. But, she was holdin' another precious bundle too, so's I carried ya down most the way.......*Rosumbra*."

Eleanor frowned. The name sparked not a single memory.

Despite his earlier yarn though, she believed him all the same. How else could Althea have made it down to the lower village with two little ones in tow? Eleanor had never thought about her having had help before, but it made perfect sense.

"Ro*sum*bra" she murmured, feeling its hollowness against her tongue. An umbra rose was a delicate blossom the color of blood. It dwelt entirely in shadow, she knew, and was meant to be pruned back year after year, like most of the flowers Borrac favored. How typical of him to name her so! Contrarily, Nodd had renamed her

C. A. Morgan

for a heartier bloom, one that was not only beautiful, but wild and free, and thrived in the sunlight. And like her, one that could weather anything, even the harshest winter in these mountains.

"No..." she said, shaking her head. "Rosumbra is dead. I'm Eleanor."

Gord resisted the urge to reach for her hand. *A strong name for a strong ewe*, he thought. He might not know her whole story yet, but from what he did know, it was no wonder she was a little rough around the edges. He picked up a stick and snapped it in two, adding it to the fire. Borrac had done his best to break her, and for that he would make him pay. But it was good to know she was made of stronger stuff – like eleanor. *It's perfect for her,* he admitted, *and she's perfect for me.*

## *Chapter 11 – If Looks Could Kill*

Once she realized she wasn't going to be eaten after all, Lureli felt much better. Then she got mad.

"Let go of me, you...*amphibian!*"

Somehow Tad had managed to tunnel all the way over from his bubble enclosure to hers, and in the same amount of time it took her to manage a shallow hole! Sure, she knew that Anuran could burrow, but that was just ridiculous. And so was his strength! Even her Mer litter bearers would have dropped her by now, and they were as brawny as they came. Tad's stick-thin arms must be solid muscle.

Both of them seemed equally covered with sand, though Tad's lower extremities remained buried from the waist down. The hole he came up through had all but disappeared with her thrashing; if anyone had been around to see them it would appear a squat child with extra long arms carried her.

"I said, put me down!" Lureli ordered sternly.

But Tad only smiled and tightened his grip.

"Are you deaf?" she asked. "Where are your ears?" She strained to see them. The lock he had on her made it almost impossible to move, but really, where else could they be but on his head? She looked him right in the eyes and scowled. His grin split his face from...well, not from ear to ear, unless that was what those round, swirly things were.

There was one sure way to find out.

Exchanging her scowl for a sweeter-than-arame smile, Lureli leaned in as if to kiss his cheek. Instead, she put her mouth directly over one of the discs and yelled as loudly as she could – *"HWAAAAAAH!"*

The next thing she knew she was picking herself up off the sand. Tad's webbed fingers had flown up to the sides of his head covering what were indeed ears. He keened, rocking back and forth like beach grass in a fickle wind.

"Well" she said, feeling only slightly guilty, "that will teach you to listen." It was unlikely he would be hearing anything out of that particular ear for days, but by the way he was carrying on you would think she had killed him. Sorry tears welled in his eyes, and he looked like an injured lover.

*What a tadpole!* She thought, brushing off the sand and retreating as far away as she could. Leaning against the glass, she slid down it facing him, and feeling very self-satisfied. *Bet you won't try that again!*

Tad averted his gaze. His shoulders slumped and his hands dropped to his sides, lying atop the sand. Then sighing, he worked his spindly legs the rest of the way out, and once freed, hopped to the opposite side of the enclosure and squatted there, not meeting her eye. They stayed that way, intentionally ignoring one another until Lureli could no longer bear the lack of attention.

"So..." she said, "what's a frog like you doing in a sea like this?"

She didn't really expect an answer. But Anuran, as it turned out, were extremely quick to forgive and equally loquacious. It was all the invitation Tad needed. He hopped over to her side of the bubble - keeping a respectful distance when her palms went up - and began to regale her with his own adventures in his own distinct brand of Common, pieced together from who knows where.

"*Yuuuuuup*, Miss ogda seen - so madder she was! Skinnered me 'bout, she did – brrrrrrawk!" His sentences came out like one long croak, and each time he took a breath his neck bulged with reserved air. "Slippery her be, and chaaaaange uppin', issa swimmer once den not – wanda her you more-den-me wanda slurp flies! None for me dat, and no you for dat snake! Haaaaaah! Her chasen dis hopper waaaaaay round da lake. Taddy, he bouts gots away, den tricksie she been – *yuuuuup* – was some fat skeeter, and dats so tasty Tad chasin dat bug. And den" he wagged his head remorsefully, "she do gotsa dis hopper."

Lureli knew exactly how he felt. Japhra had somehow always known just what her weaknesses were too, and had never hesitated to use them against her. The difference was that she deserved what she got, while he should have remained an innocent bystander, not a pawn in her evil schemes. She wished once again that she never taken him from his home in Lake Mirth. Poor Tad.

"But why bring you here?" Lureli wondered.

He shrugged his froggy shoulders. "Fishin' - dats'a guess. Brrrrrrawk."

For her, no doubt. And now here they were, bait and quarry, trapped in the same blasted bubble. Japhra could show up at any moment, and she was the one person Lureli hoped to never see again! Tad might manage to wriggle his way to freedom, but she would never be able to follow him out through the sand like that; it would crush her. She sighed. It was doubtful she could convince him to leave now anyhow. As they spoke he had edged closer and closer, and was now so close they were nearly touching. He gazed dreamily up at her. She had about as much chance of discouraging his attention as a whale did lamprey! Just then her stomach growled and Tad's eyes rolled toward her middle, then back into his head in a swoon. A shiver ran over him and he gurgled blissfully, leaning nearer still.

Lureli thought she might be sick.

"Touch me once more and…and I'll scream!"

For once she had more attention than she wanted, and it was no fun at all. Like a small child, she had had to remind him over and over again, hoping that eventually it would sink in. She understood that he just wanted to be near her, and was trying her best to be patient, really she was. But the least little encouragement on her part drove all reprimands from his pointy, large head. The stupid frog knew no boundaries - how could he be so th?! She was beginning to understand what suffocation felt like!

They had been playing this uncomfortable game of tag for hours, and Lureli didn't know how much longer she could keep it up. Her stomach felt shrunken to the size of krill, which she would gladly eat her weight in if she had the chance. Dry didn't come close to describing how parched her throat was, let alone her skin. Tad was probably equally dehydrated, though he seemed not to notice. But she didn't dare sit still long enough to try to hollow out another hole with that great big, green barnacle around. To him, it would represent an open invitation.

But oh, how exhausted she was!

She did her best to stifle a yawn. Tad yawned back at her.

*He must be sleepy too*, she thought, hatching an idea. *Maybe if he drifts off first...*

It took another hour of endless dodging and yawning, fake and otherwise on her part, but eventually Tad succumbed. And just in time too, for, watching his eyelids finally flutter shut, she felt hers growing too heavy to hold open.

\*\*\*\*\*\*

Lureli woke gradually from her stupor. Her eyes roamed back and forth beneath their lids, a smile playing over her lips as she rolled onto her side. She settled back in, the sand shifting to fit her form. The dream she was enjoying slowly morphed into semi-awareness as she reached up to rub the sleep from her eyes, and encountered a skinny arm. It was flung carelessly over her side. She patted it, confused; it twitched and she startled. But when the arm tightened around her drawing her closer, she sighed and relaxed into it. At least the parts of their skin that touched were moist.

"My, my, my…what a cozy s-sssssscene!"

Lureli's eyes flew open. As she tried to scramble to her own feet, her gown tangled around Tad's flippered ones, and she tripped backwards on top of him.

"Brrrrrrrraaaaawk!" His huge inflating air sack pushed her off onto the sand. Caught up in the shimmering fabric of her gown, he tried to hop away and fell flat on his face. Rolling over, he got even more twisted up in it. Pulling and falling, and struggling to get back up again, finally the pair righted themselves. They stood, panting, two bundles of exhausted nerves.

"It's her!" Lureli cried, gasping for breath.

Tad didn't have to guess who she meant. But Japhra was nowhere to be seen. They circled each other, searching for her. She could take the shape of any creature, so it was impossible to know what to expect, but nothing moved within, or outside, the enclosure. Tad looked at Lureli questioningly.

"She's here somewhere, I know she is! I can feel her watching..."

Tad's eyes grew even wider and his head sunk lower between his shoulder blades. His eyeballs roved independently of one another; no nasty creature would sneak up on him! But after turning every stone and digging up every little bump in the sand, they didn't turn up so much as a clam. Japhra wasn't inside their bubble, and as far as they could tell was nowhere near it on the outside.

"Maybe it was a dream..." mumbled Lureli, though unconvinced. Then a new thought entered her head. "I'm imagining things out of desperation; no one's ever going to come. Maybe everyone's forgotten about us." She was so worn down by hunger, thirst, and everything else that she could no longer hold her emotions in check. She began to tremble, and then great sobs of self pity shook her shoulders, while her dry eyes burned. She sank heavily onto the sand.

Tad squatted behind her not knowing what to do. Slowly, he inched his way forward. A calming rumble billowed his throat as he reached out and patted her back in sympathy. When eventually his arms encircled her and drew her head toward his chest, and then pulled her onto his lap, she was still too distraught to care. Rocking gently back and forth, he stroked her hair and crooned.

Outside the bubble, two smallish eyes opened on the sea floor behind them. A wave rippled the sand, and

C. A. Morgan

the outline of a flounder was for a moment visible before the sediment settled back to disguise it once more. The eyes narrowed, and then closed.

## *Chapter 12 – A Rose of Another Color*

With his belly full and his thirst for conversation nearly slaked, Dornub clambered to his hooves. His story of how he'd first met her was still ringing in Eleanor's ears as he continued with the tale.

"Dinnit ya ever wonder 'ow ol´ Nodd knew this cave were 'ere?" he asked, thumping himself on the chest and not waiting for an answer. "So's ya see, I been makin' use of it longer 'n you been breathin'. It's where I were 'eaded when I run into Gord 'ere, innit, so's I woulda found ya any'ow. But you an' me, we gots history 'ere…"

He rambled on for a bit until Gord stood and made an elaborate show of stretching and yawning, and he finally took the hint. "Now, you'll pardon me," he said abruptly "-but I'll be taking m'self off to bed. Don't let me disturb yer peace. I always liked the 'idden space in the back better, if yous don't mind, and I sleeps like a rock. G'night t' ya."

With that he retrieved his lantern and pack, and retreated toward the rear of the cave. Grabbing a spare blanket or two from the pile, he disappeared through a narrow crevice into the adjoining chamber.

Eleanor stood to watch him go, both dreading and anticipating what the rest of the night might bring. She hoped he was right and no one else was coming down the mountain after him. Either way, with him tucked away in the second cavern, she and Gord would have a little more time alone together. Her cheeks grew warm, and she knew it wasn't her fever returning. Twiddling with the wool along her thigh, she shifted nervously from hoof to hoof, pretending to be concentrating when really, she could hardly think at all. Gord started poking the fire, not meeting her eye. *He's nervous, too,* she realized, though she couldn't imagine why. In this game he definitely had the advantage. Her lack of confidence made her feel like an imposter, uncomfortable in her own wool. She had waited so long for a ram worthy of her attention, but now that he was finally here, she had no idea where to begin. He, on the other hand, would not have waited for her. Or had he?

"Eleanor," Gord said softly, stepping toward her. She looked up. "Why didn't you leave already if you were in such a hurry to get back? Sure, I know you were recuperating; that's why I've kept my distance. But you've been getting steadily better. You could have left a day or two ago. Why have you waited this long?"

His questioning took her by surprise. "I...um..." she stammered uncharacteristically.

"I think I know the answer," he hurried on, rescuing her from her discomfort. "I hope it's because you want to be with me as much as I want to be with you."

She started to object, but he raised a hand to her lips, gently silencing her. He looked her directly in the eye. "You may think there have been others before you, but there haven't been. That's not to say I wasn't ever tempted, but it's not the way we do things on my mountain. And even if it was, *I* wouldn't have. I want it to be all or nothing."

"But when you kissed me-"

"That was my horns talking. This is my heart."

Taking her hand he leaned in, his lips brushing lightly against hers. When she didn't protest he kissed her again, still tentatively, asking not taking. She held herself stiffly, enjoying his kisses, wanting them, but also wanting so much more and not trusting herself. When his lips left hers to trail across her cheek, her brow, the bridge of her nose, his breath and beard tickled her skin. The sensation was all so exquisitely new. Her ache grew almost unbearable as he raised his head to gaze into her eyes, and she saw that he felt it too. She shivered then, melting against him as he drew her close, giving herself up to a pleasure so long denied.

Eventually they parted, both of them flushed and breathing hard. It would be so easy to get carried away, to forget about Dornub in the next room, to give themselves to each other not caring what came next. But that was not what either of them really wanted, what they had both waited for. Gord came to his senses first, holding her at arm's length while he stilled his own racing pulse. Eleanor, confused by his sudden restraint started to turn away, embarrassed. But he refused to let go of her. She looked back at him. His eyes bored into hers with such intensity, and a passion that burned to match hers.

"Not yet" he whispered hoarsely. "Not like this. I need to know, Eleanor of Cor, that I am the only one for you, now and always."

Eleanor licked her tender, bruised lips, still tasting his. She tried to speak, but no words would come – what was happening to her? She had always been in control - except for her temper - needing no one and choosing to let so few in. Nodd, Althea, Lavina and the twins; she had cared for them and her villagers, guarding them as fiercely as she guarded her heart, but she had never really allowed herself to love even them. Was there room in her heart now for Gord?

*Yes*, a small voice answered inside her head, *room for him, and to spare.* Arguing with her conscience, she wondered - *but should I really let him in?* And again, that small voice – *Yes!* Eleanor felt something release inside her and slowly, timidly almost, she nodded.

Gord broke into a huge grin. Eleanor blushed, and then laughed out loud as he scooped her up, twirling her around the cave and crowing like a cock. Dornub stumbled back in rubbing his eyes, and smiling when he saw them.

"Guess you'll be needin' me 'elp tying that knot after all!" he said.

## Chapter 13 – Who is Who

Elazar was smitten. Even his wingtips tingled at the sight of her. Surely she must read his thoughts, he hoped, as a rosy blush stained her cheeks, adding an extra glow to her already vibrant aura.

They were still at table, prismed light dancing throughout the crystal banquet hall and across the sumptuously laid board. Azadhar was, of course, seated at its head. His stepmother, Jacharra sat to his father's left, and Elazar himself at his right hand. Aridhina had been placed two settings down and across from him, between his sisters. Ladhelle, as his assumed intended, was to have been seated next to him, though somehow his brother Rachazar had managed to insert himself between them. Would that it had been Aridhina – *ch'ara*, but she was lovely! Blindness may have dimmed her eyes, but certainly not her beauty, nor for that matter her spark. What a fiery-fly, that one! She had done nothing but contradict him throughout the meal, almost as if she was purposefully trying to earn his disapproval. But, try though she might, it was hopeless. After this night, he would love no other. Ladhelle was beautiful and kind, it was true, but in wit could hold no candle to her. While dullness in a comely wife might be commendable to some, with the exciting plans he had in mind, he would need someone of equal passion to share his mission. And it was clear Aridhina supported his views, no matter how vehemently she denied it. Yes, her arrival was perfectly timed - how fortuitous!

His royal father would surely not disapprove of the match since no formal promise had been made to Ladhelle. Jacharra, however, might be another story altogether. Since it was unlikely that Azadhar would outlast his young wife – Elazar's third stepmother - she must pacified if there was to be peace with her throughout his own reign. Without it, all he hoped to accomplish, his dream, would be unattainable. His first task now that he had returned from his questanna was to convince Azadhar of its worth. The second would be to earn fair Aridhina's affection, and third, to convince his stepmother of his choice of bride.

It would not be the first time that someone in his line had married outside of the royal houses. His father's last two wives had been common as well, and in fact, should he himself have settled on Ladhelle, Elazar would have been introducing still more common blood into the royal line. Yet, no one in recollection had ever married a Naturra, not that Aridhina appeared as such. If not Naturra though, where did she hail from? She claimed no knowledge of her former life, so his father informed him, but she had astounding ideas about the future. She could not be Kandharran; surely he would have noticed her before now no matter how much the city's population had swelled.

It did not matter, in truth. She was here now. And soon, he hoped, she would agree to be his.


Aryelle's head spun, and not from the blaiz either; her crystal cup stilled brimmed with the potent decoction. She had sipped only water throughout the meal, knowing she would need to keep her wits about her. If only he would stop looking at her like that her pulse might stop racing! She could *feel* his stare as surely as others might see it; feel its probing weight as he plied her with questions about herself and her opinions. The answers she had practiced on others of the royal household seemed inadequate to him. He wanted more from her, more than she was willing, or even able, to divulge. Odd though it seemed, she could feel his interest pique with each cool rebuff she threw his way. Like scent, various other emotions wafted off the rest of those gathered: good humor, admiration, and mild resentment from the family; thinly veiled hostility from the Naturra servants. Coupled with his charmed curiosity, it created a turmoil of emotion too heady for comfort.

She ate sparingly, which was all she could manage with the ominous roiling of her stomach. Finally she excused herself, waving off all offers of company, and fled to the gardens thankful to have made her escape. Surely Elazar would not leave a feast held in his honor to follow her, nor would the rest of his family. With only one wrong turn which landed her briefly back in the laundry, Aryelle made her way outside, and sighed with relief. She often strolled here in the cool of the evening; it was the only place she could relax enough to think clearly. And thinking was definitely what was required now.

The enclosed formal gardens were actually quite simple, cultivated blooms giving way to groomed, segmented plots of woodland flowers between hedges that ran as straight as crisscrossed staffs. The aromas alone were breathtaking; how this layout compared to the future, exquisite beauty of Ladhonna's handiwork mattered little to someone who couldn't see. Walking unguided was easy for her here, much more so than in the maze of meandering corridors within Azadhar's residence, which could be so achingly familiar, then suddenly not. The pathways were bordered by waist-high shrubbery, a feature absent in her time. By brushing one hand along the trimmed hedges, turning alternately left and right, she would soon reach the tall, curved outer hedge which kept out the encroaching wilderness. Though she dared not wander alone out there, she felt drawn now to be as near the forest as possible, and as far away from *him*.

Elazar was going to be a problem. She had known it from the first, but what she hadn't known was how visceral a reaction she would have to him! It was almost as if he was herself in another form. His wit and willfulness mirrored hers so closely, time and gender notwithstanding, he could have *been* her. And vain though it sounded even to her ears, she was attracted to him.

What a tangled web!

If only she had confessed to Azadhar in the first place, told him who she really was, perhaps he would have understood, and possibly, even been able to help her return to her own time. But the charade had gone on far too long for her to turn back now. Azadhar was fair, but he was not a ruler to be toyed with. She would have to fix this herself somehow, and soon. In the meantime, she was going to have to steer clear of his son.

According to history, Elazar and Aridhina had married after a whirlwind romance. Their time together was brief however, ending in tragedy when Elazar was - *would be!* – killed in a Naturra uprising. Why that must be so she could not fathom. From her lessons she knew that he would attempt to reunite the two factions of Empaya, something she was still hoping to accomplish in her own time. It would be left to Aridhina, pregnant with twins, to carry on his mission. Slow progress would be made over the next few generations, but the Reign of Shadow would set things back even further. Her father Elazarin would all but abandon the cause. And she would pick it up again.

Had Mandlebrot sent her here to learn from the mistakes of the past? Or, by becoming Aridhina, was she meant to alter the river of time?

She wandered for some time mulling these mysteries. So troubling were her thoughts that Aryelle didn't hear, or otherwise sense, anyone approaching her until a hand touched her lightly on the shoulder, and she practically jumped out of her wings.

"*Dher na'phra!*" she cried, turning. "You scared the breath from me!" And then, reaching out with T'sura, she registered surprise, "It is you!"

"Yes, it is me!" The Naturra girl whom she had first encountered in the forest sounded as hostile as ever. "I saw you leaving the laundry, and followed you as soon as my duties ended. The head laundress thought you were me, and gave me quite the tongue lashing for shirking. She thought I was playing dress up with the finery."

"I remember your brother saying that you looked a bit like me. But what are you doing here? Is Lorian with you?" Surely Aryelle could not blamed her for her plight any more than before.

"Lorian is the only thing that stands between our siblings and starvation. Our parents both spend their days fetching for others, and now I, too, must labor for the Kandharra. But it is you who have much to explain! I have heard rumors about you, rumors that say you do not belong to the city as you claimed; that you were found... *and* that you have a new name."

"That is right. The El 'Kandhar himself dubbed me 'Aridhina' for the blue of my eyes." Aryelle didn't know why, but a shiver ran through her. "Aridhina means 'sky encircling the soul'-"

"I know what it means!"

"It is a beautiful name, really."

"And you cannot have it; it is already taken!"

"Surely there are many Aridhinas."

"I knew when first I saw you that you were not to be trusted!"

Aryelle was taken aback. "You are mistaken! I have never meant you harm."

"All the same," she announced, "you have. The name is mine!"

Aryelle's muddled thoughts made her slow to comprehend. She was unused to being accused; the blood pounding through her temples was too loud, too rapid for coherent thought.

Perhaps thinking that she had not understood, the girl repeated herself. "It is my name, given me by my parents."

"What are they called?" Aryelle asked, reaching for something, anything that made sense.

She answered reluctantly. "My father is Jolarian. Lodhina is my mother. My name comes from theirs, as is customary. And while you may take the life I might have had, you will not take my name!"

C. A. Morgan

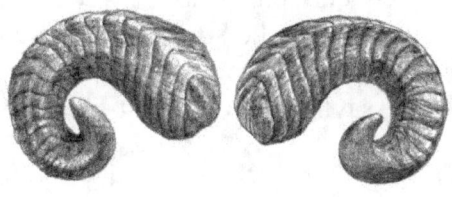

## *Chapter 14 – Tying the Knot*

After congratulating the happy young couple, Dornub hobbled back to bed. Morning would be soon enough to get the job done he told them, confiding that they should spend a bit more time getting acquainted, since they probably wouldn't be doing much talking once he left. Taking him at his word, Gord and Eleanor spent the rest of the night reliving their favorite stories for one another, and baring their souls. Eventually they fell asleep wrapped in each other's arms.

Early the next morning as promised, Dornub shook them both awake. After each had taken a few private minutes outside, they scraped together a sparse, cold breakfast from the cave's dwindling food cache. Dornub's hooves were no longer paining him so he said, and soon it neared time for him to leave. After a brief rummage through his pack, he came up with a length of rawhide cord. Eleanor and Gord stood solemnly before him, holding hands as he wrapped the cord snugly around their wrists and tied it off.

Taking their clasped hands between his he asked them, "Is it yer wish to be so tied, always and only to each other?" When they both started to answer, he interrupted them, saying, "Well, don't tell me! Tell each other!"

They turned and looked into one another's eyes. Gord smiled, and Eleanor practically glowed, happier than she could ever remember being. There was no moment but this, and all else fell away as she spoke the words newly written in her heart, "I choose you, Gord of Hope, to be mine."

And his heart answered, "I choose you, Eleanor of Cor, to be mine, always and forevermore."

"Then so be it, an' may it be a fruitful union too!" exclaimed Dornub, laughing, and they laughed along with him. "An' now, I'll be off!" he said, winking. "You can cut the cord when the day is up, but not yer promise."

They said their goodbyes, but neither one bothered to look up as he actually exited the cave, having eyes only for each other. If they had, they would have seen the flutter of wings as he flew into the open sky. It was just beginning to snow.

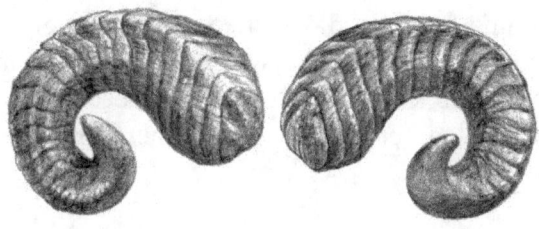

## Chapter 15 – Consummation

They kissed briefly, and then Gord swept Eleanor off her feet and carried her toward the back of the cave. Her head rested against his strong shoulder while the muscles of his broad chest flexed, and her mind raced ahead. But when he tried to squeeze through to the back chamber with her in his arms, they found they couldn't fit. Awkwardly, he set her down, and they shuffled single file through the narrow passageway.

Eleanor stepped into the chamber, stopped abruptly, and gasped. By the warm glow of Dornub's lantern, she saw that the peddler had prepared a beautiful bridal chamber for them. Little bottles and various metal trinkets twinkled with reflected light from a host of niches along the chamber walls, shimmering like far-flung constellations. A soft nest of blankets – she hadn't noticed there were fewer in the pile outside – was spread out in the center, the perfect size for two. To top it all off, and though it was entirely the wrong season for them, a small vase of her namesake flower graced the bedside.

Behind her, Gord whistled appreciatively. "May Cor, and all the gods, bless whatever happens here," he whispered. He kissed the top of her head, and sidling around her, led her further inside where their marriage bed awaited.


Later, curled in the comfort of one another's arms, they lay quietly talking. It had taken some interesting maneuvering to get comfortable with their wrists still bound, but they had somehow managed. Eleanor twirled a finger of her free hand in the thick hair of Gord's chest, nibbling playfully on his shoulder when he commented on her surprising lack of inhibition.

"Just because I waited for you, doesn't mean I wasn't interested!" she reminded him. "And what about you? For a ram who claims he's never done more than kiss a ewe, you sure seem to know what you're doing!" She blushed, remembering.

"It was worth the wait!" His eyes twinkled merrily. "But...how is it I am favored with all of these blushes? Perhaps Rosumbra does suit you as a name."

"And perhaps you'd prefer sleeping alone tonight!" she threatened.

"You could saw off my horns and I wouldn't mind as much!" he cried in mock alarm. "I take it all back!"

"All of it?" She rolled over to straddle him, sitting on his belly and pressing her forehead against his so tightly that his enormous horns could almost have been hers. A smirk belied her fierce stare, and sitting tall again, she broke into a full grin. He reached up and tickled her, delighted to find her extremely ticklish, and refusing to stop until she squealed for mercy. Taking advantage of her weakness he rolled atop her, and she squirmed helplessly beneath him. His lips pressed against hers again, and this time she did bite him, but only lightly.

"Ouch!" he complained, leaning back. "What did you do that for?"

"Just to keep you guessing," she laughed. "Tell me you would rather be bored."

After a moment he joined in laughing. "Oh, Eleanor, how have I ever gotten along so long without you?"

"I dunno. But I can't imagine you ever doing it again!"

"Me either." he agreed. Then pausing, he said "But seriously, my little warrior, I would not want you to be alone again if anything ever happened to me."

"Pah!" she scoffed, "I'm rather good at it. Besides, I'm not so sure I'll ever get used to sleeping with these big ol' horns of yours!" She reached up to rattle one and he grabbed hold of her wrist, startling her. Opening her hand, he kissed her palm and brought it to up to his cheek, his gaze so tender that she felt her heart melt. This was no time for teasing. He still wanted to take care of her. And now that they were tied, he always would. It would take some getting used to. She let her hand fall back to his chest, and his eyes shifted from her face to her shoulder.

"Tell me about this," he said, tracing her tattoo with the tip of his finger.

At his touch, a memory jolted through her, and she bucked him onto the floor of the cave in a desperate attempt to stand, unmindful of the cord that bound them. Bent over him, unable to breathe, she felt the walls begin to close in around her.

In choosing Gord, she had utterly forgotten one thing: She was not free to choose. She was already Chosen.

## *Chapter 16 – Live Bait*

Tad was a perfect gentleman.

When Lureli awoke a second time she found herself still snuggled in his lap, feeling relaxed and refreshed. He smiled sweetly down at her, undemanding and totally harmless, and she realized that she now felt safe in his arms. The novelty of it unlocked a door in her heart. Perhaps she could trust him as a friend, the one thing she'd never let herself do with a man. It was worth a try since there was no one else around. She still had problems; her way of thinking through things was to do it aloud, preferably with a sounding board. Not that she wanted his advice, but he had already proven his ears worked. She had a feeling he would be a good listener, too. So, through what would have been tears of self-pity had she been able to make them, she found herself pouring out her desperate tale, beginning with her mother's death and the part she now realized she had played in it. Her confession broke her own heart, softening it at the same time, and for once she heard herself as others must. Poisonous years of self-loathing worked their way to the surface as she rambled on, something she had never admitted to herself. So much had befallen her through her own poor choices, and now that she was opening up about it, the unresolved guilt she had carried for so long floated away like foam, along with her former life as a self-destructive victim. Emptied, her whole outlook brightened. Certainly some things were beyond her control, some wounds not self-inflicted, but she had wallowed long enough. It was time to pick herself up out of the mire and be her mother's daughter again – strong, independent, and ready to face life whether above or below the surface. Even life in a bubble.

Tad soaked up her words, and her change in attitude toward him. When she finally stopped speaking, he croaked, "Yuuuuuuup, that's right, but my legs are numb now, so if you wouldn't mind getting off...?"

"Tad! You can talk like a normal person!" Lureli exclaimed, jumping up.

"Yuuuuuuup. Whose ears are good ones now?" His satisfied grin turned into a grimace as he stretched out his sore muscles. Standing fully erect, he bowed stiffly at the waist.

She inclined her head in return, a rare blush staining her cheeks. "Thank you for listening. And I'm sorry about earlier. You just wouldn't let go and-"

"You gave me an earful and I deserved it – yuuuuuuup. I'll be good now, I promise." He crossed his arms over his chest. "Hands to self, and self to helping, that's what Taddy's here for."

"Oh, Tad!" she said, throwing her arms around him.

It was his turn to go red, an interesting combination with his green skin. His big eyes rolled back and forth and he stood stock still, not daring to breathe, but his grin said it all. When at last she pulled away, he swooned, blissfully content. It was clear there was nowhere in all Emrysia he would rather be.

That bubble was easily burst. "Now, let's concentrate on getting out of here, shall we?" said Lureli with renewed determination.

Tad sighed. "Yuuuuuuup."

Now that her mind was clear, it didn't take long for an idea to spark. How much easier it would be to dig right against the glass, and why hadn't she thought of that in the first place? She knew the enclosure wasn't solid beneath the sand; otherwise Tad would never have gotten in. She had been trying to dig in the very center of it, creating far more work for herself than was necessary, but all they really had to do was follow the glass down far enough and, hopefully, squeeze out underneath. They set to work immediately.

Tad, who was great at burrowing, turned out to be horrible at digging large, open holes. Using mostly his feet and not his hands, instead of emptying it, the excess sand filled back in around him, burying him up as he went. After a few minutes of this, Lureli bade him watch as she worked, thinking he would eventually catch on. It was awful at first. Her fingers were still raw from digging earlier. Then, remembering her bundle of belongings, she ran over and pawed through it, recovering the Aurrac horn cup. It would make a perfect scoop! She tossed the rest aside and began scooping sand out of the hole and dumping it to one side for Tad to brush away.

Sooner than she would have imagined they had a deepish crater, several feet wide and big enough to climb into. With Tad around she had no fear of it collapsing, even when the sand at the bottom began to get soupy, knowing he would pull her free if it fell in on her. As before, the slurry felt lovely, but having a friend she could count on was even more refreshing.

Suddenly Lureli felt the glass give way to sand, and knew she had reached the bottom edge of it. She began digging furiously, unmindful that the hole was rapidly filling in from the bottom. Tad, pushing away the wet sand as quickly as she scooped it out, looked up just in time to see the sea come rushing in. The force of it lifted Lureli off her feet as a powerful jet siphoned into the enclosure. Soaked in sea water, for an instant she was transformed, scales and fin replacing pale legs in a twinkling, and then changing back again as she hit the sand.

The sea continued to pour in, covering the floor of the enclosure, and Lureli was delirious with joy. She splashed in delight. Tad hopped in happy circles around her, dipping his head under once the water level grew deeper: one foot, two feet, three feet deep and more.

Soon it was deep enough to swim, and Lureli's tailfin reappeared for good. The two of them frolicked playfully in the circling current.

Their joyful abandon was short lived. Lureli was first to realize what was happening. As the water rose it was replacing breathable air - all well and good for her since she couldn't drown, but Tad was an amphibian, and would only be able to stay under so long. They had to get out of here! She tried to warn him in her native tongue so as to be understood under water, but he only shook his head. Pantomiming, she pointed toward the dwindling pocket of air above them, took his webbed hand, pulled him toward it.

"Ahhhh" he sighed as his head broke the surface. "Lovvvvvve it! Come on, let's swim some more! Tag – brrrrrawk – you're it!"

"Tad, the air is running out. What about breathing?"

"Who needs to breathe?"

"You do, don't you?"

"Yuuuuuuup, I suppose I do, since you say so."

"Well then, let's get out of here. We can find you a place on shore where I can visit. The water seems to be slowing down now-"

"But Taddy wants to stay here with you always!"

"No, Tad, I can't stay here either. I don't belong in a bubble. I belong in the sea with my people! And, you belong with yours...oh! Oh, Tad! You don't have people anymore, do you?"

"Miss can be my people," he said hopefully.

"I would love to be your people, Tad," she said, bobbing in the water. "But first we have to get out of here. Let's see if we can swim out through the hole we made, okay?"

"Nope, won't be able to," he said.

"We have to try," she insisted. "Come on, I need your help."

Reluctantly, he agreed. Taking a deep breath in the dwindling pocket of air, he followed her down to the bottom of the enclosure. Sand swirled where seawater continued to seep in, but the hole was gone. Lureli looked at Tad, and her eyes began to fill with panic. He held up his hands in a gesture meant to calm, and pointed back toward the surface. Lureli shook her head. She began to claw at the sand, but the seawater only pumped in faster. When she stopped, the sand settled back to a slow roil.

There would be no more digging.

Tad took her by the hand and led her back to the top of the bubble where they could talk.

"We're still trapped!" Lureli wailed once her head rose above water level. The pocket of remaining air was half the size as before. "Oh, no! Water is going to keep seeping in, Tad; what are we going to do?!"

"Be happy?" he answered.

"No, this is serious! We've got to think! Maybe you can stand to stay here until you die, but not me!" She looked around wildly, searching for some way out that they may have overlooked, but there was nothing. Eventually she hung her head in defeat. It was hopeless.

Tad reached over and stroked her cheek. Tenderly, he cupped her chin to make her look at him. "Miss won't die. Taddy will never let that happen. Brrrrrawk – we'll wait it out. There will be enough air, you'll see. Someone will come - brrrrrawk. It will be alright."

Searching deep into his caring eyes, she tried hard to believe him.

Elsewhere under the sea, seated on his coral throne with trident in hand, Orpheas felt a shifting of the current, and looked up.

C. A. Morgan

## *Chapter 17 – Trapped*

"Hurry, Ladhelle!"

"I am coming, Dharra, keep your wings tucked! She may not have even gone this way."

"She did too. She always seeks the gardens nearest the forest, though how she could prefer that smelly old wilderness over the scent salons I will never know! And do not call me Dharra! Short names are vulgar."

The duo's approach sent the real Aridhina scurrying while Aryelle turned her head to listen. As they turned toward the hedgerow, the Naturra girl disappeared around the topiary at the other end of the row. There was no calling for her to wait; Aryelle was dumbstruck.

"See, I told you she would be here!" said Jadharra triumphantly. She circled, inspecting her like a prize trophy.

"Are you unwell, Ari?" asked Ladhelle, finally catching up. "You look ashen."

"I...I am...not, um, unwell" she stammered, "though I believe I need to lie down..."

"Quickly, Dharra, take her other arm. There, there – something has shaken you. Can you tell us what it is?"

Aryelle only shook her head. The hand she held out to her was trembling so badly that the other girl took and tucked it under her arm to still it. Jadharra went around to her other side, and they supported her between them. The girls exchanged worried looks as they helped their friend back to her rooms, several flytes up in the royal residence. She spoke not once the entire time. Though neither girl was adept at discerning what ailed her, both knew something was horribly wrong. When Aryelle refused offer of their continued company at her door, they hurried off to inform the El'Kandhar of her worrisome state.


Azadhar and his heir had withdrawn after the feast to the El'Kandhar's study, and were embroiled in a fierce game of valleo. The game board - a wide-brimmed, shallow burl bowl - was smoothed to a glassy finish and riddled with evenly gouged, round depressions. It balanced on a solid concave pedestal, gliding this way and that at the slightest pressure from the two competitors, who faced off over it with their fingers resting along its rim. The skittle – a round, green-picked valleo nut - skipped around the edges as the bowl tilted to and fro, bringing shouts of glee or groans of defeat, depending on who was defending or challenging. Elazar had just scored against his father when Jadharra burst into the room uninvited. Ladhelle hovered just outside the door.

"Dadher, you must do something! Aridhina has a secret and she will not tell!"

"Eh, what is this?" he asked not looking up from his game. "A secret? M'yana, everyone has secrets."

"What Jadharra means, sire, is the secret is making her ill," Ladhelle filled in timidly from the doorway.

The skittle settled into a hole and Azadhar gave a triumphant bark. "Hah!" He turned then to look at them. "Come in, child, come in. Ill, you say? She looked well enough at dinner, would you not say so, my son?"

"Very well, Father - exceedingly well even."

Azadhar's lips twitched in amusement. The boy was transparent as ever. It was good that his motives were so pure. He glanced at Ladhelle, and then probed a bit further with his mind, undetected by her. There was no jealously there; that was good. There would be no contesting the match on her end, at least. And now, since Aridhina was a full revolution older, there need be no waiting! That was sure to please Elazar as much as it did him. His second son would certainly be happy with this new development, too. Ah, things were settling themselves quite nicely. Soon most of his children would be wed, and none too soon. He wasn't getting any younger.

"Perhaps she is love-struck," he said, grinning. "My handsome heir, newly returned, might have something to do with that."

"Bleh! No, Dadher," said Jadharra, "she is not pining for Elazar. Not every commoner wants to marry a royal! She dreaded even meeting him."

Elazar frowned. "Why would she do that?"

"Who knows? She acts so strangely sometimes, like the world is coming to an end and she alone must save it! Perhaps she is too busy for love with all of her trying."

"I will go speak with her-"

"Nay, leave her be, Elazar," advised Azadhar. "She is bright; she will figure out what is bothering her, and then she will tell us herself. That one is not afraid to speak her mind, and I like her all the more for it. Less silliness." He dismissed the two girls with a flick of his hand, and they left the room twittering. Azadhar smiled, ever the indulgent parent, and turned his attention back to his son. "She would make a fine addition to this family," he added, winking, and spun the valleo bowl on its stand challenging him to another match.

Night fell heavily on Aryelle's heart. After hours of pacing her chamber (and two more stubbed toes!) her burden felt no lighter. Spring had fled headlong into winter, not summer; the days lengthening for others, but not for her. All was night and no light, it seemed, could penetrate this present darkness; instead, it grew blacker. It would continue to do so too, unless she put an end to it. Armed with that knowledge, she knew what she must do. Or undo, to be more accurate. She must stop pretending. Lies, like termites, multiplied exponentially; they corrupted from within unless caught early. She would go to Azadhar, confess her deception, and try to set things right before the whole tree came tumbling down. Hopefully it wasn't too late.

*If only I find him alone*, she thought, silently opening her door. Barefoot and in a simple silk sleeping shift, she tiptoed into the polished corridor. Taking her bearings, she concentrated. T'sura confirmed for her that one else was near. Thankful for the privacy of the royal quarters, she turned in the direction of the El'Kandhar's study and felt her way along. After all this time, there were few corridors she was confident enough to walk alone, but this was one of them. She had spent many an enjoyable afternoon in that comfortable room discussing the Kandharra's relationship with the Naturra, and the last time she had ventured there, it was at the El'Kandhar's behest to consult with him on a particularly tricky passage in the Book of Illumination. Honored that he had trusted her so completely as to seek her counsel, she balked now at the thought that she must betray that trust, and almost turned back.

Instead, turning left as the corridor came to a "T", she continued on past three closed doors, entering a completely glassed-in hallway that dipped and rose along the contours of the branch on which it was built. The slow growing valleo hadn't altered overmuch, though the city itself had greatly expanded by her day. This had been (would be?) one of her favorite places as

C. A. Morgan

a child, providing unlimited hours of entertainment. She and Karril had held races here, rolling everything possible up and down its slopes - including themselves, wrapped in the pods of their own wings. She found it much less entertaining now that she was blind and unsure of her footing, though somehow she managed.

Just as she reached the top of the slope where the floor began to level out again, a large object slammed into the glass beside her head and ricocheted off. Reflexively she ducked, a gasp escaping her lips as she shied away from the glass. It must have been a large bird, or bat more like, since she knew full well it must be dark. Calling herself silly, she straightened and took another step. A second something – this time a rock! - crashed through the glass, sailing past just in front of her, and spraying shattered glass across the floor. Shaken, she let out a little cry as another rock hit the glass behind her – cracking, though not breaking it.

Aryelle froze, not knowing what to do. Rocks did not fling themselves at glass hallways. Someone was throwing them - someone who was purposefully trying to hurt her! But who? And, more importantly, why?

She crouched down, making herself a smaller target as yet another rock rebounded off the glass. She was too exposed, that much she knew, and she must get out of this hallway! She leaned forward intending to crawl the rest of the way, but putting weight on her hand, a jagged shard bit painfully in her palm. A deep gash opened. Blood splattered as, unthinking, she shook the shard free. Now blood poured from the wound, painting the hallway crimson.

A solid wall and safety lay just ahead, the way littered with glass, and slick now with her blood. Terrified and alone, in utter darkness, she could not tell how badly she was hurt, or whether it was fear or blood loss that was making her so dizzy. Clutching her wounded hand, she slid backward to the valley in the middle of the hallway. But as she tried to scamper up the opposite side back the way she had come, another rock sailed through the glass, strewing its shrapnel before her. With her heart pounding out of her chest, she slid back to the center – trapped, and the perfect target!

Whimpering and covered in blood, she curled into a tight ball and hoped for someone to save her.

C. A. Morgan

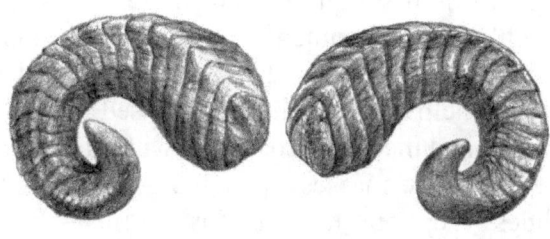

## *Chapter 18 – Till Death We Part*

Eleanor awoke drenched in sweat and bellowing her outrage.

"Whoa, little one, settle down! Everything is fine. You are still right here with me." Gord leaned over her, stroking her hair and murmuring softly. Eleanor turned her head and tried to get her bearings, focusing finally on his concerned face, which she could just make out in the dimmed light of the lantern. She stared at him in disbelief, and then threw both arms around him, clinging like a frightened child.

The dream had been too real, too frightening. She shuddered recalling it.

Borrac, his leg still broken, was riding on a litter carried by the children of the lower village, and he was still after her. He whipped and beat the children, trying to make them go faster. When they couldn't keep up, they started falling one by one along the trailside. But he would not be thwarted. He stood up on the litter – it looked like Lureli's – and started shouting pure gibberish, which she could somehow understand. In his arrogance, he was calling on the gods of this and every mountain to help him. He shook his raised fist, thundering at them, and they, in turn, shook with fury, throwing down their bulky masses upon the Aurrac clanherds. Landslides, eruptions, furious dust storms - on every single peak and hillside the clans suffered. None were spared the devastation. Afterwards, she wandered from mountain to mountain, village to village, and everywhere there was wailing and ruin. In one of the villages, someone recognized her from the games. He – it looked like Nashor - called to the other villagers, all of them stained with birthmarks just like Nodd's. Those who were able to hurled stones at her, driving her from their midst; she ran until, suddenly, she was in the cave again, kissing Gord, loving him...and then the cave walls disappeared. The angry mob rained boulders down on top of them. She managed to back away, but Gord was crushed before her very eyes. She reached out for him, and instead found herself falling backward, ever deeper into a dark and endless well. In the wet, black night that surrounded her, Aryelle and Lureli led angry hordes of their own peoples, who slashed at her with swords until her blood had soaked them all. And ringing through it all, the sound of Borrac's insane laughter...

"It was only a dream, my love, only a dream." Gord kissed her tenderly. If shaken himself by what she described, he did not show it, trying only to comfort her. "Don't concern yourself with dreams – only what's real; with you and me. Come" he said, rolling out of bed. "Let's step outside and get some fresh air. We've been cooped up for too long and with little but love in our bellies. Hunting will do you good."

"No!" she cried vehemently. "We have to stay inside! We can't go out there!"

"Eleanor! You're just being silly now; where's my strong warrior?"

"I am not silly!" she snapped, embarrassed that he should find her weak. She stood up where she was, the blankets in a puddle around her ankles. "I just...it shook me, that's all."

"I can see that," he said, stepping back toward her "but really, there's nothing to fear. You're just worried about your village, and in a few days we'll see for ourselves that everything is just fine." He reached out to tuck a loose strand of hair behind her ear. Dangling from his wrist was the broken cord.

Both of them stared, and then looked toward her arm and the matching end of the cord. Gord tried to shrug it off. "I guess we got a little carried away, huh? It must have been almost worn through. I didn't even notice."

The small hairs on the back of Eleanor's neck prickled. She wasn't superstitious, she never had been, but the coincidence was more than disturbing. Maybe it was a sign. "I'm sorry, Gord. I should have known better. We never should have let Dornub tie the knot for us."

"What!? You think this means something? It doesn't!"

"But I'm one of the Chosen-"

"I heard that prophesy too, and I don't believe it any more than you do! You said yourself Accora was a fool, and that you never intended on going along with it."

"The fairy and mermaid-"

"You don't owe them a thing. This means nothing to us - his prophesy means nothing! Now, come on!" he said. Turning his back on her he kicked aside the blankets, and started toward the passage to the front cavern.

"But-"

"No buts!" he proclaimed, turning to face her. "You are mine now; we-" he qualified, his tone mellowing, "-belong to each other. I never should have talked of dying before. That's what got you thinking like this."

Eleanor wasn't sure why his words rankled, but for some reason they did. She wasn't being irrational; Borrac was still after her. And, even if she didn't believe in Accora's prophesy, Mandelbrot was real. The Connectedness Locus was real. The *danger* was real. And somewhere out there, Aryelle and Lureli were still counting on her to call them back together. While it was true, her main concern right now was him, he wasn't her only one. Belonging to him was what she wanted more than anything; if she was going to have to face what was to come, she wanted to do it with him still by her side. There was only one way she could think of to keep him safe.

"You're right," she conceded, "it was just a dream. But...I don't want to go outside just yet. Come back to bed."

The lantern began to sputter. Soon the cave would be left in total darkness, and then they would have to feel their way out. Eleanor put on her most seductive smile and held her hand out to him. And he came to her.

Sometime during the night, Gord woke up to a chamber that was gloomier than a tomb. He couldn't even see Eleanor's head resting on his shoulder, though he felt her chin digging into it. He shifted, and she rolled over in her sleep, snoring softly. He lay for a while beside her in the dark, hands folded under his head while he thought. She had almost convinced him, but not quite. Responding to his love making, throwing herself into it even, she had seemed to enjoy it as much as he did. Even so, he could tell she was distracted.

It wasn't like her to be so frightened by a dream. Weakness was not something she tolerated well in herself or others. He was the same way. Illness was one thing; everyone got sick occasionally. And he had actually enjoyed caring for her, watching her health return, but this dream business was another story. How could he help when she was being so ridiculous? He had thought she was stronger than that, but obviously she had a softer side too. He had to say, he preferred her rough edges, though he supposed it would be nice to have her need him a little bit. When they had lambs of their own, he could count on her to protect them fiercely, but there would still be room for him as her protector.

He decided not to wake her now that she was sleeping so peacefully, but neither did he want to have her wake up and not be able to see anything in this pitch black. If he felt his way quietly to the outer chamber, there would probably be enough light for him there to get a fire going. When she woke, its glow would tell her where he was, and lead her through the passage into the other chamber. Carefully, so as not to disturb her, he tucked the blanket in around her and rolled out of bed. He nearly tipped over the dark lantern, but caught it just in time. Picking it up, he carried it with him, treading as lightly as he could over the uneven surface. He staggered in the direction memory led, the click of his hooves on the rocky cave floor sounding like drum beats to his ears. Eleanor snored on. Luck was with him, and his outstretched hands found the opening almost immediately. He squeezed through.

The fire started easily enough. Well banked nearly a day ago, there were still a few coals to work with. The stacked wood was well seasoned, and caught flame at once. He built up a roaring blaze, for it had grown chilly in the caves. Once the fire was made, he puttered around waiting for Eleanor to wake up. He folded the blankets from where they had slept singly, and put a pot of soaked grains near the fire to simmer. They were near the end of their stores, and he thought with longing on the food cache he had built up for the villagers. When she still hadn't roused by the time breakfast was ready, he decided the call of nature could wait no longer, and stepped outside.


Eleanor awoke to the sound of thunder so loud the mountain shook with it. She sat up, rubbing her eyes, letting them adjust to the flickering light that was coming from the outer chamber. Gord must have started a fire. *Good,* she thought as the rumbling continued. It must be storming outside - snow thunder, a rarity. Maybe they were already snowed in, and she would have to agree to spend an extra day here where they could be alone - *if* he asked nicely. Dornub would be slowed down by the storm too, so it would pose no problem. In fact, she began to look forward to it. She yawned and stretched, a smile playing across her lips as she recalled the previous night. Day *and* night, she reminded herself. Their lovemaking had been playful and fierce, and later, slow and tender. It had not completely erased the nightmare from her mind, but with a full night's rest in Gord's arms, she realized that he was right. It was nothing to worry about.

She could smell the wood fire now and...was that porridge burning? Oh well, it was about time he hung up his apron and let her do a little of the cooking, not that the result would be much better. She forced herself to stay put a little while longer just to prove she wasn't worried by his absence, then rolled off the bed and tidied it. After that, she made her way to the outer chamber. A fire burned steadily in the pit, though with a bit more smoke than usual, but Gord was nowhere to be seen. Chiding herself for the sudden rush of panic she felt, she forced herself to think calmly. He had started the fire and breakfast, and then most likely stepped outside to relieve himself. Cor knew, she felt the need too. Eleanor moved toward the opening, noticing how little light was streaming through the mottled fleece hanging. The storm had quieted now, though it might not yet be over. Gord was likely just outside if snow was still coming down. She would try not to embarrass him. After waiting several moments, when he failed to come back inside, she decided her need was greater. She pulled aside the fleece. Instead of her mate, found herself staring at a solid wall of white.

## *Chapter 19 – Bigger Fish*

At last the sea stopped leaking in. There was only a
head's height or so of breathable air left. And, when the
sand finally settled and the water cleared, the seafloor
beneath them was level. Not even a depression remained to mark where their hole had been.

Now they had all the water they needed, yet their
situation seemed even more hopeless. Despite that, they
made a tasty snack of the few little fishes that had been
sucked in along with the sea water, enough to stave off
their gnawing hunger. To conserve air, and to distract
herself from fretting about their circumstances, Lureli
decided to teach Tad Glisseon. Maybe he was right, and
help was on the way; at least he would be able to com-
municate with them. Besides, it would pass the time.
Keeping her head underwater so that she wouldn't use
up his limited air supply, she would say a phrase in her

native tongue and wait for his reply. His hearing was amazing both above and below the surface, and he was a remarkably quick study. In a matter of hours they were able to converse almost as fluidly underwater as above. What's more, now that Tad didn't have to keep refilling his air sack midsentence, he began to stay under for longer and longer periods, soaking up everything she had to say, fascinated with her every word. Eventually, while regaling him with a funny story about an overly amorous moray eel, it dawned on her that he wasn't holding his breath anymore. He was breathing underwater! Hope swelled in her chest - she didn't even care how he was doing it. They weren't out of the water just yet, but at least he wasn't going to drown.

Things started to look a little less bleak. Now that Tad understood Glisseon, the time was passing so much more quickly. In fact, Tad the Gentleman was such good company that she realized she was actually enjoying herself. She could even entertain the idea of being stranded here with him for a few more days if necessary. Though she hoped it wouldn't be so, the thought made her smile.

Tad caught her smiling and grinned back. His pupils widened till they filled his eyes, and she could see herself reflected in them.

That's when she noticed his color.

Despite his grin, Tad was beginning to look decidedly peaked. No longer a healthy emerald green, he could now only be described as pale puce. Maybe that was normal for Anuran, she tried to convince herself. Or maybe his sickly shade was the physical manifestation of being lovesick. Or - she hated to even consider this possibility - maybe the salt water was finally getting to him. What if his kind were only suited for life in fresh water?

A fleeting shadow passed over the enclosure. Lureli blinked, and wondered if she was seeing things. Then out of the corner of her eye she saw another dark shape dart past, first one way, then the other. Finally; something was moving out there. Someone was coming for them at last. She craned her head trying to see who it was.

Suddenly, a tentacle twice as thick as her waist slapped against the side of their bubble and stuck there. It was followed by another, and another, until they were engulfed in the writhing, puckered grasp of a giant squid! Strange, luminescent colors rippled up and down its spearheaded body. The size of it was enormous! Unblinking, its giant eye peered in at them.

Lureli squealed. Not quite the rescue she was hoping for, but this creature - a cephalopod - was no stranger to her. Squid of its size were quite rare, and fiercely territorial. They were also determined hunters, and extremely good problem solvers, as anyone from the undersea realm could tell you. Lureli was almost certain she had seen this particular one before, lurking in the shadows near the Asylum. Its powerful arms could pry open any shell; she had seen its viselike grip in action, stealing lobsters from Glisseon traps. If there was a seam or crevice, it was sure to find a purchase, and once it did, then watch out! If it was able to free them, they would have to swim for their lives.

But...with nothing to grab onto she was certain it would be unable to breach their bubble. Here inside the smooth, solid glass dome, there was really nothing to worry about.

Until Tad went berserk.

Ping-ponging off the glass as each suckered tentacle slapped against it, Tad grew ever more frantic. Swimming in crazed circles that stirred up another whirlpool, he searched for somewhere to hide. Lureli called out for him to stop, but it was no use. He was terrified of snakes, and this creature was a writhing nest of them! When its abdomen pressed against the glass revealing a horrifying claw-like beak that opened menacingly, he nearly fainted dead away. Instead, he started to burrow.

Choking on sediment, Lureli reached out and grabbed him, not letting go even when he struggled to get away. Her hair caught in the current, streaming around them both. Over and over she called his name, but his glazed eyes barely registered that he heard. Finally he went limp in her arms, and she knew he was going into shock.

Outside, the giant squid slid over and around - such a strange shell! It could see but not reach them. It was hungry, and wouldn't give up easily, not with its prey so beautifully displayed. It would find a way in.

Had she known better, Lureli would have been more worried, but she only frowned, wishing it would simply go away, and stop scaring Tad. She needed him to stay with her. Without him she'd be lost. She had to calm him down, make him see that they were safe, at least for the time being. Sitting on the seabed as the sediment settled around them, she stroked his pale face, shielding it against her bosom. Softly she crooned into his ear, soothing songs of the sea that her parents had sung to her. No fears, no worries, such were the songs of the Glisseon, songs that men were irresistibly drawn to. Songs to send unsuspecting sailors to their watery demise, she realized suddenly, and stopped singing.

What was she doing?

Tad blinked, seeing her again, adoring her as before. His eyes locked on hers, and in them she saw trust and utter devotion. But that had always been there, hadn't it?

Realizing what she had done, she felt sick. Was she really any better than that stupid squid? She had never really thought about it before; the Glisseon preyed on men, not for food, but for attention. Singing their songs they made slaves of those who survived, harnessing them for labor and protection as much as anything else, holding them captive through enchantment. And when the time was right, they made them over into Glisseon. The survival of their race depended on it. They never even considered whether or not it was right.

Looking at Tad, his feet still buried in sand, she saw him as if for the first time. She had taken him away from all he had ever known without even thinking. It was her fault he was here. It was Lake Mirth all over again, though she hadn't meant to enslave him, really. She just didn't want to be alone.

She saw how sick he looked, even sicker than she felt, as he smiled wanly up at her. And for once, she had the most unselfish thought of her life.

"Tad...you have to go. I think the seawater is making you sick."

"I'm fine wherever you are," Tad managed to croak, though his gaze wandered to what was happening outside, and he shuddered.

"No, listen to me!" she said, following his gaze. "I know you want to stay here with me. And I know you're afraid of the giant squid, too. But if you don't get out, get back to the surface and dry land with fresh water, you'll die! I couldn't bear that on my conscience."

"But, Miss-"

"No buts, Tad. Burrow out of here, and come up far enough away that you aren't seen. Head for the shelf, due east. This squid... is my friend. I'll distract it for you. I won't let it hurt you."

"I could never leave you here alone! I love you!" He struggled to right himself.

Rising, she turned away. "I don't love you, Tad. I never will."

"But-"

"Just leave already! Leave or I'll scream so loud and high the glass will shatter! I can do it, even underwater, you know. The squid will get you; it'll get us both!"

With that she began pushing him toward the sea floor, beating his head and chest with her fists when he resisted. He threw up his arms to protect himself, and she flicked sand over him with her tail. Outside, the squid slid over the dome in agitation.

"Go away, Tad! Get out! That's an order!"

With one long, last heartbreaking look, Tad gave up and continued to burrow. Sand settled in around him. In no time at all, he was up to his knees, then his waist, and finally his thick neck. Then he was gone.

Watching him go, she knew it was for the best. Even so, Lureli's heart was nearly breaking. He would never know it now, but in her own way, she loved him more than she had ever loved anyone. The funny thing about living underwater, she thought, watching the shifting sand grow still, is that no one can tell when you cry.

Outside the bubble, the giant squid went wild with frustration. One of them had escaped; might not the other? It writhed in fury, following Lureli's every movement. But instead of disappearing, she swam to the farthest point from where her friend had burrowed out, and leaned against the side of the glass dome. The squid tightened its grip, redoubling its efforts.

Lureli slid to the sand and waited.

C. A. Morgan

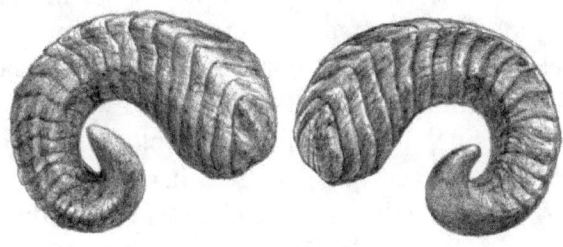

## *Chapter 20 – Buried Alive*

She dug until her fingers bled, screaming Gord's name, cursing the gods and Borrac most of all. The fire she smothered with snow when the smoke got so thick on the cave's ceiling that she feared she would suffocate. Fearing it had already used up too much air and that she would die before she got to him, she dug even faster.

Eventually she wore herself out, and fell asleep leaning against the snow. She woke with a start after just a few moments. Wrapping her hands with strips torn from the fleece doorway hanging, she used whatever else she could find to dig with: the horn cup he had first given her to sip from; their shared spoon; the pot blackened by fire with charred remnants of the last meal he had prepared still clinging to it. She dug until she knew it was nightfall by the intense darkness seeping through the snow, and then, in total gloom, dug into the night.

When morning came she was still digging, widening the hole she had managed to hollow in hopes that she would find Gord safe in some depression against the rocky mountainside. As the sun rose higher and she burrowed further, she was surrounded by light on almost every side, and still she felt no closer to reaching the snow's surface. She sensed her mind slipping, thinking this was what it looked like when the mountain peak was in the clouds. She began to drift, to imagine that cloud was all it was. Or...maybe she was already dead and didn't know it. She was certainly cold. Wasn't it supposed to be more pleasant where the gods dwelt? She vaguely remembered cursing them, but couldn't for the life of her remember why. She wondered; if she *was* dead, was she allowed to build a fire? She wandered back inside the cave and saw the fire pit swimming with melted snow. It wasn't so bad in here, though; less cold, and the dim light more soothing. Maybe she should just wrap up in a blanket, lie down, and rest awhile. Then she could dig some more. But...why?

Her eyes drifted shut, and she leaned against the cave wall. Being dead sure was strange, she thought as she fell into a deep and troubled sleep.

## *Chapter 21 – Thy Father's Will*

"You were very fortunate."

"She was more than fortunate! 'Fate's hand guides the most unlikely instruments' - is that not how the saying goes? How ironic; instead of driving you away, they drove you straight into Elazar's arms!" Ladhelle's smile was beatific.

It was mid-summer again, and the lush gardens were in full bloom. The three girls were wandering the garden pathways, not straying far from the Mother Tree. Since the attack, Aryelle had grown nervous about venturing too far from safety. Talk about irony! She had suffered so many trials since leaving her sheltered life behind, and faced far greater dangers, yet all it took was an unknown assailant throwing stones to reduce her to the helplessness of a fallen hatchling.

"We all knew you two were well-suited," Ladhelle continued. "I, for one, am glad that you know it now, too.

Aryelle blushed prettily, crimson cheeks to rosy wingtips. She could hardly believe that she and Elazar were betrothed - how far from her original intent that night!

When Elazar left his father's study and found her curled in a pool of her own lifeblood amid all that shattered glass, he had scooped her into his arms unmindful of his own safety. As she clung to him like a terrified infant, he ran back to his father's study, where the two of them performed the assumption that would save her.

She owed Elazar her life; how could she not give him her heart?

The future would take care of itself, she rationalized. Who was she to think that she possessed the power to change anything, unless, of course, she was meant to? No action of hers would matter later, because later there could be no comparison. If Elazar had not found her in time, there would have been no future for her, this one or otherwise. She was alive right now, and that was what counted.

Though she might never see him again, she knew her father would understand.

Besides, she could see again! The assumption had healed more than just her injuries. Amazing, yet true, the T'sura had vanished along with the rest of her wounds. In her day, such was unheard of. She was later told that under normal circumstances they would have asked her first, since some with the T'sura felt that they had earned it. There were benefits after all, though that way of thinking was an unpopular one. But it was why no one had offered to heal her of it before. Elazar however, had taken it upon himself to "fix" this one little flaw in the helpmate of his dreams whilst he had the opportunity. Aryelle couldn't be more grateful! The El'Kandhar and his heir were powerful healers indeed! All were in this time. Even children were encouraged to use their light, instead of saving it for themselves, and grew all the more accomplished for their practice. Contrary to what she had been taught, spending one's light did not cause it to burn out; it made one's flame grow brighter. And now, with vision restored and her own bright flame still blazing, she fit right in. Mandelbrot had sent her back in time to have her eyes opened that she might see again, yes, but also opened to the fact that this was where she truly belonged!

Part of the reason that the city was open to outsiders, she began to realize, was so that the luminaries would have more opportunities to grow their skills. It was both logical and mutually beneficial. It also explained why the Naturra were merely tolerated; they did not need healing since they healed themselves. No one questioned the delight the Kandharra took in their own healing abilities. Aryelle recognized their vanity and accepted it – for the time being. She herself would not succumb again to healing merely for vanity's sake, and perhaps it would be her lot to make them see their folly. Since her own assumption though, she had been privileged to witness and participate in many others, and could feel her skill growing. She had even learned to

C. A. Morgan

call upon the light to shield herself and others from harm, a skill practically lost in her own time. If only she had known how before! Then again, it may not have mattered, as she was taken by surprise.

"Father is still trying to discover who attacked you," said Jadharra. "We know they were Naturra; there are rumors of an all out revolt brewing, but no one knows why you were singled out." She plucked a gaillardia blossom and began to tug off the flame-like petals one by one, tossing them aside.

"Well…" said Ladhelle, "I think I might know. The Naturra have always resented you being here and calling yourself Empayan. They do not claim you, and though you might not remember where you come from, you are certainly not from the city itself or someone would have recognized you. They wonder who you are and what you are doing here."

"How do you know? Who have you been talking to?" Jadharra asked skeptically.

It was Ladhelle's turn to blush. Aryelle guessed that she had been paying attention to the maids' gossip. No wonder she did not want to say. Jadharra adamantly refused to believe that anything a Naturra said was worth repeating. How could she be so different from her brother? Elazar not only went out of his way to interact with the Naturra, he even occasionally dirtied his hands working alongside them. Perhaps that was why one of them had tried to scare her off. Azadhar had begun the work of improving relations by bringing them back into the city; with Elazar posed to be the next El'Kandhar, he was in a position to effect even greater change. If they thought she shared the views of most Kandharra, and had gained both his favor *and* his ear, they might think their future was in jeopardy.

But Elazar was not the one that would keep that flame burning, Aridhina was – *she would be!* History was clear; the task of reuniting the Empaya was not a simple one. It would take many lifetimes to achieve. Still an unfinished dream in her own time, was she up to what would be demanded of her in this one? Would she be able to break through to both the Naturra and Kandharra, setting their reunification in motion? Would she in fact change history? And what of the other Aridhina? Was she truly the one meant for the life she was leading? She did not know, and perhaps she never would. Aryelle had not run into her since that fateful night, though admittedly she had not visited the laundry again either. She was trying to avoid the fact that if she stayed in this time, as she now intended to do, Aridhina would remain just as she was; a servant whose name and life she may have stolen.

"Well," continued Jadharra when neither of them responded, "I would rather Father make an example of one of them, guilty or not, and just get it over with. We cannot have this tension ruining the wedding. Oh! I forgot to tell you, Ari. Mother said you should come for a fitting. I cannot keep standing in for you, you know. Your wedding robes will end up far too short!"

"Nor I!" cried Ladhelle, who was glad to have so narrowly escaped them.

So far, Aryelle had put off thinking about the actual wedding as much as possible. Would that it was enough to have contracted with Elazar! At first, it was all that mattered, and she convinced herself that she was happy. She might not actually love him, though she was fond of him, but thinking about marriage meant thinking about bearing his children, which led, sorrowfully, to thoughts of losing him before they even took their first breath. Twins would be conceived on their marriage bed, should written history remained unaltered – twins that would grow up fatherless. It was the part of this future that she hated thinking about, part she could never admit to foreseeing.

"Please, Ladhelle, just this once," Aryelle begged of her. "I promise that next time I will go myself, but you know how uncomfortable Jacharra makes me. I think she tells the seamstress to jab me on purpose."

"You really must make peace with her, Ari. She will be your mother soon, too."

Aryelle batted her lovely green eyes, and Ladhelle capitulated.

"Alright, just this once… though if I take a needle for you, it will cost you your wings!"

Both girls hurried off, leaving Aryelle alone with her thoughts, which had begun to grow increasingly dark. She strolled a while, glancing occasionally over her shoulder, before settling onto an ornate bench surrounded by the perfume of a thousand orchids. The scent salons really were lovely, she admitted, as she watched a large moth settle onto one particularly delicate pink petal. While blind, she had found them overpowering, but now that she could see the fragile beauty behind it, she could appreciate their heady fragrance.

She sat awhile before she realized the smell was making her head ache. Or was it her racing mind? Abruptly she stood up to leave, and the moth fluttered away.

"Ah, a rose among the weeds!" exclaimed Elazar, turning into the far end of the path and coming toward her. His wings gave a little flutter as if he would fly, but thinking better of it, he broke into a trot instead. "What are you doing out here all alone?"

He had become a bit overprotective of her, which was understandable, she supposed. But nervous as she was herself about a repeat attack, she had always chaffed at such treatment. This time however, she bit her lip as he took her hand and kissed it.

"What? No barbed retort?" he teased playfully. "Who is this green-eyed maiden impersonating my Aridhina?"

Innocent enough words. Still, she pulled her hand away, choking back a sob.

"My dear one, *mi'qua!* What is wrong? Have I said something to offend?"

Aryelle collected herself enough to answer, "No, I just..." but words escaped her. Instead, she reached out and stroked his cheek with genuine affection, an act which brought on real tears. How often would she be reminded of her charade? How many times would she miss him ere he was actually gone?

Elazar was beside himself. He had just come from seeing Ladhelle in wedding robes - and looking quite lovely, too - to find his betrothed, his willful Aridhina, practically blubbering herself silly. Where had that strong young woman gone?

He took both of her hands in his this time, speaking with great patience. "I suppose you are as jittery as any bride, even more so that we are to be wed so soon. I do not mind so terribly, do you? Father does not believe in the customary waiting period. 'When your heart knows what it wants, my boy, you must take it!' he says. I suppose that is why he has had so many wives! But not to worry, Aridhina," he said as he realized that he was rambling. "Should I ever lose you, I would never love another!"

His words were like a dagger. Aryelle could no longer contain her tears as fresh guilt washed over her. She tore free and ran back to the Mother Tree, leaving him shaking his head after her.

******

"How can you say she is not the one after all? What could have happened to change your heart?" Azadhar was dumbfounded. He had loved each of his wives fiercely, even though it had never taken long before new love filled his heart after their passing.

"My heart has not changed," said Elazar, though admittedly it had perhaps cooled a bit. "But Aridhina is not herself of late. The attack was one thing, though I found it hard to believe she had never learned to shield herself. Uncontrollable weeping every time she looks at me is quite another. I cannot have her falling apart when things get difficult-" he plowed ahead sensing Azadhar's objection, "-as you know well they will."

He was right, of course, about the Naturra and about Aridhina. Azadhar had seen for himself how bad it was getting, and pitied the girl. What was it about her? She was a mystery, practically falling out of the blue, knowing things no outsider should know - *by his wings!* She knew things hidden to even him! Perhaps such things were troubling her now.

"Let me speak to her first, before you make any rash decisions," he said. "But know this: you must marry, and soon, my son. It may not be long ere my own T'sura sets in, and I wish to see my grandchildren first! I will be the first of our line to do so, thanks to marrying your mother so young. Don't spoil that pleasure for me."

"And if not Aridhina?"

Azadhar pondered, and finally answered him. "Ladhelle looked lovely in her robes, you said?"

"Yes, but-"

"Well, if the robes fit..."

C. A. Morgan

## Chapter 22 – A Surprise Catch

Lureli didn't have to wait long.

The giant squid's grip was even stronger than she could have imagined. Fierce determination, fueled by years of having that which it most wanted beyond its grasp, augmented its strength. It squeezed the glass bubble with more force than a vise. When that failed, it repositioned its hold. Several of its suckered limbs released their hold at once, suctioning back against the glass in an elegant and terrifying caress. Then, ever so slowly, it began to turn the glass to the left.

Lureli felt the dome shift and looked up. The squid's hypnotic gaze pinned her in place. The glass inched left and stopped, then right, and then left again. The monstrous creature was working it back and forth in the sand, testing it like a screw - and now it knew which way to twist! In one fluid motion it leaned into the turn, spinning the dome up and out of the sand. For a moment, it clung to the glass still wrapped in its tentacles. Turning the bowl over and finding it empty, it looked for what would fill it.

Too late, Lureli realized she was free of her glass prison. The squid dropped the bowl, jetting toward her like a silver spear. She darted away, but the squid was faster. A tentacle shot out, lassoing her around the waist; another circled her tailfin, squeezing. She struggled, punching and clawing at them, flailing with all her strength, but to no avail. The tentacles merely tightened, drawing her toward the squid's yawning beak. She bucked in terror.

But this particular squid was not hungry for mermaid.

"Welcome home, Lureli. S-ssssso nice to s-ssssee you!" it said in perfect Glisseon.

"Japhra!" cried Lureli, still helpless in her grasp.

"Yesssss…"

Close up, she could see the squirming host that was constantly in motion across the shapeshifter's skin, and stopped her struggling; it was no use - she was still trapped. Japhra wanted a bigger fish, and now *she* was to be the bait.

"Ah, so you've guessssed. Let's-sss go find Orpheas, shall we? We are sure by now he would give jusssst about anything to s-sssave his precious-ssss daughter!"

"Indeed, I would!" the sea king bellowed, swimming up behind them out of the murky blue depths. He stopped just short of them, glaring, so close that to

Lureli it looked as though he filled up half the sea. His powerful tail flicked in agitation, and his trident glowed an ominous, fiery red. Flanking him on either side were - Jorda, Crispin, Katri, Jaim and Dani! – her loyal Mer servants and their youngest brother, all of them now shape-changed into Glisseon. Still, their combined brawn could be no match against the squid's great mass.

Japhra turned, squeezing Lureli even tighter. She felt ribs crack, and gasped with pain.

"Release her!" Orpheas commanded, and surprisingly, Japhra complied.

"As you wish, Your Majesty," she said, relinquishing her prize. Rolling from her tentacled grasp and sinking to the sea floor, Lureli groaned in agony. Dani rushed to her side as her father and the rest remained to confront Japhra.

"So it *was* you who has been terrorizing the Glisseon - how dare you return!" Orpheas shook with barely restrained anger, his wrath so fearsome that even the former Mer cringed. "You've tried my patience once too often, you poisonous wretch! First my queen, and now my daughter – how dare you?!" he repeated.

"We thought you might missss ussss-" Her many arms drifted sinuously open as if to embrace him.

He was not drawn in. "You are no longer welcome in this realm!"

"Tsk-tssssk" she said, retracting like an anemone. "We thought you learned your lesss-son with dear Vivianne." Pulsing with vivid color, she flowed around him as his head turned, following her every movement.

"Fool!" she cried. "As unrepentant as she was - how we thrilled to be finally rid of her! And now, your daughter – sss-so, sss-so lovely! - has returned to ussss what is rightfully ourssss. We were meant to rule and now *We* shall, with or without you, my king!" And from some hidden fold of squid-flesh, one of her tentacles drew forth Vivianne's coral headpiece, and slid it over the tip of her pointy head.

Blind with rage, Orpheas raised his glowing trident, but Japhra was quicker. A tentacle whipped out, curling around his trident and wrenching it from his powerful fist. Three others followed, encircling his body and head in tight coils, and they began to squeeze. The former Mer, weaponless yet still mighty, fell upon Japhra. Just as quickly, her remaining tentacles wrapped around each of them. Dragged like rags through the water in every direction, they struggled helplessly in her grasp.

Japhra drew Orpheas toward one giant eye and gloated, "Such a puny little starfish! S-sssso weak, s-sssso fragile. One s-sssnap, and I could end your miserable life! However…you missssed witnessing Vivianne's final momentsss, and they were s-sssso very moving! Thissss time you may watch, before *you* die, too."

She turned him around, forcing him to look on as she oozed her way toward Lureli. The others twisted in her grasp.

"Wait - Noooo!" he cried. "You have already won! You have me, and Vivianne's crown: Isn't that what you wanted? Please... I'll give you anything, just let my daughter go!"

It broke Lureli's heart to hear her father reduced to begging, her pain even stronger than her fear. But Japhra was no longer interested in bargaining. With a look of pure malice, she pointed Orpheas' trident in her direction. Dani, crouching protectively over her, looked up trembling, but refused to move. He was all that stood in the way.

His brothers screamed in silent horror as a bolt of pure heat sizzled through the water, blasting a wide hole in his back. He died instantly.

The captives struggled all the more desperately, but Japhra ignored them, prodding Dani's fallen body with the trident, and rolling him aside of her intended victim.

Suddenly, right beside Lureli, a webbed hand burst out of the sand. In its clasp was a simple stone blade. Rising from the sea floor like a pale phoenix, Tad drove the knife through the end of Japhra's tentacle, pinning it to Dani's burned flesh. She howled her pain and surprise, her remaining tentacles flailing violently through the water with force enough to shift the tide. The trident slipped from her loosened grasp, yet her crushing grip on the captives only increased. Tugging on her injured limb, she tried to free it of the dead weight. Her thrashing stirred the sea like a typhoon.

Shielding his face from the sting of sand and struggling to stay upright, Tad stretched out his arms, reaching for the trident. With his legs still buried in sand, he couldn't quite touch it. Swallowing her pain, Lureli rolled over and grabbed it herself. The trident glowed red in her unfamiliar hands, searing her skin, but still she held on. Rolling back onto her side, she aimed at Japhra's giant squid eye.

The sea sizzled as a bolt of lightning heat struck Japhra, momentarily blinding them all. Reflexively, Japhra's tentacles uncurled, releasing her captives. In the same instant, a jet of black ink clouded the water.

The trident fell from Lureli's blistered hands, and when the water cleared enough to see, Japhra was nowhere in sight.

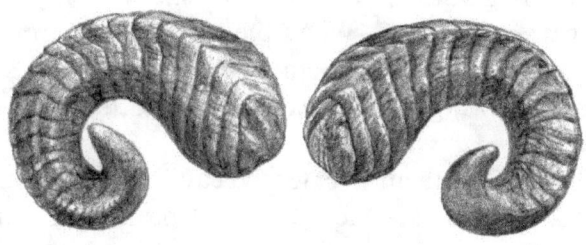

## Chapter 23 – No Time to Die

They found Eleanor a week later, emaciated and lying in her own waste, surely only hours from death.

Weakly, she raised her head from the cold stone floor of the cave and peered up at them without recognition. She was nearly unrecognizable herself. One eye was totally swollen shut. Her face and hair were the same filthy shade, the latter hanging in knotted streaks about her exposed shoulders. Her wool, once soft and white, was matted with feces, vomit and blood. The fleece covering she had torn from the doorway only partially covered her now, and was torn and similarly soiled. She lay beside a pile of dirty snow, obviously her only sustenance for days. Her uncontrollable shivering had melted the patch where it touched her, so she was wet as well, though it was freezing in the cave. There were neatly folded blankets along the far wall, but it appeared she hadn't strayed more than a few feet from the entrance. Except…she had somehow managed to scrape a room-sized hollow in the snow outside before finally giving up, unaware that she was only a foot or two from freedom. When the rescue party from the lower village - nine of them in all - reached the slope and began to dig, they broke through to her almost at once.

The first of them to enter the cave had a big, purple birthmark across his face. He knelt beside her, pulled his tunic over his head and, lifting her head gently, shoved the rolled garment beneath it. He spoke to her in hushed tones, as if he knew her well. A second ram approached. He looked like the first, only more muscular, and without blemish. He directed two older rams coming up behind him to get rid of the snow and filth, then walked away. Another hurried past and began to build a fire. Two ewes filed in and began bustling about the cave, scouring it for anything they could use. The muscular ram came close again, piling clean blankets over her and then, wrinkling his nose, left to help the others.

"The important thing is to get her warmed up," she heard him say. "Then we'll see about getting her clean and her wounds tended. Luckily, we have plenty of food with us; there isn't a scrap left in this cave."

Though she had become inured to it, the smell was slightly better for everyone else once Eleanor was covered, and the rest of her mess cleaned up and tossed outside. Then, for a while it was even worse as the interior air began to warm up. Only the tang of wood smoke made it bearable.

"Eleanor," said the birth-marked ram softly, and trying not to breathe too deeply, "can you drink this?" He put a horn of water to her lips and watched it trickle between them, but she made no move to swallow. "Eleanor, you must drink. Please, do it for me!"

Her cracked lips bled as she tried to speak, but no words came out. Ever so slightly she shook her head.

"Leave her to me," said one of the ewes, gently pushing him out of the way. "We will take good care of her, Camellia and me. Go outside and help Throck, and take the others with you. There is still plenty of snow to clear before we can bring the sled down."

Leaving them to it, he left the cave with the other rams. Eleanor still refused to drink. The ewes carefully washed her instead, starting with her face and exposing as little of her skin to the air as possible. The rags she had wrapped around her hands were so crusted with dried blood and filth that her arms seemed to end in clubs. She was too weak to do any more than protest mildly. Since the water came from skins carried under their tunics next to their bodies, it was quite warm, and actually pleasant. By the time they finished their chore, she had stopped shivering.

*They won't have to wash my corpse*, she thought, *I'm ready now to bury.*

A new ram appeared at the cave door. As she once more refused to drink, he and the others pushed a wooden and wax-stiffened felt sled right up next to the opening. A slight figure slowly rose from it, moving stiffly. Eleanor watched through half-closed lids as the figure approached. Where there had been no recogni-

C. A. Morgan

tion of the others, this face, so different from the rest, was immediately identifiable, though she had doubted she would ever see it again. Through parched lips she whispered one word before unconsciousness took her.
"Karril..."

## Chapter 24 – Broken Promises

Time for Aryelle since her betrothal was announced was like soaring the currents; one moment floating carefree and exultant, the next plunging toward the ground and praying for another gust to lift her skyward.

She supposed it was a good thing Ladhelle had taken that final fitting for her, and not Jadharra. Aryelle's robes fit perfectly, and even Jacharra was more amenable to the match than previously, perhaps now envisioning a happy marriage for her own son, Rachazar with Ladhelle - and a houseful of potential grandchildren to come.

But was Aryelle's own match happy?

Elazar was still attentive, though a bit distant in recent days. Knowing how her tears worried him, she had somehow managed to keep her emotions under control -

at least, she had not again succumbed in front of him. But more and more often, she caught him looking at Ladhelle with new respect in his eyes. The girl had bloomed now that less was being asked of her, and her confidence grew daily. Being *Domina Dhe'zudo* – the heir's intended – had never sat well with her; now that she was free of that burden she positively glowed. It was the look of someone in love with the world. Aryelle knew she did not look the same way, and wondered if her betrothed was regretting his choice of a bride.

Lately, she missed her own time more than ever, and had all but forgotten her pact with Eleanor and Lureli. She wanted nothing more than to be safely back in her own time, in her father's house, surrounded by those she loved. Yet here she was, home without really being home, she thought wryly. And, she had promised to stay.

A knock on her door startled her. Who would be calling on her this late? She rarely ventured out of her rooms after dark anymore, and the rest of the household respected her need for solitude. She moved to the door and leaned her head against it, sensing who it was on the other side.

"Elazar, come in," she said, finally opening the door. She stepped aside so that he could enter. He did so hesitantly, as if concerned that someone would come upon them and misunderstand. A shadow clouded his face, and did not kiss her cheek though she offered it. "Do not worry," she said, "I will leave the door open wide enough for you to flee." Her attempted witticism sounded as feeble as it felt.

"Aridhina, there is something we must discuss," he said seriously.

So... the charade was becoming too much for both of them. He looked so uncomfortable that Aryelle took pity on him. "I know why you have come."

For a moment they stared into each other's eyes. Regret passed between them like a shared, sad memory.

"You know about my work with the Naturra, and my need for someone by my side who can share in that work. I thought you were that someone...but..."

"But, you no longer do."

"My father spoke with you?"

"He did. And, I told him that this fragile Aridhina was not whom she seemed." It was the closest thing to the truth she could bring herself to say.

"So he told me. And also that you still do not remember where you come from. I thought that if I could help you to remember, help you to see your past, it might help us to see our future together."

*Oh, no!* thought Aryelle. This was something she had not even considered. When Azadhar came to her and she had been unable to confess after all, he must have assumed that her indecision was due to a lack of confidence in herself, like Ladhelle.

"I know you mean to help, but truly, Elazar, where I come from is only part of it. I do not think that in knowing you would feel any more comfort. Nor would I," she answered earnestly.

"Then...?"

"Then" she said, taking his hands in hers with strengthening resolve, "things will be better with us, you will see. I will be able to face what I must." She thought fleetingly of the pain she would feel at his passing, the emptiness she would have to endure. The lonely revolutions till, as history witnessed, she would love and marry again.

"Face it you may, but not I. Not with you at my side, I am afraid." He bowed his head, and when he looked up at her again his heart was heavy. "I am sorry, Aridhina."

She turned away, feeling the weight of his rejection, and knowing that nothing she could say would convince him to change his mind. Nothing but the truth, a truth that would inflict a wound from which there would be no healing. She could not bring herself to do it.

The door closed softly behind him as he left.

## Chapter 25 – His Father's Son

When his cousin, Aryelle and the others vanished, Karril was left reeling in stunned disbelief. One moment, Nodd was calling out to them to come see what he had found, and the next, Karril was alone in the Maze of Ages, the hieroglyph chamber that housed the Stone of Seeing. Had they somehow disappeared into the Stone? He circled it again and again, his terrified face reflecting off its myriad facets, his desperate cries echoing through the empty chamber. Alas, even Rona was gone without a trace. The other praircat could offer no explanation. Such had never happened to visitors before - nope-nope. But out of sight, out of mind, they said; praircat disappeared suddenly all the time. Maybe they would come back, maybe not. If he wanted to stay, he was more than welcome. Since Rona had gone off again with Reena so near whelping, wouldn't he like to stick around and help?

Not knowing what else to do, Karril had stayed with the praircat and waited, keeping vigil alternately beside the Stone and, when their constant petting grew too overwhelming, at the edge of the warren where it touched the northern prairie. Reena's pups made their appearance, and still there was no sign of them. When roving packs of Wulfen and nameless rabid creatures began threatening the warren, he built fires and posted a watch at every tunnel, organizing the praircat into effective teams who could collapse and seal off the warren in an instant. He waited all through the long autumn into months normally grown cold, and had just about given up hope of anything ever being normal again when strange vibrations began emanating from the Stone, and images on the Maze walls to selectively glow. It was not constant, but whenever it happened all of the praircat would rush to see what part of the Maze was glowing, abandoning their posts and crowding into the chamber, ooh-ing and ahh-ing until the vibrations stopped. It was maddening! And futile too, since nothing useful ever came of it. How was he to protect them from their enemies if they wouldn't keep to their watch?

Winter finally began to spit snow, and he knew he would have to spend it with them. No longer a sheltered juvenile setting out on a new adventure, he had shouldered responsibility for more than he ever imagined he could, and far too much in his own estimation. Though weary beyond belief, he continued to man his post faithfully. Except…just that once when the vibrations began, he was already fast asleep.

And that is when the Wulfen attacked.

They came from the south in broad daylight, and entered the underground network of tunnels undetected. By the time their menacing snarls and the praircats' helpless yipping alerted him, the damage was already done. He entered the Stone's chamber a frightened boy; in outraged horror at what he found there, he became a madman. Screaming, and with an aura brilliant as the noon-day sun, he chased the Wulfen from the warren. They ran from his blazing fury full-bellied, with tails between their legs.

His guilt was immeasurable. He could not blame the Wulfen, who were but changling beasts, only doing as their perverse nature dictated. But he should have prevented it. And so, knowing he was no longer of any use there, he decided to go after them. Leaving behind a note of explanation in case his cousin returned, he took only Elazaryn's bel for company, and what food he could carry. The Wulfen were headed north, directly toward Mt. Cor. Perhaps he could get ahead of them somehow, and if need be, warn the lower villagers.

He realized his plan was flawed when it began to snow in earnest. His clothing was not suitable for such harsh weather, and with his wings bound as they had been this entire time, they would be useless for flight. He considered returning to the warren, but hadn't the stomach to face it again. He thought also of the Swamps of Dire, which lay somewhere off to the west; there would at least be shelter there…but no. He plowed onward, following the Wulfens' tracks by Bel's dimming light, until he fell too far behind and the snow obliterated them. And still he kept moving. When the skies finally cleared he realized just how far he had drifted off course. By then he could navigate by keeping Mt. Cor in his sight. Hopefully, the Wulfen had veered around the mountain, and were no longer headed toward the lower village.

By the time he stumbled into the cluster of grass huts, his feet and fingers were black with frostbite. Only recently returned themselves, the villagers took him in. Althea and Lavina nursed him back to health, though there was little they could do for those bits the weather gods had claimed. He never explained why he did not just heal himself, but shared with them what he knew of Eleanor and Nodd's travels. They commiserated over his losses, and their own.

******

Karril healed Eleanor just as his father had all those years ago. Though grave, her condition was not too taxing on his growing abilities, and physically she would be just fine. What she needed most had already been done for her. Rest and proper nourishment would take care of the rest, but her mental state was another matter. Karril felt out of his league in that attempt, nor would he invade her privacy by probing her mind, and had the wisdom to let time work its own healing.

She recognized the others now. It was Jode who had found her, and his twin, Nashor, and others from the lower village. Once Silene and Camellia had gotten her to eat and drink, Karril begged Eleanor to tell him what had become of Aryelle and the rest. Though all she wanted to do was sleep, grudgingly she filled him in. There were gaps, of course, and he quizzed her unmercifully, needing to know more of her fantastic tale and what had befallen his cousin. Finally spent, she fell silent. He told her his own story then, adding that about a week ago, a strange ram had shown up at the lower village. Her eyes lit up at that, but once he described Dornub, she sank back into sullenness.

"He told us we might find you here, and showed us how to make contraptions for walking on top of the deep snow to get to you. No one thought we would need them, but when we reached the northern slope and saw how buried it was, we were grateful he had. Only, as you can see, I am not so good at walking these days."

She ignored the obvious. "He didn't say anything about Gord, did he?" *Maybe*, she dared hope.

Karril looked at her strangely. "No one has seen Gord since the Upper Village," he said, "unless you have…?"

Eleanor didn't answer. That was it, then; Gord had died in the avalanche after all. She knew it must be so by how dead she felt inside. After a moment though, she asked after Nodd.

"No sign of him, or Accora either. You said this Mandelbrot fellow was going to send them home?"

"That's what Lureli said."

"But you did not hear it yourself?"
She was done talking. "No."
Karril took the hint.
"Then maybe he sent them both to the Upper Village. That is where Nodd was from, right?" He stood up, wobbling a little and not expecting an answer, and went to see what Jode and Nashor were doing.

The glimmer of hope died almost the instant it sparked. Eleanor didn't think she could feel pain worse than losing Gord, but she was wrong. This added a whole new layer. If Borrac had Nodd, then he was a dead ram.

## *Chapter 26 – Too Little, Too Late*

"She's gone!" cried Lureli waving away what she could of the dissipating ink.

"It's a big sea; she could be anywhere, be anything," Orpheas said unnecessarily, but to Lureli it barely registered. It hurt to move, and hurt even more when he swam over and wrapped his powerful arms around her. She winced, and her father winced with her, holding her more gently, but not willing to let go.

"I thought I had lost you," he murmured, stroking her hair. "I could hardly forgive myself for sending you away. Come; let's get you home. My men and I will find Japhra once you're safe and looked after. It's time we were rid of her once and for all!" Glancing over her head at Dani's ruined body, he shook his head sadly. "Such a shame…"

Dani's brothers had swum over and were solemnly lifting him from the sea floor. They would not leave him to feed the fish, but would take him to the surface first, and give him a proper sendoff such as they had not been able to do for their other brother, Fransi. Lureli choked back a sob. She wished she could go with them, though only in part. As indebted as she was to them all, she remembered there was another she owed even more.

"Tad, where are you?" she called, searching both sea and sea floor from the shelter of her father's arms.

The others moved aside and she saw him. Sediment had settled over the frogman where he lay; on his back, knees bent, his lower legs still stuck fast in the sand. He tried to sit up, and one of the brothers reached down and grabbed him by his arms, pulling him free. He shook hands between both of his, and then bent to retrieve an object from the sand. Straightening as though he had forgotten he could swim, he ran in slow motion toward Lureli and the sea king. In one hand he brandished the trident, but rather than attacking, he threw his arms around them both in a tremendous hug. Orpheas raised a dubious eyebrow.

"Oh, Tad, you were so brave!" exclaimed Lureli, hugging him in return. "But you look terrible! We still need to get you to dry land."

"Look!" he said as if he hadn't heard. "Taddy brought presents!" He held Orpheas' trident out to him. In his other hand was the Aurrac cup. It was half full of sand, and protruding out of the top of the horn was a slender razor clam. "For you. It's all that is left of your collection."

Lureli reached for his gift.

"NO!" boomed Orpheas, knocking the cup from Tad's hand. It sank slowly, and as it did, the clamshell opened. But instead of revealing the enclosed clam, a milky, transparent jellyfish ballooned up and out of it - Japhra!

Orpheas reached for his trident, shoving Lureli out of the way. Tad dove on top of her, knocking her further aside as the jelly pulsed toward Orpheas' face. The sea king ducked, but not soon enough.

"Aiiiiieee!" He grimaced. Painful stings lit up the skin of his upper arm and chest where the jelly trailed over it. Luckily, he dodged the worst of it. Gritting his teeth, he called for the rest of them to swim to safety.

Lureli froze as her father speared the jelly with his trident, twirling it in upon itself like seaweed, and grinding it into the sea floor. All at once, it became a manta ray, its whip tail sliding through the trident's tines to escape. Gliding over the sand just out of reach, it circled back toward them and became a snapping barracuda, its ferocious jaws lined with jagged teeth. Orpheas fought it off as Tad pushed Lureli behind him. She peeked around his shoulder to see Japhra shift yet again, this time into a giant creature so ancient and foul that she found she could not name it. The brothers cowered, and even Orpheas blanched. Towering over them, it was all gaping jaws and hideous fangs, with row after row of razor sharp teeth. Its scales were the shade of rotted kelp, and the sea grew rank from the bilious cloud that hung in the water surrounding it.

"Take whatever form you will, Japhra; this day will be your last!" Orpheas bellowed. He waved his mighty arm and a wall of spinning sand rose up from the sea floor to separate them. From behind its shield he turned to Lureli and said, "Swim away, daughter - now!" And kissing her quickly, he added to Tad, "Take care of her, Anuran!"

Not waiting to see if they obeyed, he dove through the sand wall with a fierce battle cry.

*"Fath-!"* was all she got out before Tad grabbed her painfully around the ribs and pulled her away, swimming for all he was worth. Lureli struggled free to swim alongside him, and glancing back, saw the former Mer join in the fight. The sea around them churned, and the beast's head broke through, snarling and snapping in her direction till they beat it back. Lureli flinched and, with a flick of her tailfin, swam upward toward safety, leaving Tad to follow in her wake.

They hadn't swum far before Tad slowed to a crawl. Lureli looked back and saw he was much worse. The battle raged on below them. Already two more of the brothers appeared to be hurt. And now she was torn. Should she go back and try to help, or see Tad safely to shore? He didn't look as if he could make it on his own and besides, she feared he wouldn't leave without her. To stay would mean his death for certain.

Waving her arm, she urged him onward. They swam a bit farther, and he fell further behind. When she looked back a second time, what she saw scared her nearly as much as the monstrous creature Japhra had become. Tad had gone as white as a pearl, and was starting to bloat like a rotted corpse. His body was taking in sea water, but not filtering it or letting it pass through. All that salt was poisoning him. As she swam back to him, his eyes rolled back in his head and he ceased swimming altogether.

"Oh, no! Tad! Please don't give up - *please!* Don't leave me!" She threw an arm around his middle and swam as hard as she could. He patted her on the back and opened his eyes to smile wanly at her.

"Okay," he croaked.

"Hold on," she said, dragging him up through the water. "I think I know a shortcut."

C. A. Morgan

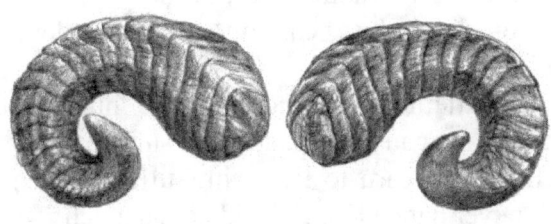

*Chapter 27 – The Prodigal Daughter*

Nashor and Jode loaded Eleanor into the sled, tucking the blankets in around her. Healed, and with a little food and fresh water in her she was functioning much better, but she was still weak and they weren't taking any chances. In spirit, too, she appeared wounded. Neither of the rams had ever seen this side of her before, and worried almost as much about her despondency as they had at finding her so near death.

Karril squeezed into the sled at her side. Going downhill was too great a challenge for his balance now that several of his toes were missing. It wasn't until he sat down, though, that Eleanor noticed his hands, still bandaged with frostbite. She looked at her own, no longer a mark on them.

"Why don't you do something about that?" she asked with her usual bluntness, though not as if she really cared.

Karril looked down at his hands. "I do not know. Maybe so that it remains a part of me."

"You should just heal yourself and be done with it. I would."

Her bitterness did not surprise him, though he questioned its cause. Yes, she had suffered, but they all had. Better to learn to live with suffering than to pretend it never happened. He told her as much.

"Sounds like something Nodd would say."

"You should listen to him more."

"Thanks for the advice, but I'll wait until he tells me so himself," she said turning away. She looked back at the cave as the sled began to move, and heaviness settled in her chest. She had known such happiness there, and had lost it all too soon. She would survive, of course; she must now - but she would never be the same. Silently, she said goodbye. *Gods take you, Gord, though I wish they never had...or that they had taken me too.*

They rode the rest of the way in silence, pulled by Nashor, Jode and the other Aurrac rams in turn, all of them wearing what looked like woven drying racks strapped to their hooves. They were following the path broken in by their trip upslope, so the going was relatively easy. At times the sled even had to be held back; but for a way to steer and room for them all, they could have careened all the way to the bottom. As it was, they set off at a brisk trot and kept it up. Near dusk, they left the snow pack created by the avalanche, and Eleanor turned to look back up the snowy slope one last time.

Somewhere up there, her only love was frozen as cold as the hole in her heart.

That night they camped under the stars, huddled for warmth around the campfire. Eleanor cringed at the thought of sleeping so near any other ram. Nashor tried to sidle up behind her, and she moved away, causing Jode to frown when she squeezed in between him and Silene. His twin was used to being rebuffed by her though, and when Camellia – a pretty young thing despite her blanched looks - batted her pink eyes at the handsome ram, Nashor smiled and went to snuggle with her.

And so it went. It took almost three days to reach the lower village. As they approached it, something clicked in Eleanor's brain. Karril was asleep in the sled beside her, so she asked Jode, who was walking just behind them instead. "When did Dornub come?"

"About a week and a half ago, close as I can tell," he answered. "I don't remember when exactly. Why?"

"It couldn't have been that long. It took him nearly a week to get to the caves from the summit, and he didn't have those contraptions you're wearing now. The north face is the shortest route. If he came down the same way we did, he would have still been on the slope when the avalanche occurred. He would have been buried too."

"So, he must have crossed to the southern slope further up."

She shook her head. "Trail's easier the way we came. At least, it would've been without all that extra snow. Why would he have left it? And even so, he couldn't have gotten to you that fast either way unless he flew."

"Then maybe he did.... and maybe praircats will grow horns!" Jode countered. He was still a little miffed at not being able to snuggle Silene all the way down. Besides, who was she to worry about such details when she had not even thanked them yet for trudging through all of that snow to get her? If she was sound enough to argue, she must be feeling better. Had he been pulling the sled, she would be getting out and walking the rest of the way, no matter how close they were.

There was no time for that, though, as doors flew open and the villagers poured from their homes to welcome them. Elders held back, waiting their turn as the sled was surrounded by cheering youngsters. Outfitted in colorful, warm tunics, they swarmed over the lot, waking Karril, who greeted everyone enthusiastically. Eleanor, for once, found she could not bear the attention; their din made her want to run and hide. She pushed them off without a word of excuse, and struggling to her hooves, pawed her way through the crowd. But when Althea and Lavina waddled out of Nodd's house awash in joyful tears, she hurried toward them. Instead of avoiding their hugs and kisses as she always had, she allowed herself to be engulfed in their twin embrace, finding comfort in their ample arms.

\*\*\*\*\*\*

A month passed. The village was quiet, most of the villagers staying indoors through the worst winter any of them could remember, despite it having gotten such a late start. The air grew ever colder as one month stretched into two. Eleanor barely poked her nose outside, spending her days with the sisters, though she usually wasn't much help at all. There were plenty of empty rooms in Nodd's house she could've chosen to spend her time in. However, though she still avoided the other villagers, ever since she came back Eleanor hated to be alone. Instead, she sat listlessly in the corner of the warm kitchen, contributing to the work and conversation only when put to directly.

Althea watched her brood, but for once kept her tongue. She almost preferred the girl argumentative. If Nodd were back, he'd know what was ailing her, unless of course, it was the fact that she was here, and he was not. As the months came and went it was more of the same. In private, Althea consulted with her sister. It had been a long time since she had wintered with her own daughter; for years now the girl had spent the dreary, cold months at the peak. But Lavina was just as clueless.

Jode and Silene had tied the knot shortly after their return to the village, and now shared a small hut of their own a stone's throw away. One uncharacteristically mild afternoon, Althea plodded over to ask Jode if he had any idea on how to help snap her out of it.

"I'm plum outa ideas," she admitted. "Nodd spent more time with her these last few years than I ever did. What d'ya think is ailing her?"

"I dunno. She's been different since we found her, almost like she died inside that cave."

"Can't ya take her huntin' or somethin'?" she pleaded.

"I've offered," he said. "She's not interested. She won't even traipse this far to see us. And I know Karril has asked her to come help him and Nashor teach the children to read Common, too, though I don't know what good it will do any of them down here where there's no books to speak of. But she don't wanna be around the young'uns at all."

Althea pondered. "Did ya see anything strange up there in the cave?"

Jode took his time answering, and when he did, it was not the answer she was expecting. "The front cave was pretty much as we left it at the start of winter, except for the mess she made. I didn't see it myself, but the back cavern looked... I guess 'strange' is as good a word as any. Silene said that when she lifted a lantern inside to check it out, there was stars a twinklin' all around like the open night sky. That..." he paused, deciding whether to share the rest, "-and a bed in the middle. It was made up fer two, and a vase of dead flowers stood beside it. She couldn't tell if it had been used, though it didn't look it. She didn't touch anything. Said it had the air – you're gonna think this is strange, too - but, it had the air of a shrine."

Althea did think it strange, almost as strange as them coming home to a full food cache! Dornub hadn't mentioned either thing when he came, so it wasn't him, and Eleanor hadn't said a word about anyone else being up there with her. Then again, her daughter hadn't offered much information at all since her return. She hated to pry now that the girl was at least willing to spend time in her company; it could drive her away. But if it was some stray ram she was pining for, well, she just might have a little advice worth sharing, provided Eleanor was willing to receive it.

With at least a little more to go on, Althea said her goodbyes, thanking Jode and inviting him and Silene over for supper. "You sure are gettin' plump mighty quick, missy" she said patting Silene's slightly rounded belly on her way out. "Cor-whee! Could be ya got twins a bakin' in there, wouldn't surprise me none. That Jode sure do take after his sire! Lordy, I miss 'im! Still... them lambs'll be somethin' t' look forward to. First of our own."

"They won't be spring lambs, Althea, so keep your wool on," Silene teased good-naturedly. "And don't be gettin' any ideas; I'm a nursin' 'em myself!"

They all laughed.

When she got home, Althea found Eleanor sitting in the kitchen, chopping roots alongside her aunt while Lavina prattled on. At first glance she appeared to be listening, but anyone with half a mind could tell hers was somewhere else.

"Sister," said Althea, unwrapping her headscarf, and Lavina looked up from what she was doing. "Why don'tcha take a basket of fresh oatcakes out t' Nashor and the fairy boy? They is schoolin' the young'uns outside today, and I s'pects they'd appreciate a little treat."

"Yes, indeedy! It'll be a right treat fer me t' poke my own nose outside, too. Been cooped up so long, I can't stand the smell o' my own wool!" she laughed, winking at Althea. "How 'bout you, Eleanor? Wanna come along?"

"I'm fine" she answered.

"Fine as hooch, but ale is better!" hooted Lavina.

"It would do ya good...?" she coaxed.

"I said I'm fine."

The sisters exchanged glances. "That's alright, I could use ya right here," said Althea as Lavina waddled out with the basket on her arm.

She waited a while before she dared to broach the subject, and when she did, she tip-toed around it in typical fashion. "Shore am happy to have ya back where ya belong," she said, grabbing Lavina's knife and a turnip and beginning to chop.

Eleanor glanced up. She could feel something coming. She weighed whether or not she should go catch up with her aunt.

"Ya know, Nodd an' me, we always wanted what was best fer ya. You was always his favorite. Near broke both our hearts when they took ya up top, away from yer clan."

Eleanor kept chopping. "I came back whenever I could."

"That ya shore did. Yer a good girl, always was. Don't s'pect I ever told ya often enough, bein' so busy with them babies all the time."

"It was fine."

"I s'pect someday you'll be wantin' lambs of yer own."

"I suspect not."

"Cor, there ain't nothing like a wee babe wrappin' their arms 'round ya! That soft wool an' those chubby creases... I always loved a'nursin' 'em. They smelled so good! And you was always so good with them young'uns, too. I'd hate t' see ya miss outa havin' yer own."

"That'll never happen," said Eleanor quietly.

"What'cha mean?" asked Althea innocently. "Ain't ya never thought about it? Never been sweet on nobody?"

"No." Eleanor lied.

"No beau up top? Huh? I seen Nashor look yer way a time or two – what about him? Only, you best jump on that one right quick if yer interested, or you'll lose out to that flirt, Camellia. She been winkin' those pretty pink eyes at 'im ever since ya got back!"

"She can have him."

"You weren't..." Althea grew suddenly speechless.

After a moment Eleanor looked up from her chopping. Her mother had gone pale. "Weren't what?" she asked.

"You ain't pining fer..." Althea could hardly bring herself to say it, "-fer Borrac, are ya? Ellie, he's a beast!"

Eleanor slammed down her knife, and looked at her dam as if she'd grown an extra set of horns. How could she think something so foul? How could she know her so little? Disgusted, she headed for the door.

C. A. Morgan

"Aw, Ellie, I didn't mean-" Althea called after her. The slamming door cut her off.

Eleanor stood outside, shivering in the shadow of the doorway, not wanting to venture further, but unwilling to go back in and face her dam. To be honest, she knew why Althea didn't know her. She just demonstrated it - she would never let her in. Nodd had been able to break down her walls occasionally, and though her broken heart wished otherwise, she had invited Gord in too, but never Althea. She had always slammed the door in her face, first out of resentment at having to share her with so many others, and later, out of plain old dislike of having her stick her nose into things. She had kept her at arm's length her entire life, despite Althea's repeated attempts to get close to her. No wonder she thought so poorly of her.

Eleanor turned around and rested her forehead against the cool of the door. Why couldn't she go back to the way things were? Why was caring so hard? Inside she could hear Althea crying softly, berating herself even though she had done no wrong. Althea didn't think poorly of her she admitted; she loved her, and was probably afraid of losing her all over again. She might have already lost Nodd - *her* only love - just like she had lost Gord. How then, could she be so cruel and continue to shut her mother out? They might be all each of them had left.

Taking a deep breath, and heaving and even bigger sigh, Eleanor opened the door and went back inside.

## Chapter 28 – Time to Wound, Time to Heal

Days passed. Nothing, yet everything, had changed. Aryelle had never been more miserable in her life. She was supposed to be a healer. Instead she was wounding everyone around her. A pall descended over the royal household. Jacharra became even more self-righteous, going out of her way to cast doubt upon Aryelle's character. Elazar kept busy and out of her way; the few times they did come into contact were awkward and uncomfortable. Now that his betrothal to Ladhelle was reconfirmed, Rachazar and Jadharra were both angry with her. And poor Ladhelle! Her resigned acceptance of a fate chosen for her was heartbreaking after how hopeful and happy she had been. Only good natured Azadhar remained as jovial as ever. But then, he was

C. A. Morgan

the only one still getting what he wanted. If only he knew...

Aryelle alone realized the full portent of what their altered fates meant for the future. Not only would *her* bloodline never come to be, but Karril's as well, and countless other luminaries whose ancestors would themselves never be born. The termites had won. The house was crumbling.

She could no longer bear to stay here and witness. Somehow she had to get back to her own time. Otherwise, guilt would overwhelm her.

But was that even possible now?

She had searched and searched for answers, wandering the gardens for hours at a time. Mandelbrot had taken the key, not that she knew how to use it, nor, she realized, would she even recognize it should it suddenly present itself. Recalling the words of Accora's prophesy was no help; she was not the one bearing the mark, the one who would call them home. She could think of no way out of this mess, and grew more desperate with each passing hour. The rest of Azadhar's household was on edge along with her. Here in this time she was no more than a blight. What made her think she had ever been anything else?

The Reign of Shadow had followed her through time.

Try as she might she could make no sense of it. Mandelbrot had to have sent her here for a reason. It could not have been to make all of *this* happen! Somehow, some way, there was a solution that was escaping her, something that she was overlooking. Desperately, she searched her mind, peering into the long forgotten corners of her memory where shadowy and cobwebbed images floated just out of reach. Finally, she stopped searching, and let the light within guide her.

And just like that she knew what she must do.

She could not answer this riddle, but she knew someone who might.

The laundry smelled fresh as ever, and was so steamy that Aryelle's wings began to wilt the moment she entered the room. The Naturra workers kept their wings and hair bound, of course, and she envied them for that as she wandered among them, tentatively searching. Would she even recognize her? One of them brushed by her carrying a bundle of silken robes twice the size of her bound wings, so large that she appeared to be headless. Aryelle stepped back out of the way, and was left with the fleeting impression of a walking, valleo drum hammer, carrying its own heavy drum. Anger wafted off her like perfume. Had she been the one to throw the stones? Or had it been another, or any number of others? Too many weary, perspiring faces were turned her way, hostility written across every one.

*"An tortisse ana probo shusse n'et dhin; andhe'zuan dhinna!* - A fair turtle to poke her nose outside her fancy shell; have you lost your way?"

"Aridhina" Aryelle said, recognizing the voice, and relieved she would not have to ask any of the others where to find her. "I have come to see you." Catching sight of the girl's face as she dumped her heavy load

C. A. Morgan

into an open washtub, she could not have been more
astounded. It was like looking into a mirrored glass! For
all that it had shown her, T'sura had kept her from seeing the obvious.

Aridhina, nonplussed, pushed the wisps of hair out
of her eyes and proceeded scrubbing. "Have you come
to return what was stolen?" she asked.

It took a moment for Aryelle to respond, and when
she did her words surprised both of them. "Will you
walk with me in the gardens?"

Aryelle was sure the other girl would refuse. Then
Aridhina spoke to the woman at the washtub next to her
who, when pressed, grunted her assent. As she shook
the sudsy water off her hands, wringing them on the
front of her robe, Aryelle noticed how reddened and
chapped they had become. Guiltily, she hid her own
smooth hands in the soft folds of her robe. Another
glaring worker helped Aridhina shrug off her sweaty
bindings. Aryelle nodded her thanks with eyes down-
cast, and led the way outside.

They walked without talking, Aridhina treading in
Aryelle's footsteps. Only when they neared the farthest
corner of the garden where few Kandharra ever ventured did Aryelle finally turn and confront her. "You
did not tell me we shared a face!" she cried.

Aridhina just stared at her and shrugged. "You
heard Lorian say we look alike."

"A 'bit like you' is what he said - not your exact
double! You even have green eyes!"

"But *you* did not then."

Aryelle's head spun. So this was why the Naturra all hated her so. They saw that Elazar might actually have chosen Aridhina – *the real Aridhina* – if not for her. And oh, with her fierce will what she could have done for them! Instead, Aryelle had ruined things for everyone. "It *was* you..."

"No, not me," answered Aridhina mistaking her meaning. She raised her chin in defiance. "I know who did throw those stones, but nothing you say will ever persuade me to reveal them. And do not even think of trying to probe my mind! You will gain no entry there, thief!"

How the girl must hate her! How she must chafe at the very sight of her, living in the El'Kandhar's residence, living the life of luxury that might have been - *would have certainly been* hers. Could it still be somehow? Aryelle wanted to know who her attacker was, and would have tried to read her thoughts regardless, but what did it matter when there was so much more at stake? She had never intentionally hurt anyone. Was it possible there still a chance to fix this? She knew she must try. First though, she must convince Aridhina to trust her if she was ever to help her take her rightful place.

"My name is still Aryelle," she said in apology, "and I do not want what you think I have stolen. I want to be your friend. We have more in common than you might think."

"And I know more than you think!" Aridhina retorted. "You *are* from Ka'Andharra – a different Ka'Andharra than this, but Ka'Andharra nonetheless.

You are of Azadhar's line. I know that someday you will return to this Ka'Andharra...but you will never rule it!"

She might be right, of course. She had always known it. Thoughts of Lureli and Eleanor – the other Chosen – came rushing back, along with the reason they must someday be reunited. If they were to save Emrysia from the evil that threatened in her time, they might be required to sacrifice the lives they had previously known. Aryelle knew, too, that the girl had not read this in her thoughts; she would have known had she tried. So, how did she know?

"I know these things because I am meant to know them, and you are not!" she continued, answering her unasked question. "You came here to take what was destined for me, and because of it, you cannot even see your own road clearly. Even with T'sura you could not see it. You do not know where to look."

"Then show me."

"It is all around you." She gestured eloquently, angrily; the broad sweep of her arm encompassed the entire garden. "This place is more than it seems. You have never walked the whole of it, have you? No Kandharra ever does. Yet, the Naturra do so often. We do it while you are sleeping, dreaming of your petty pleasures that you did nothing to provide - so arrogant, so superior! Well, we too have hidden wisdom, and we created these paths to guide us in its use."

Aryelle looked all around her. They stood near the outermost corner of the gardens. A few paces behind her lay the gated passage to the wilderness beyond. To

her left and right, the path zigzagged back and forth between lush blooms and foliage, hedges folding upon
themselves in rows of fluctuating length, with the
Mother Tree at the heart of it.

It was a labyrinth.

How could she have missed it? It was configured
differently, and was so much larger than the labyrinth
Ladhonna had created............no! Ladhonna had not
created it. Naturra workers had! Aridhina was right; she
had never walked either in its entirety. Before she had
no need, and blind and preoccupied, she had not recognized this one for what it was. Later, she had been too
afraid to venture far from the inner gardens.

"The labyrinth-"

"We call it 'The Way'."

"You saw all of those things while walking The
Way? What more did you see?"

Aridhina scowled, and then answered reluctantly.
"At first I saw only good things for my people. I saw
myself helping to heal the Empaya, Azadhar's son at
my side. I turned again, and I saw myself with a child at
each breast. But when I turned back the way I had
come, I saw that *you* were keeping this from happening.
I saw you in a Ka'Andharra different from this one, one
where the Naturra are still not treated with respect. Are
you a spirit come to spoil the future? Tell me! How can
you steal all of this from me and still claim to be my
friend?"

Aryelle had no answer, so asked instead, "Did you
see anything else?"

"No."

215

"When did you see all of this?"

"The night I followed you."

That was the night of her attack. "The Way…" Aryelle looked up, musing.

"It shows what might be, not necessarily what is," said Aridhina interrupting her thoughts. Her face grew slightly less hard, but her next words hit Aryelle like so many stones. "No one will cry if you leave, but all will if you stay."

If only she *could* leave.

"I am sorry," said Aryelle softly, ashamed at not being able to comply, or to do what she most wanted to do. She bowed her head, filled with remorse. Then submitting to whatever fate would follow, she lowered to one knee, bending forward, and offered Aridhina her wings. "I wish I knew which turn my path - and yours - will take," she whispered with her face toward the ground, "but I do not know, not for certain. I only know that our desire to help our people is one and the same. The Ka'Andharra I come from is different, it is true. If it is to ever change for the better, it will be because we both decide to help make it so."

Aridhina stood over her indecisive, wanting and yet not wanting to reach out and wrench the very wings from the interloper's back, and who could fault her? Then, with head still bowed and movements slow and unsure, Aryelle reached up, offering her hand as well.

Reluctantly, Aridhina took it.

The moment she did so the ground dropped out from under them. The gardens and labyrinthine paths vanished. Aryelle clutched Aridhina's hand as a blinding current pulsed between them, fusing them momentarily together in a flash of brilliant light. Suddenly they were outside of Ka'Andharra; back in New Forest, with everything around them just as it was before, as if they had ever left it. Oh, but they had! Aridhina, her eyes wild with fear, looked around in disbelief. Aryelle, kneeling there in all her finery, had known much stranger things, and was quicker to catch on. She could hear a small group coming toward them through the fresh-scented forest. No less afraid, but understanding infinitely more how this could be, she knew now without a doubt why she had been sent.

Taking advantage of the other girl's shock, she pulled her off balance and unto the ground beside her. There would be no time to bind her, but she must not be allowed to fly away! As Aridhina cursed her, struggling to right herself, Aryelle grabbed one of the girl's wings, and, gritting her teeth, tore it from side to side ensuring that she would never get off the ground. Quickly Aryelle staggered to her feet, ignoring Aridhina's cries of pain and outrage, and raced to the nearest tree. Behind it she found the net, stashed – was it only moments ago? - by its owner for safekeeping. She threw it over the howling girl.

"Trust me," she cried, "and remember; I do this for the Empaya! Tell them what you told me - that with only one wing, no one flies!" Then, not daring to look back, she darted deeper into the forest.

Hiding behind a large beechnut tree, she watched as a group of Kandharran Elders came into view and took the injured foundling, Aridhina, back toward the treeborn city.

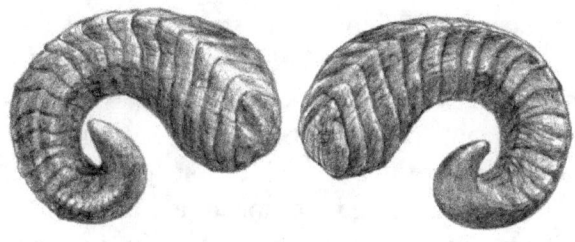

## *Chapter 29 – An Early Spring*

Though she hadn't really expected to, once she confided in Althea, Eleanor felt a bit better. She had done it only for her mother's sake, and it was true Althea was almost giddy at sharing her prodigal daughter's confidence, despite their shared losses. What she hadn't counted on was how much easier it was to think about Gord knowing that someone else knew about him too. Maybe it was because, in talking about him, she was able to relive the good moments. Also, Althea's optimism was catchy. She was convinced both he and Nodd were still alive somewhere, even if they couldn't be with them right now. Eleanor knew better, but what harm was there in letting her think so? At times, she almost believed it herself.

Like her mood, the weather in the weeks that followed couldn't make up its mind, fluctuating between fair days and stormy skies that left everything coated in diamond-slick ice. Most Aurrac opted to stay inside this time of year; to slip and fall could mean a broken leg. The enforced confinement usually drove Eleanor mad, but for once she was content to stay safely put. She and Althea were getting along better than they had in years, and the days settled into a peaceful routine of work and activities meant to keep the doldrums at bay. Often it was just the three of them - Eleanor, her dam, and her aunt. Though Karril and Nashor joined them for meals, most of the time they kept themselves busy away from the women's chatter. Eleanor was actually learning to knit, something she had never deign attempt before. Althea was an excellent teacher, and though Eleanor doubted she would ever get very good at it, she did learn how to laugh at her missed stitches and uneven rows, rather than scowl. She even started a blanket for one of Jode and Silene's expected little ones.

"I pity the lamb that gets stuck with this," she rued one day as the three of them sat knitting.

"Me too," teased Althea. "That's why I'm a making an extra one! Them twins won't hafta share everythin' like me and mine did." By the wistful look in her eyes, Eleanor could tell she had just thought of Nodd.

"I liked sharin' with you, sister," Lavina piped in. Her needlework was just as fine as Althea's, but today she was busy making herself a new halter instead. Not looking up from her own flying fingers, she was oblivious to her sister's frown.

"I'm going to have to knit myself one of those," said Eleanor, changing the subject. She looked down at her own chest. "This chamois one of mine is getting too snug. Too many oatcakes and too much sitting around with you two, and pretty soon folks will be thinking we're triplets!"

The sisters sized each other up and burst out laughing.

"It'll take a fair share more'n that t' give ya as fine a figger as ours, Cor-whee!" hooted Althea. "These jugs don't grow on skinny little missies like you, sweetie."

"Yer loss, too," added Lavina good-naturedly. "Nodd, he couldn't keep his hands off 'em, either set!"

"Whoa! That's more than I want to hear!" said Eleanor, tossing down her knitting. She got up and walked over to the window. Earlier it had looked menacing outside, but now the sky had cleared, and the day appeared fine.

"I think…" began Eleanor musing, "-yes! I think I will go hunting today."

Althea looked up in surprise. Lavina, who was biting off a knot in her yarn, went slack-jawed.

"What?" asked Eleanor, shrugging her shoulders, "Did you really think I was going to stay holed up in here forever? I'm no praircat, and between the two of you, there's not much room for another domestic goddess!"

The sisters, sitting side by side, each looked at their mirror image and howled. Eleanor laughed along with them, wiping tears from her eyes. Althea, who was less concerned about the ice than her daughter's renewed interest, told her "Get on with ya then! An' bring us home somethin' other'n coney – a big fat beaver maybe. I could use some more lard rendered." She looked back at her sister and snorted, and they began to laugh all over again.

Eleanor found her spare bow and quiver in the low thatched room off the kitchen. She grabbed a knife off the table and strapped it to her foreleg. Normally, she would have also wrapped her arm to protect it from the bowstring and Hornet, her peregrine falcon, whose sharp talons had gashed her more than once. It struck her that this was the first time she had thought of her hunting partner since fall, but then again, she hadn't had the urge to hunt all winter. Not that she usually did; confined Aurrac rams were not the best citizens, so patrol members were kept busy keeping the peace during the colder months. She was fairly certain that this winter had been much worse up top. She pulled a warm tunic over her head, glad she no longer shared that responsibility.

Once outside, she paused to fill her lungs with sweet, fresh air before setting out. There was a southern breeze and it was warmer than she expected. A fine day indeed, she thought, testing the wind and heading into it. Before long she had to stop and shed her tunic. The sun felt good on her bare skin, which was nearly as pale as Camellia's after winter's long confinement. Thinking about Camellia made her think of Nashor. The two, if she was reading the situation right, would soon be tying the knot. And that, of course, brought Gord to mind, not that he was ever far from it. She felt her heart clench, and almost turned around. But taking a deep breath and steeling herself against her emotions, she dropped her tunic in the melting snow and headed out to find fresh game.

She avoided the flat prairie where the softening snow was still ankle deep, keeping to the slope and lower elevations along the river, in the opposite direction from where she knew a beaver's lodge to be. Today she wanted a bit more challenge. As early birds trilled from the surrounding bushes, she stepped carefully nearer the stream's edge lest she tread on thin ice and take an unwelcome plunge. In places, a thin layer of ice still covered the rock-strewn river, though mostly, even that had melted. Little rivulets ran from nearby patches of slush to feed it, a sure sign of the coming spring. Soon the river would be roaring with more spring melt than its banks could hold, but for now, its tinkling music filled her appreciative ears. In other years, watchers would be posted, on the lookout for floating baskets that might hold a squalling, blemished newborn - the only kind that was ever sent to them from up top. But with the news of Borrac's new policy, no one bothered.

Eleanor was just about to head further upstream when she heard a far-off cry. She looked up, craning her head toward the sky. There, circling overhead...could it be? She looked around for something - anything - to wrap around her arm, and coming up empty-handed, quickly removed her quiver and dumped its contents on the snow. She thrust her arm into it and raised it to the sky just as Hornet lowered his tail feathers to slow his descent. He landed on her arm with a happy skreah.

A lump formed in her throat as she reached up with her other hand to stroke his dark head. A patch of feathers was missing along one side of it, perhaps from a scrape with some unwilling prey. "Nice to see you, old friend," she said, "though you've looked better. That makes two of us, I guess." She stroked him for a few moments, but with no way to tether him, he soon decided there were more interesting things to do and, spreading his wings, he lifted off.

Eleanor watched him rise into the sky and circle, waiting for her to flush some game. Then, as she bent to retrieve her arrows, something drifting past in the river caught her eye. At first the bobbing basket didn't register, and then she heard a loud wail.

"What in Cor's name...?" She looked around, but this time there was nothing to improvise. The basket had floated out of reach. It would be too heavy to send Hornet after – that much she knew. Besides, its contents were too precious to risk being dropped midflight. Slinging her quiver quickly over her shoulder, Eleanor followed along the river's edge as it bumped its way toward the village, calling for help at the top of her lungs.

Villagers heard and spilled out of their homes. Breathless with trying to keep up, Eleanor pointed toward the floating basket. As heads turned and everyone else stopped to stare, Jode jumped into action. He grabbed an overturned wash barrel and clothesline pole. Tossing the barrel into the water he climbed aboard, poling his way out to the middle of the widening river to retrieve the basket.

Though caught off guard, none of them was overly surprised to see the basket's lid pop open and three arms thrash out of it. Poor little buggar; extra limbs were an especially unacceptable deformity up top. They crowded around as Jode hauled it ashore under one arm. He sat the basket on the slushy snow, and reaching in, lifted out not one, but two tiny babies wrapped up together, one with an arm still tucked tightly by its side.

"Is they fused t'gether?" asked Althea, hurrying over as fast as her hooves would take her. She nearly slipped on the ice.

Jode placed the bundled babies, both howling now with hunger, into her open arms. She began to unwrap them.

"Cor's horns – what have we here?" she gasped, and collapsed onto the slushy snow.

Two perfect Aurrac lambs stared up at her.

C. A. Morgan

## Chapter 30 – Unexpected Help

The mouth of the underwater tunnel appeared before them, about halfway up the cliff face. Lureli swam past it, shuddering and wishing Tad could go faster. Eventually, despite his slow crawl, they reached the top of the drop-off, and the shoreline appeared. They swam toward it until it became too shallow.

Struggling under his added weight, Lureli helped Tad stumble ashore through the lightly falling rain. A flock of seagulls scattered noisily into the leaden sky as she flopped him over onto the wet sand, gasping for breath. She was only tired, but Tad, poor thing, was barely alive. There was hope now that he was out of the salt water though; at least, that's what Lureli told herself. She rolled him over and pried open one of his eyes as the curious gulls returned to shore.

"Still here," he croaked hoarsely.

"Oh, Tad..." she whispered back, blinking away her salty tears. Cradling his head in her lap she stroked his swollen cheeks. A lone seagull, more daring than the rest, wandered in closer. It watched them for a moment, and then darted in to peck at Tad's bloated, white foot.

"Shoo - *shoo!*" Lureli said, waving it away. "Get out of here! Leave him alone, you horrid thing!"

"Well, that's no way to greet an old friend!" cried the gull, lifting off.

For an instant, Lureli was gripped with terror. Then she recognized the voice. "Wait! Mandelbrot - come back! I didn't realize it was you. You've got to help us!"

The Lydian shape-shifter settled back onto the sand. He waddled over leaving a trail of wet footprints. "Pretty convincing, aye?" Another gull waddled in close behind him, and he turned on it, hissing.

"I thought for a moment that you were Japhra," Lureli told him.

"I believe she's still busy right where you left her. But don't worry-" he rushed on, "Your father will take care of her. You have your own troubles just now," he said, bobbing his gull head toward Tad.

"Can you help him?"

"You're a princess; he's a frog... Does he really matter all that much to you?"

She looked down at Tad's pasty, swollen face. His eyes were closed again, but his lips were curled in a contented smile. Amazingly, he was still beautiful to her. "I'd give up my tailfin for him," she whispered softly.

"You already have," said Mandelbrot.

Lureli glanced down at her lap. She hadn't even noticed she had legs again.

"It's not permanent, you know. It never was. You've always been able to dwell on both land and in the sea, you just didn't realize it. Japhra lied."

She shook her head. "It doesn't matter now. All that matters is that I don't lose Tad. He's my best friend, and...I love him."

"To save him, then, lose him is what you may have to do."

"What do you mean?"

"Your bundle of belongings was with you in the Asylum, yes? But not your valise; it's waiting for you in that cave," he said, pointing toward an opening in a familiar, rocky outcrop further ashore. "Ah, I see you remember," he added as she paled.

"Wh- what is it doing in there? How does that help?" Fear crept into her stomach - not again! Was it just another trap?

"I brought it for you. You said yourself that the Glisseon never die from disease or old age. Maybe one of your potions could help him. Of course, if you're not sure which one, you really ought to try them out on yourself first. In his weakened condition, he might react poorly to the wrong one. In fact, you might even kill him outright. But...I think you know which one."

Lureli nodded slowly. "Will you fetch it here?"

Mandelbrot scratched an itch under a wing with his beak, and then wagged his head at her. "Sorry-" he answered. "I'm running late." As she looked on he changed before her eyes into a long-eared, white rabbit - too much like Japhra for comfort - and bounding away, he was gone.

It began to rain harder.

"Tad. Tad, come on," she said. "Let's get you to the cave. Everything is going to be all right."

She patted his cheeks, but he was sinking into unconsciousness. She would have to leave him where he was. Maybe, though, the rain would help wash some of the salt away. Gently, she rolled his head off her lap and stood up. Planting a kiss on his topknot, she bolted for the cave entrance. Nearly there, she looked back. Gulls were darting toward Tad's still body to peck at him – oh, no! She couldn't leave him alone and unprotected! Waving her arms she screamed at them, running back as they scattered. She grabbed one of Tad's arms and began dragging him over the sand, but she couldn't move fast enough. A few of the more persistent gulls followed, and more than once she had to drop his arm to chase them away. Finally, they reached the cave entrance and she dragged him inside. The gulls gave up, rejoining their flock.

The cave's interior was dimmer than she remembered. As her eyes adjusted, she recognized it as the same, but the feeling it elicited was even more desperate. Then, she spied her valise and dropped Tad where he lay, running to pick it up. She hesitated: What if she had already drunk what she needed during her most recent binge? Throwing the case open, she quickly found the bottle she was looking for among the rest, and breathed a sigh of relief. The bottle was small and round, and pink as salmon. One swallow of its contents and Tad should be good as new. It was what they gave the Mer that they might not drown once they came to live beneath the sea; it freed them from disease and enchantment as well. She remembered that the last time she had used it was to save the luminaries in Wellwood Forest. There should be just enough left...

Hurrying back to where she left him, she fell to the ground and drew Tad's head into her lap. She pulled the bottle's stopper and tipped it into his slack mouth. A few drops trickled out. She waited, but nothing happened.

"Tad... Tad, swallow it."

He lay limp as seaweed. Maybe it wasn't enough. She shook the bottle and another drop or two fell between his lips. She held her trembling hand above them, holding her breath as she felt for his.

"Come on, Tad! Don't do this to me! Don't you dare give up now! I'm not giving up on you - no, I'm not, not ever!" She dropped the bottle and threw herself across his chest, sobbing as though her heart would break. She was too late.

Poor innocent Tad, whose only fault had been in loving her. She cried until not a single tear was left.

The wan daylight faded. Though the least she should do was keep vigil over his body, Lureli knew she couldn't stay here. She was so, so sad, and so very weary. How could she go on without her friend? Eventually, exhaustion took over and still clinging to him she drifted off, moaning in her sleep. She didn't feel his arms as they closed slowly around her.

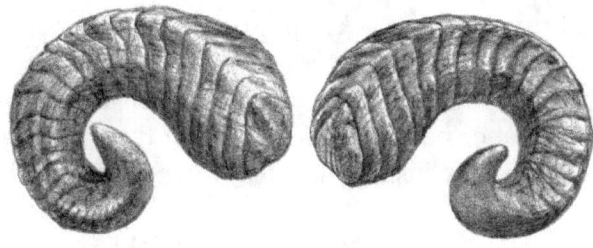

## *Chapter 31 – Comeuppance*

Things were quiet for a while, and then over the next few weeks, as temperatures warmed and the river flooded its banks, the village swelled with new arrivals. A few, though not many, had birthmarks or deformities, blemishes that would have made them unacceptable in any year up top. But like the first set of twins they pulled from the water, most were perfectly perfect. It seemed the Upper Villagers, though they weren't good at keeping Borrac's new law, were good at keeping secrets. These lambs must have been conceived before the Chieftain separated the ewes from their rams. How they had hidden them, or gotten them to the river without getting caught, was a mystery.

And then, one day, the mystery was solved...

Several villagers were at Nodd's house helping with the babies that morning. The other ewes had all dried up long ago, and all they could do was cuddle and coddle, but there was plenty of that to go around. Althea's breasts though, were used to the yearly need and provided milk in abundance. As soon as one wee lamb finished suckling, another was placed on the opposite breast. Eleanor had just wandered into the room where Althea was in constant demand when Camellia burst through the other door.

"Nashor sent me - he says come quick!"

Normally, Eleanor avoided Camellia, not because she disliked her (though she did), but because her girlish glow reminded her too painfully of her own loss. This time, however, hearing the urgency in her voice, she put that aside and followed her out the door toward the river. Hornet, tethered to his perch just outside the door ruffled his feathers, ready for action. Eleanor stroked his head as she walked by. "Maybe later," she promised and kept going.

It was lambing season. Since Nashor had never helped with lambing, he had volunteered for constant river duty while the other rams were busy shepherding their growing flock. He had rigged a draw net across the water so as to easily pull the bobbing baskets ashore. Several days had passed now with no more floating babies; today he would have drawn in the nets for good. Instead, he had awoken to a river chock full of baskets. Around his feet were more than two score, all with lids still latched shut.

"Are you waiting for me to open these?" Eleanor asked. Gooseflesh rose on her arms as she realized suddenly that not a peep was coming from any of them. Her stomach flipped, queasy and settled. She reached toward one of the baskets and felt his hand restraining her.

"Go home, Camellia," Nashor said, looking meaningfully at Eleanor. "I'll come around later,"

"But-"

"Go home, I said!"

"Well, ya don't have to show off them horns; I know ya got 'em!" She flounced off in a huff, but he paid her no heed. They had bigger problems.

"So, what's-" began Eleanor.

"You don't want to look," he cut her off. "But if anyone needs proof Borrac is mad, here it is."

"What?"

"Heads, Eleanor - severed heads in all of them!" Nashor nearly choked as he spat out the news. "Rams and ewes…and I know of some them. You do too."

Eleanor took a step back. That made no sense. The only Aurrac she knew up top were members of the patrol. She didn't associate with anyone else up there, and even them rarely. Suddenly, she had to see for herself. She opened the basket she'd reached for. Just as Nashor had said, it held the gruesome, severed head of a young ram who had been her subordinate. Accusing, terror-filled eyes stared up at her, and she almost dropped it. Slowly, she set it down, reclosing the lid. Morbid curiosity drove her to open another. She immediately regretted her decision. Its macabre contents, the head and

C. A. Morgan

hands of the ewe who had dressed her hair at Borrac's summit complex, were bruised and swollen.

"Don't, Eleanor!" said Nashor, hoping to make her stop. "Don't torture yourself."

But it was too late, she had to see them now, had to know who else she knew. One after another, she flipped open their lids. Another young guard, and an older one who had shown her the ropes when she first made patrol. Sickening with each, she continued: The pretty little ewe who sold chaga on the corner near the barracks, another who hawked wares she had no interest in but had passed by daily, another young ram, and the prostitute she had once offered her gloves to when she found her walking home late one night from the Chieftain's complex. And yet more patrol rams.

How could this be? How could he? The ewes – yes, despicable as it was; there were ways to tell who had disobeyed his edict, and he would have been furious. But why would Borrac kill off his own patrol?

"I'm guessing they're the parents of those little ones inside," said Nashor, as sickened as she was.

Eleanor opened one last basket. Inside was the head of a ram who defied Nashor's logic. Above his frilly, blood-soaked collar, Gorron's rouged cheeks stood out against his bloodless face.

"No" whispered Eleanor, her throat raw with bile. "This is more personal."

\*\*\*\*\*\*

"I tell you, he sent this as a direct message to me! He may or may not have caught some of them breaking his law, but those baskets hold the heads of every single person I ever knew up top! He wants me to know what he's capable of. What he'll do to all of you down here if I don't go back!" Eleanor screamed at them.

The village elders had gathered at Throck's small house in a room ill-fitted for their needs, but with Althea housing a full nursery at Nodd's house, it was the next largest, private space in the village where they could congregate. Crammed into every corner, there was much grumbling and head-butting as they tried to decide what course to take. It was obvious now that Borrac was not going to just leave them peaceably alone. The general consensus was that he must have either allowed or sent those wee ones himself to be a burden on them, to slow them down should they try to leave the mountain, though some argued that it was just spite. Either way, there were more mouths to feed than ever. With the rest of it, well, he was sending a message loud and clear, to them and to his own herd up top. And if he could terrorize his own villagers without conscience, what would he do to them when he finally came down off his mountain, as they were sure he soon must? How could they possibly prevent it?

Angry protests arose at every suggestion. More than once someone lamented Nodd's absence. He had seen them through terrible times before, and was the only one with sense enough to lead this ramshackle herd. As more murmured grumblings were layered with whispers of Nodd's name, Eleanor grew fed up.

"Nodd is not here, got that? Nobody wishes he was more than me! For all we know, he's Borrac's prisoner," she announced to loud objections. "We can at least be thankful his head wasn't in one of those baskets! But, there's no guarantee it won't soon be."

"Ya didn't say nothin' 'bout thinkin' Nodd was up top before!" The accusation was flung from the crowded far corner of the room.

"What good would it have done?" she countered, trying to see who had spoken. "The passes have been snowed shut all winter. What do you think we're going to do now that they are thawing - storm the top? A handful of used up rams and greenhorns, with few weapons and even less training? Even without those he butchered, Borrac's got more patrol than we have villagers, young and old! We can't fight him; we can only hide, and maybe not even that now. That's just what Nodd would tell you if he were here."

"Then what do you suggest?" asked Throck impatiently. Even here they weren't used to taking orders from a ewe.

Eleanor shook her head. "I wish I knew. The only thing I can think of is to just offer myself to him. It's what he expects me to do. It's what he wants."

A chorus of emphatic "No!" rose around the room, and Eleanor looked around gratefully. But that still didn't solve their problem.

Just then there was knock at the open doorway. Karril edged in uninvited, followed by Nashor and

Jode. A few rams shifted to make room, standing practically horn to horn as Karril's wings brushed past them. The three of them made their way to where Eleanor stood.

"You tell them, Nashor," Karril prompted, stepping aside to let him by.

Nashor cleared his throat and squared his shoulders, and for the first time ever, Eleanor looked at him and saw his father. He was exactly what Nodd would've been without his disfigurement, she thought. If only he had his horns...

"We have a plan," he announced to her astonishment. He glanced at Jode, who nodded his encouragement, and continued. "We heard what you said about Nodd...*our sire*...but we don't think Borrac will kill him; if he has him, he'll keep him for bait. It will be several weeks yet before the passes are clear. Borrac won't be fool enough to attempt coming down them with the weather still so unpredictable; that doesn't mean we have to just sit here and wait for him either. Jode has offered to go to the foothills of the next mountain to rally more rams to fight with us. After the massacre of their chieftains, we figure most everyone will be looking for a fight. From there, we can send out runners to the clanherds on the other mountains. I'll stay here and continue training the villagers," he said, surprising Eleanor again, "and that's not all-"

"What do you mean – continue? You've been training the youngsters to fight?" she asked.

Nashor actually blushed. "The older ones, too - yes; ewes and rams. Along with reading, we've been having regular sparring lessons." He looked around the room, addressing the gathering. "You all already knew how to fight, you just needed practice. I know we can't beat him alone, but we may not be as alone as you think-"

Karril piped in, barely containing his excitement. "I will go to the Naturra. The Kandharra might not be willing to fight, but the Naturra know what it is like to be oppressed. I believe they will help. The Mer may as well, if we can get word to them."

Eleanor frowned at him. He seemed taller than she remembered, but he was still slight, and unsteady on his injured feet. "And just how are you going to find them?" she asked. This so-called plan of theirs was rife with holes.

"You will take me."

"Me? No, I won't," she objected. "If there is fighting to be done, I will be here to do it."

"We will be back before the fighting begins, because first, we are going back to Rona's warren-"

"Leave Rona out of this. He's had enough trouble, don't you think?"

"No one thinks so more," Karril agreed soberly. "But we need the Maze of Ages! We can locate the Naturra quicker that way. The praircat showed me how to read the chamber walls while we were waiting for you, and I know they have settlements on this side of the forest."

"And you think they're going to jump up and help us? Who dropped you on your head?" she snarled.

"I do not think so; I know. I have seen it in a dream."

"Oh... so now we're going to go chasing dreams, are we? Sorry, I've had my fill of lost causes."

"Eleanor."

"What?" She turned, exasperated, toward Jode. "He's filled your heads with wool and nonsense! There is no way-"

"Eleanor!" boomed Nashor and Jode together, startling themselves and everyone in the room. They looked at one another, and then Nashor nodded for his twin to continue. Jode reached into a pouch that hung from a cord around his neck, and pulled out an even bigger surprise.

"Dornub gave this to me," he said, holding out his hand. "He told me it would come in handy when I needed t' convince ya of something important. I think this is it."

Lying in his open palm was a small, crystal vial, the key to the Stone of Seeing.

Eleanor was flabbergasted. "How did you... how did he get-? Oh, never mind! This changes nothing!"

"He also said to tell ya you got a job t' do, and it's time t' do it. Oh, and that he had a different name once, too. Said it was...Mandelrot, or some such thing. Said you'd recognize it."

Eleanor sat down hard right on Throck's lap. In any other circumstances, he might have been delighted, but she was clearly in shock.

"Somebody get her a horn of ale - quick!" he shouted.

A few moments later, a brimming horn was thrust into her trembling hand. She gulped the brew down. When asked if she wanted another, she shook her head. What she really wanted she could not have; to wake up from this nightmare. To escape being Chosen.

## Chapter 32 – Show Me the Way

As the forest darkened around her, Aryelle remained hidden with her back pressed against the smooth bark of the beechnut. She faced west, soaking up the last of the fading light and waiting until long after they were gone before she moved. For the first time ever, she was alone in the forest as it came alive with the night chorus of nocturnal creatures. She listened, breathing in the sweet musk, and feeling the weight of the last months slip from her narrow shoulders. No longer afraid for the immediate future, she would relish this one moment of freedom for full measure before she must pick up the yoke that was rightfully hers.

But now, how to do that? The time was surely near, she could feel it. Nothing more could be left for her to accomplish in this time. The real Aridhina would soon take her rightful place, her wings healed, and she would be stronger and wiser for having suffered at her hands. The divided Empaya though, would remain unchanged until they both did as they must. Would Aridhina have done her part without her? Would she complete her own role in her day? If she could only be there to see the Empaya reunited!

When it was full dark, she finally stepped from her hiding place. The night was cool, but not uncomfortably so. Hunger gnawed for the first time in weeks, which only helped to heighten her awareness. She made a decision. Holding her skirts high to keep them from snagging, she walked slowly back toward the glow of the treeborn city.

There *was* one more thing she must do.

She had never completed her questanna. Now, in this time, she would seek her true path. She would walk The Way.

## *Chapter 33 – Where to Now?*

"You're alive!"

*"Yuuuuuuup!"* Tad smiled at Lureli as she startled awake, still wrapped in his arms. His color was perfect, and he looked as if nothing bad had ever happened to him. Lureli hugged him as hard as she could, and sat up. Another night had passed, and daylight was streaming in through the openings in the cave.

She hugged him, and then gave him her most serious look. "I have to tell you something, Tad. But first, let's just spend the day together."

The clouds parted as they left the cave. They spent the day talking and playing on the beach, wandering the dunes for hours. Though Lureli occasionally dipped into the sea, she made sure Tad stayed well clear of it. They ventured further inland and came across a rippling stream, and she watched him splash there, but did not

C. A. Morgan

join in. Hand in hand, they walked back to the shore to admire the sunset. Leaning her head against his shoulder as they sat side by side, she finally said what she had avoided telling him all day.

"Tad... I have to go now."

"Where are we going?" he asked.

"Just me, Tad; I'm going. You have to stay here, or go home to Lake Mirth. Go home, like me, but not *with* me."

"But-" the argument caught in his throat. He looked at her sadly. "You're never coming back, are you?"

"Never is a long time, Tad - who knows what adventures await? But you need to get on with your life, not spend it waiting around for me. You can take more tadpoles – your siblings - from Lake Mirth and warm them up. Watch them grow up! I'll always cherish the time we spent together, every single moment of it. And, I'll always remember you as my dear, dear friend." She kissed his topknot one last time, and before he could see her tears, she waded into the sunset waters and dove in.

Swimming to the drop-off without turning back was the hardest thing Lureli had ever done. When the shelf opened below her, she hesitated, but only for the slightest instant, before thinking of her father and home. She turned and headed toward both, not knowing if either would still be there. She had swum halfway down the cliff, her landmark – the tunnel - yawning before her, when she heard a voice call out to her.

*Lureli...*

Was that Tad? Or was her mind playing tricks?

*Luuu-re-liii, come ba-ack...*

No, that voice - it couldn't be! It belonged to her mother, and it was coming from in there! Lureli shook her head in disbelief, yet wanting desperately to believe. She leaned her head into the open mouth of the tunnel. Then, against all reason she swam just a short distance into it, making sure she could still see the exit. Was it really her mother? What if she wasn't actually gone - only trapped here in the tunnels all these years? She swam in a bit further, and stopped.

What if it was Japhra?

She had to know either way. If Japhra, then that meant her father was dead, and she could never safely return home. But, if it *was* Vivianne after all, and she was just waiting for her to come to her...well, she may not ever find this exit again, but they could certainly make it back to the cave, and home from there. They might all be together, a family again! And just maybe the three of them could someday travel to Lake Mirth to visit Tad. Before she even knew that she had, Lureli swam around a bend. The tunnel glowed further ahead, but it was only the luminescence of the walls. She looked back-

*Lureli, follow the sound of my voice; it will lead you to me...*

And so she let it.

C. A. Morgan

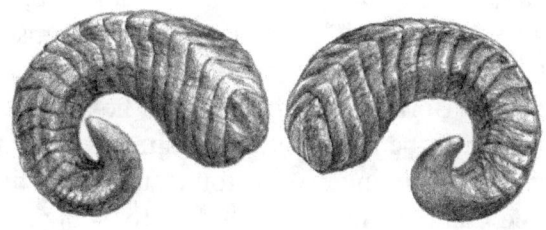

## Chapter 34 – The Mother of All Storms

As it turned out, runners to the other clanherds were unnecessary. Jode (and Silene, who wouldn't allow him to leave her behind) headed out early the next morning toward the base village on Mt. Forge. Unlike Nodd's disgraced castaways, the lower villages on every other mountain were peopled with average, ordinary Aurrac who just preferred living away from the larger herd at the top. Like Nodd's villagers, they were mostly shepherds and farmers, and peaceable enough, though all Aurrac rams liked a good fight.

The second mountain in the Aurrac range was much smaller than Mt. Cor, and the two of them left knowing it would only take them a day or so to reach it. They never got that far. After half a day's travel, the expectant young couple pulled up short when met by a makeshift army of disgruntled rams from all twelve other clanherds, already on their way to challenge the Head Chieftain.

Leading them was a big horned ram who, on his last visit to the arena, had witnessed for himself the Head Chieftain's obvious madness. In the bloodbath that followed Borrac's pronouncement, he had seen that something must be done to depose him. He returned to his own clan, sending word around to other villages, nooks and crannies in these hills to rally support. More rams, he said, would likely be joining them when the rest of the passes cleared - in fact, they could count on it. They were headed to the southern slope of Mt. Cor – Nodd's village – and would wait there for others to arrive. If Borrac didn't come down to meet them, they would storm the peak by the time summer blew in. And a mighty storm it would be!

Jode promised their support. Knowing they could move more quickly alone than with the accompanying army, he and Silene hurried back to share the good news with their fellow villagers. They arrived home near dusk to find yet another surprise waiting. The western prairie surrounding their small village was teeming with small armies of what appeared to be luminaries and Mer. Though in separate camps, there was definitely some mingling among the two. It was an encouraging sight.

Karril came rushing out of Nodd's house to greet them. "I told her they would come!" he cried, anticipating Jode's questions. "We did not even have to ask - Dornub went to them! Mostly Naturra, scores of Mer, and there is even a handful of Kandharra inside; they are not here to fight, though. They have come to take me home with them," he continued apologetically. "They brought word that my cousin has returned, and best of all, my mother is home safe! We will be leaving soon to go back, but my uncle has vowed to help. More Kandharra are already on their way! Even though such is not our custom, Gaelen said they have been training all winter to aid you in your struggle!" Karril beamed.

"It may be too late by the time they git here, but it's more than I dared t' hope," said Jode, sending his weary spouse home to rest. The Naturra could fight well. When he tried to imagine what kind of fighters the fairer luminaries would be, he couldn't. At least they'd be around to help clean up the bloody mess afterward. He gestured toward the encampments. "I would'a loved t' seen Eleanor's face when they showed up."

"She was not here. We were supposed to leave for Rona's warren, but she left without me before day-break, and no one knows where she went. Hornet is gone, too. Nashor guessed she must be hunting."

"He's probably right. She most likely needed some time to come t' grips with it all. The two of you won't have to go now. She'll come t' her senses and come 'round before nightfall, most like. And then, won't she be surprised?"

\*\*\*\*\*\*

Eleanor was surprised alright, but the army she was looking at wasn't on her side, or anyone else's for that matter.

She had not gone hunting as Nashor suspected, but had headed out due south toward Rona's warren following the same route she and Nodd took to escort the luminaries and Lureli home. This time however, she had left Karril behind on purpose, the crystal key hanging in a pouch around her neck. Her thoughts were divided between then and now, and her frustration grew with each mile. If Borrac's rule was the Reign of Shadow Aryelle spoke of, there was no doubt that evil was winning. It didn't matter that Nashor had been training them; the villagers would never be ready for the coming battle. What she did now might be the only thing that would tip the scales in their favor. If there was any hope for this present darkness to pass, it lay in her – no, *them* - following their common destiny, instead of fighting against it. So she hoped, and anyhow, she knew it could be avoided no longer. But submission didn't come easy.

Fueled by anger she pushed herself, running until a stitch burned in her side and then settling into a quick, cantering gait that was easier to maintain. By the time the sun was low in the sky, Rona's warren came into sight. So did another, less welcome scene. Camped just this side of the clustered hillocks was a pack of untransformed Wulfen, larger than any she had ever encountered. Reflexively, she flattened herself against the ground. Thank Cor she had spotted them first! Usually Wulfen traveled solo, in mated pairs, or family groups; this horde resembled an army. Creeping closer, she spied on them, and when she had to duck down, her ears told her more than she wanted to know. They didn't seem to care who heard them. Snarling hostilities among themselves, she listened as they tortured and then devoured some poor, pitiful creature. Dangerous as they were even now in human form, she could only imagine the nightmare they would inflict if they were still this near the village when the full moon rose.

Oh, why did they have to be here now? She had hoped to get this over with, to do whatever prophesy would have them do and return to Mt. Cor before the fighting began.

Skirting around to the south, she approached the warren silently from the far side, ducking into a hidden tunnel just as two rather drunken Wulfen stumbled by. She caught the words "Dezrot" and "Aurrac" amid their harsh laughter, but could understand no more of their garbled conversation.

Making her way underground through the warren, she had plenty of time to rue her decision. If the Wulfen were headed toward her village, she needed to get back there and warn them. Hang prophesy! Hang being chosen! Self-consciously, she rubbed her shoulder where Nodd's tattoo - the symbol that she was the one destined to bring the Chosen together - adorned her shoulder. Well, here she was, following destiny's call. She just hoped the others would be quick about it!

Rona and his pups were nowhere to be found underground. Maybe they had moved off in search of another warren to join. She hoped so anyhow, and that they weren't the meal the Wulfen had just enjoyed. Of all of them, Rona deserved the lot that had befallen him the least.

Peeking out from one of the tunnels, she saw that the Wulfen were breaking camp and moving off. Relief flooded through her; they were headed eastward, and not north toward her village. Good, she thought, let them steer clear of the mountains. There were plenty of slobears, poothas, and other beasts of the prairie to prey upon - even teumessian fox. The Aurrac had enough to worry about right now with Borrac.

And, she had a job to do.

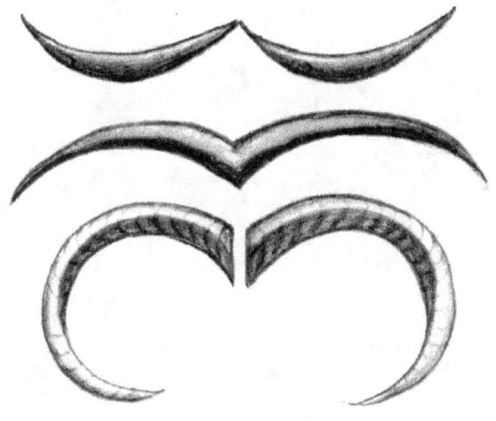

## *Chapter 35 – The Call*

Further and further in she swam. She saw no other living creature, only followed the voice as it called to her. Time took on no meaning, and Lureli no longer knew if she was asleep and dreaming, or awake chasing a dream. She closed her eyes, guided by sound alone, and felt herself swimming through the void of the Connectedness Locus, felt another presence guiding her. She opened them...

-and looked up at Eleanor.

"It took you long enough to get here."

"Nooooooo!" she cried. "Not yet!"

C. A. Morgan

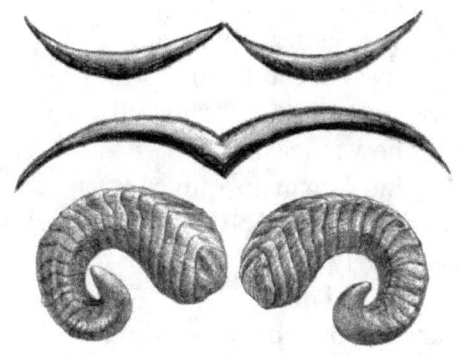

## Chapter 36 – The Eldest of Them All

"Well then, where is Aryelle? Why isn't she back yet?" Lureli was more than a little frustrated at finding herself back at Rona's warren, and with the timing of it, but mostly at being there alone with Eleanor. They were standing outside in the first rays of morning sunlight. The moment she opened her eyes and saw that she was next to the Stone of Seeing, she had bolted up the tunnel. Now Eleanor was trying none too patiently to explain.

"I had to get you back first. I thought you might resist coming."

"You were right! I never even made it home! It's not fair!"

Eleanor snorted. "Who said any of this was fair? Do you think I enjoy seeing my people slaughter each

C. A. Morgan

other? Do you think…" she swallowed a painful lump, "do you think I asked for any of this?"

"No, but…my father, my men-"

"-are as good as dead to you, if they aren't already! Get that through your thick fish skull! We're all we've got, *sister*, for now at least."

Lureli's chin began to quiver. One lone, fat tear rolled down her cheek. "But you tricked me!" she squeaked accusingly.

"Yeah? How'd I do that?"

"You know how; by pretending to be my dead mother!"

Eleanor looked at her as if she'd just grown horns. "What do you mean? I didn't trick you. I didn't even know your mother was dead! All I did was come back here to the Maze of Ages and say your name – just once!" she added preemptively, since Lureli looked about to argue. She heaved an exasperated sigh and began to stomp back inside.

As much as Lureli hated being alone with Eleanor, being alone without her would be worse. She called after her. "What are you doing? Where are you going?"

Without looking back, Eleanor grunted. "I'm calling Aryelle."

Lureli gulped. "Is that really all it took?"

Eleanor returned far enough to glare at her. "I didn't even know if it would work, okay? I thought I was wasting my time on some crazy idea that prophesy planted in my head." She threw up her hands and began pacing. "I almost left. But then, I started wandering around here, trying to figure out the Maze, and where the two of you might be. I figured Aryelle could only be in her treehouse, but who knew where you might have ended up. Except-" she strode back to where Lureli stood, stopping only when they were hoof to toe. "Except I muttered your name out loud, and suddenly, here you were. Conjured up like a bad memory. It doesn't matter anymore where you were...or who you were with, or how happy they made you. All that matters is that none of us can get out of being Chosen, like it or not. We've got a job to do, so let's just do it and get it over with!"

At that very moment, Aryelle walked out of the warren. "Shall we be about it, then?" she asked.

They stared, dumbfounded. She was dressed like a fairy queen, all in colorful silks, her delicate feet swathed in fine slippers. Glowing like a lamp in the rosy morning light, her wings shimmered against the backdrop of the warren. More importantly though, they noted, she was no longer blind.

"You can see again!" cried Lureli. "How?"

"That is a long story. Perhaps someday we will have time to share our tales. Now we have more important matters to discuss."

"What are you doing here? I didn't even call you yet," blurted Eleanor.

"You must have. I heard someone clearly speak my name as I wandered the gardens," said Aryelle walking between them, "-and knew it was time to return. I turned around a hedge, and suddenly, I was here."

"Well, that's strange! I spoke one name and one name only: Lureli. I might have thought of you both, but-"

"It seems that was all it took," Aryelle told her. "As prophesy foretold, the eldest beaconed, and her sisters came. The Chosen are reunited."

"Look, not to interrupt our little 'family' reunion, but that just doesn't make sense, and I'm tired of not knowing what's going on. I'm not going anywhere else, or doing anything either of you says, until I get some answers!" Lureli planted her hands on her hips and waited.

Eleanor shot her a murderous glance and took a step toward her, but Aryelle laid a restraining hand on her arm. A look, and more, passed between the two of them.

Eleanor backed off, taking a deep breath to calm herself; why the mermaid brought out the worst in her she didn't know, but for some reason she always did. "Well then, let's get caught up so we can just get on with it, how's that sound? You first, Little Miss *Shell-fish*."

Lureli cringed at her mean-spirited pun. She was no longer the same person they had known, and she knew it. The only way to prove it to them was to share what had happened. And so, she poured out her tale, glossing over what she had already told Aryelle about her past, but filling in the gaps when needed so Eleanor could keep things straight.

"...and, here I am," she said finally. "I thought it was my mother's voice calling me, and I followed. I told myself we would be a family again, but really... I thought she was calling out to me from the beyond. I wanted to be with her *so* much, even if it meant leaving everything else behind...." she trailed off.

"You were very brave to give up Tad," said Aryelle. By this time they had settled onto the grass facing one another, and she reached over and squeezed Lureli's hand. The sun began to warm them.

"He deserved more," she whispered, falling silent.

Eleanor, reclining nearby, cleared her throat. "How touching," she said, though she obviously wasn't moved. "So what's your story, Aryelle?"

Aryelle fixed her with an emerald stare, and if either one read more in that look, they said nothing. Aryelle gave a forced smile. "Quite simple, really. Mandelbrot sent me back in time to be healed."

Eleanor chuffed. "That much is obvious!"

"Often that which needs healing most cannot be seen," Aryelle said meaningfully. She smiled encouragement at Lureli before turning her attention back to Eleanor. "Vanity and conceit have their root in pride, and I think, perhaps, we have *all* battled such in our travels. As for me, I have learned that my motives are more important than my abilities."

Eleanor's brows met in a scowl. Of all the sanctimonious claptrap-

Before the thought had fully formed, Aryelle's story flooded through her consciousness. More than just words and images, the luminarie's memories were laid open before her, beginning with the healing of the messenger, until the moment she rejoined them. All the fear and insecurities she had never let them see before - yes, the pride! - and subsequent humility. Eleanor felt as if she too was brought low before the Naturra, felt herself giving up everything to set things right. Glancing at Lureli, she realized that Aryelle was sharing this with both of them, that they were both living through it along with her. They experienced Aryelle's fear and confusion, walked with her through the ancient, elaborate gardens in the gloom of midnight, and saw her turn as if listening. They felt her resignation, and recognized their own, at finding themselves together again.

So, things were not as Aryelle would choose them to be either. Eleanor nodded curtly in acknowledgment.

Aryelle nodded back. "And what about you?"

Eleanor waited for the luminarie to plumb her mind, to pull her story from her, but she did not, and for that she was grateful. She might chose to share the whole of it with her someday, but for now, it was still too raw.

"I, too," she said slowly, "have learned to let go of what I want. If that is what you call love, then even a little of it is more powerful - *and the only thing* - that can conquer hate. That, I think, is what Mandelbrot meant for us all to learn."

"A little light to dispel the darkness," mused Aryelle, smiling. "It is one thing to hear of, and quite another to see."

"So, what now?" asked Lureli looking back and forth between them.

At that very moment, a white rabbit darted out of the nearby bushes and sat on its haunches, twitching in the midst of them. "I thought you'd never ask!"

C. A. Morgan

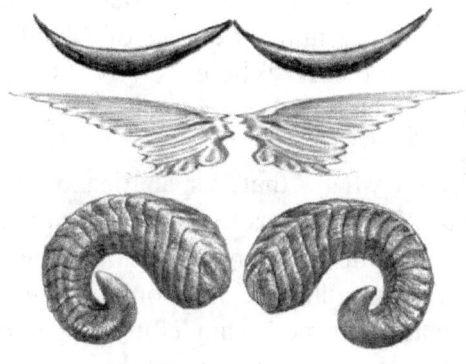

## *Chapter 37 – Reunion*

"Now that we're all back together again-" it began, blinking its beady red eyes.

"Could you please just be Anuran again?" Lureli interrupted. "It's very hard to take you seriously like that."

Mandelbrot's whiskers twitched, his long foot thumping as he scratched behind his ear. "By all means, my dear, by all means…unless, of course, someone else would prefer me in a different form. Dornub, maybe?" He grinned up at Eleanor. "No?"

She frowned, perplexed, and then as realization dawned she grimaced. She had never even suspected that Dornub was just another one of Mandelbrot's manifestations! If she had, she might never have tied the knot with Gord - and just maybe, he would still be alive today! She grew too furious for words.

Shrugging his shoulders, suddenly, instead of a white rabbit, the Anuran version of Mandelbrot was squatting before them. "Where were we? Oh, yes! Now that we're all back together again, there is just one more thing."

"Oh? And what's that?" spat Eleanor, finding her voice. "Haven't you put us through enough already?"

"Goodness, no, not anywhere near enough! And quit pouting, young lady! Gord would be the first to tell you, it's a waste of time." Mandelbrot waggled a webby finger at her. "You don't know but that you had already killed him, kissing him with that nasty cold of yours. I noticed he had a little cough when I left."

"He shouldn't have died at all!" shouted Eleanor, her flesh crawling. She hated that he should know what she was thinking, and wanted to smack the smile right off his homely green face.

"Well if he did, at least he died a happy ram. But then again, maybe he didn't. Die, that is."

"You just said he did!"

"No, I said 'if - so'. Don't you see? Choices always affect the outcome. Not everything is written in stone."

"You mean Gord might still be alive if I had chosen differently?"

"He might still be alive regardless. Things you, or he, or someone else chose might have already killed him-" at her horrified expression he hurried on, "-or might have saved him. Nothing anyone does is in a vacuum. You can't let that stop you from doing altogether; that in itself is a choice. As I hope you've learned, if you choose wisely, thinking about someone other than just yourself, at least you'll have fewer regrets."

"I know I regret ever meeting you!"

"Sorry, my dear, but you had no choice in that matter." He smiled patiently. 'Some things we can't choose for ourselves, and must just make the best of."

Eleanor's scowl deepened. At that moment, her first choice was to wring his skinny Anuran neck! "Is Gord still alive or not?" she demanded.

"That's a good question."

"What - don't you know? You seem to know everything else."

"I do, don't I?" He giggled. "At any rate, knowing isn't all it's cracked up to be. Believing is far better isn't it? It gives you something to hope for."

Eleanor lunged for him, her knife suddenly appearing in her hand. "You better hope-"

"Sister!"

Aryelle held off until the last possible moment to step between them. A sudden flash of light formed a shield of energy around both her and Mandelbrot. Eleanor's blade deflected harmlessly off of it, and went flying. The shock of its impact sent a searing pain up her arm. She jerked back in alarm, clutching her wrist as though burned. Lureli, witnessing it all in shocked silence, picked up the knife, but didn't hand it back. She sidled as near Aryelle as the glowing shield would allow.

Eleanor glared at both of them. "I may be Chosen,' she said, rubbing her arm, "but I'm not your sister, either one of you!"

"Again, not your choice!" piped Mandelbrot, stepping out from behind Aryelle. He gave her shoulder a gentle squeeze. The glow faded, and he winked his big eyes at her, one at a time. "Thank you, my dear, but you needn't have bothered. She could not have hurt me."

"That's what you think!" Eleanor said shaking her empty fist.

"Leave it, Eleanor" said Aryelle. "You said yourself we have a job to do. We need him to show us how."

"I was just getting to that," he said.

"Get on with it then" Eleanor growled, "-but I don't go anywhere without my blade." She snatched it from Lureli's grasp and stomped a few paces away, standing there with her arms crossed over her chest.

"I can see we still need to work on your diplomacy skills," Mandelbrot chastised her. "Good thing that is just what this little jaunt is for. Come along, ladies. It's time to go back to the beginning. And this time, I'll be joining you."

## *Chapter 38 – Revisited*

As the void opened into a colorful swirl of windblown foliage, they found themselves at the edge of New Forest. Crisp air hinted at frost, as if it would soon snow, though Aryelle, recognizing their surroundings, knew they were too far south for that. Ladhonna's labyrinth lay directly before them. In the rosy glow of late afternoon, the treeborn city of Ka'Andharra sprawled just beyond that, her spangled branches stretched wide in welcome - at least, for one of them. Aryelle practically whooped for joy, catching herself just in time. Would it be the same Ka'Andharra she had left; same autumn, or some future time? Would the others be welcome, too?

She turned toward the others, her beaming face sagging into befuddlement as her gaze settled upon a stranger in their midst. Lureli, noticing him at the same time, did a double-take and stepped away from him. Curly red hair and freckled skin adorned the face of the green-eyed, wingless youth. It was the messenger whose coming had started them on their way.

He smiled at them and winked.

"Mandelbrot!" Aryelle whispered in amazement. Lureli went red in the face. Eleanor just scowled.

"In person, so to speak," the young man said bowing. His clothes, though worn, were not blood-soaked or torn, and no scratches marred his chest. "I thought I should dress appropriately for the occasion. And don't bother asking; as you can see, you didn't hurt me in the least - either one of you."

"But, but...the assumption...my father-" stammered Aryelle.

"-thought he sent me back where I came from, I know. It was best to let him think so. But now he needs to know the truth, as do you."

"Despite what you said about knowing?" she asked, though she was glad now that she did. It answered so many questions.

"Oh, you are sharp, aren't you? Yes, hope is better, but knowledge is power. Elazaryn will want to know the whole story. And it will be up to you, my fierce girl," he said, turning toward Eleanor, "to convince him of your cause."

"What cause?" she growled. She had still not forgiven him.

"Why, joining the battle against darkness, of course. The front line is forming on Mt. Cor. Without the Kandharra, all will be lost."

"Get them to help overthrow Borrac? These pacifists?!" Eleanor scoffed.

"They must choose to join in the fight along with the rest. Emrysia's survival depends upon it."

"What good will they do in battle?" she challenged.

Mandelbrot dissolved into a roiling purple cloud that towered above them, but only for a moment. Resolidifying before their eyes, he frowned at her, smoothing his vest as he collected himself. When he had, he answered her tersely. "Perhaps you should ask yourself what good they have already done."

Eleanor felt punched in the gut, and lowered her gaze. She remembered then that she owed her life many times over to the luminaries' talents, and kept silent.

"And I am to reawaken in them their true power, is it not so?" asked Aryelle.

"Indeed," answered Mandelbrot, smiling from ear to ear to show his pleasure with his star pupil. "Light is its own defense. It is the darkness within which we must seek to battle."

"And what about me?" asked Lureli almost timidly. With no special power or skill to offer, not even her case full of remedies, the poor girl sounded crestfallen.

"Ah, my lovely mermaid – why don't you just sing us a song?" And with that he turned to circumvent the labyrinth, and began walking away. Aryelle gave Lureli a sympathetic squeeze and hurried after him.

Eleanor brushed past with an impatient huff. "Come along, *lovely*," she called back to her. "The rest of us have work to do."

\*\*\*\*\*\*

Whether by chance or design, they met no one as they made their way through the twisting halls and walkways toward the grand audience chamber of the El'Kandhar. Aryelle grew more nervous with each step. Pausing just outside the hall's ornately carved door, she searched the others' faces for encouragement. Eleanor jutted out her chin, urging her to just get on with it; Lureli's wide eyes grew even wider. Only Mandelbrot seemed totally at ease. His freckled face dimpled into a smile, and he gave her the thumbs up. Aryelle swallowed the lump in her throat, took a deep breath, and swung the door aside. A massive, silent throng was gathered within. It appeared they were interrupting some important event.

So, thought Eleanor, this was where everyone was hiding.

Gasps of surprise mingled with exclamations of joy as, one after another, the gathered citizenry turned to notice them. Slowly, the crowd parted to make way, and following Aryelle's lead, the newcomers began to cross the echoing marble hall.

Aryelle, fearing it all a dream and that she would awaken to find herself back in Azadhar's reign, held her breath as they approached the exalted seat of Ka'Andharra. But it was her very own father who stumbled blindly down the first few steps, as she rushed up the rest to greet him. They threw their arms around each other.

"Oh, m'yana - my Aryelle! I hardly dared to hope! But here you are, just as Kayanna predicted you would be, and all is well. Welcome home!" Elazaryn's voice shook with emotion.

Aryelle clung to him, not wanting to let go ever again. The joyful Kandharra pressed in around them. Still...all was not well, and there were others to introduce, as Mandelbrot cleared his throat to remind her.

"Dadher - my El'Kandhar," she said, bowing reverently, "there is so much to tell you! But first, come meet my friends..."

\*\*\*\*\*\*

As if one tearful reunion wasn't enough, later the questions flew fast and furious as Kayanna grilled Aryelle about Karril. Seated beside Elazaryn in his private study, Kayanna had arrived only the day before with her Naturra friends, Quinna and Jonquin. Soon Aryelle and her friends would have the pleasure of meeting them, but for now, the only other luminarie present was Gaelen, Aryelle's favorite among her father's councilors. He had given her his seat beside the El'Kandhar, directly across from her aunt, and remained standing a polite distance off to one side. Eleanor and Lureli shifted in uncomfortable silence on fern-backed chairs nearby, while Mandelbrot reclined against the narrow back of his chair, humming quietly and tracing the living limbs of the valleo around the room with his eyes.

Aryelle hung her head in shame as she relayed what had become of her young cousin, adding quickly that, according to Eleanor, he was now - or soon would be - safe in the lower village on Mt. Cor. At least...as safe as any of them were.

Hearing her name mentioned, Eleanor scowled, but held her tongue. She would speak when she must, but it was not time yet. She had been relieved of her of her knife, bow, and arrows when she entered the room, and was feeling rather naked. She would have her say about that soon enough, too!

Aryelle cringed, picking up on Eleanor's thoughts. She dreaded that they must soon relay yet more bad news, and ask her father and the rest of Ka'Andharra to trust her further.

Elazaryn sat quietly absorbing Aryelle's story while Kayanna continued to question her. Aryelle obliged. Though dying to know what had happened in Ka'Andharra in her absence, holding her father's trembling hands between her own, she deferred her questions until her aunt's were all answered. Her eyes kept returning to her father's weary face. How frail he seemed! Eventually, when it was her turn to question them, she searched his fathomless eyes.

"What happened to make you send out your Bel, Dadher?"

Elazaryn only shook his head.

"Let me answer that for you, my liege," offered Gaelen stepping forward, and Elazaryn nodded wearily.

Tears flowed freely down his cheeks as Gaelen described finding his beloved El'Kandhar in this very room, a bloody froth staining his lips, and the telltale cup of poisoned blaiz overturned on the table beside him. Desperate and alone, Elazaryn had already sent out part of his spirit - his Bel – hoping for one last contact with his precious daughter. Fortunately though, the Circle was already gathered for another assumption in the Prism Rotunda. Gaelen rushed Elazaryn to the Kandharril in his very own arms and, though challenged, they were able to save him.

"But, who would have done such a thing?" insisted Aryelle.

Gaelen frowned. "Rachaan and Ladhonna. They were watched like hawks while the evidence against them was examined," he said tartly. "Eventually, both of them were sent away, though Ladhonna still claims her innocence." He resumed the story where he left off, while Elazaryn sadly shook his head. At first it seemed their healing efforts had returned the El'Kandhar to full health, but they soon realized there was a problem. In sending out his Bel after the poison had already begun to affect him, that part of Elazaryn was now slowly growing dimmer, and would continue to do so without being assumed. And, as Aryelle could see for herself, her father's light grew dimmer along with it. There was nothing they could do.

"But, now that you have returned with his Bel…" began Gaelen, expectantly.

"She no longer bears it," whispered Elazaryn. "Karril has it now; I feel it. And there is no telling but that he may soon have great need of its light, dim though it may be."

"But, Father, we could go back for it – and him!" cried Aryelle, squeezing his hand excitedly as the thought occurred to her.

For the first time since entering the chamber, Mandelbrot spoke up. "Um - sorry, but that's not quite true," he apologized, popping out of his chair and coming toward them. "We *will* be able to go back for him, once he gets to where we know he's going. But by then, we wouldn't be able to leave with him until we were sure he didn't choose to go somewhere else in the meantime. It's very complicated, you see, and there could be lasting repercussions if we just go bobbing wildly about time and space."

"I understand," said Elazaryn, resigned. He offered them a weary smile. "It is my fault he left Ka'Andharra in the first place; I will not risk more harm befall him, or anyone else, for my sake."

"But, Father-"

"Don't worry, Aryelle" said Mandelbrot sympathetically, "It will all work out in the end."

"How can you be so sure?" asked Kayanna. Learning her son was alive but still in harm's way - and that she must leave him there - was almost more than she could bear.

"As long as these three do what needs to be done, I guarantee it," he answered with confidence.

Lureli slouched down in her chair, feeling vulnerable.

Aryelle swallowed hard. "I am sorry to have failed you..." she apologized to her father and aunt with bowed head. Looking up, she met Mandelbrot's steady eye and continued, "-but, we have a plan."

"Where have I heard that before?" muttered Eleanor. Taking her cue, she stepped forward.


"And so you say that if we send aid, this battle against your Chieftain will be won? Not only that, the Kra'nochta Empaana will come to an end?" Though impolite, Gaelen stared openly at the strange, fierce Aurrac girl, skeptically sizing her up. How could one so small be so bold? Everything she suggested was contrary to their ways: travel outside of New Forrest, concerning themselves with the affairs of other races, taking up arms – these were things no sane Kandharran would do. Yet, here she was almost demanding they do so. Still, if his El'Kandhar wished it, he would go himself.

"Well, so says Mandelbrot," answered Eleanor, weighing her words carefully. She lifted her chin in his direction and he waved, encouraging her to continue. "He also seems to think it is only part of a bigger picture. Dark times are ahead for all of us. I had never heard of the Reign of Shadow until Aryelle came along, but I can tell you this; the evil of Borrac's reign is spreading. And if he isn't stopped, it won't be either."

Elazaryn had kept his silence, allowing his two councilors to question her. But now, he slowly pulled himself to his feet and leaned toward Eleanor. "We have kept you far too long. You and our other guests will be in want of refreshment and rest. We will ponder your request overnight, and revisit it on the morrow. Is there anything you would like to add before you take your leave?"

Eleanor squared her shoulders, her short tail flicking in agitation. Though she found herself strangely drawn to the aging monarch, she was not used to being dismissed. Nor was she so sure she had convinced him of anything.

"Only this," she offered as a new thought came to her. "Long ago, a luminarie saved my life. His name was Erildhil-" she paused when Kayanna gasped, and then hurried on. "Recently, three more luminaries - including Aryelle and her cousin - saved it again. And believe it or not, this winter Karril will save it a third time. Somewhere in time, he already has. There's got to be some reason you people keep saving me. I think my being here today, asking for your help, might just be it." She backed away a step, pondering her own words.

"Thank you, my dear," said Elazaryn solemnly. "Perhaps it is time for the Kandharra to reawaken, and step out of their own shadow." With that, he summoned pages to show them to their rooms, kissing Aryelle with the promise that they would speak again later.

Everyone stood to leave. Lureli, still dejected, allowed Aryelle to take her by the hand as they followed Eleanor from the room.

"Mandelbrot, if you do not mind," asked Elazaryn, feeling for his chair and sitting back down, "I would like to have a word with you in private."

The red-haired youth had remained where he was, and answered now with an impish grin. "I was pretty sure you would."

\*\*\*\*\*\*

Aryelle practically skipped away. Her duty done by seeing Lureli comfortably settled into her rooms, she was eager to spend more time with her father.

Lureli heaved a sigh of relief. She had insisted she was fine for Aryelle's sake; now that Aryelle was gone, she could stop pretending. She wasn't fine at all. On top of everything else, she had been completely mortified when Mandelbrot revealed that *he* was the red-haired messenger! That day when he showed up on the Mer beech – it seemed a lifetime ago! - had been a particularly low day for her, from what she recalled of it. She remembered the three long scratches she had inflicted on his bare chest as he shied away from her advances, and how she had laughed at his innocence as he ran off into the forest. Oh, how she regretted all of it! And now, besides being embarrassed and miserable, she couldn't shake the feeling that she was somehow becoming invisible. There were no mirrors around for her to check...but it wasn't that kind of invisibility, anyway. It was more that everyone here seemed to look right through her, as if she had somehow ceased to exist. It had been ages since she'd done anything about her own appearance. Maybe, because she looked so aw-

ful without her make-ups, no one could stand to make
eye contact with her. Then again, even Elazaryn had
ignored her, and he was blind. She didn't mind so much
not being the center of attention, given the circumstances, but a little of it sure would be appreciated!
Lureli picked dispiritedly at the food that had been
left for her - some fruit and nuts, a few flavorless wa-
fers, and a light, clear broth that was surprisingly delicious - but she had no real appetite. The spartan room
held little interest for her either. How plain and simple
everything was, not a single unnecessary adornment.
Not exactly welcoming, she thought. All at once she
felt utterly exhausted. She flopped into the pillow-less
net bed and hugged herself. Maybe she should just try
to sleep. A little beauty rest might make her feel better.

She awoke the next morning to a loud pounding on
her door. Wiping the drool from her chin, she rolled
over and off the bed, hitting the too-close floor with a
thud. The pounding halted, resuming as she quickly
scrambled to her feet. Somebody sure was impatient to
see her. The thought made Lureli smile. Smoothing her
hair as best she could, she checked her breath and then
hurried to the door, throwing it wide. To her dismay,
only Eleanor stood on the other side. She pushed into
the room uninvited, nabbing a dragon fruit from the
serving tray as she passed by. Turning, she began tossing it back and forth between her hands. Lureli checked
the hallway. Seeing no one else there, she closed the
door and leaned against it, crossing her arms. This was
bound to be an unfriendly little visit.

"I'll get right to the point," said Eleanor brusquely. She slammed the fruit back onto the tray so hard it cracked open. "I'm going to be pretty busy for a while once Aryelle's father decides to help us, and so will she, I imagine. You're the only one who isn't necessary right now, so I want you to do something."

"And what's that?" asked Lureli, feeling more than a little offended.

"I want you to hide this and guard it," she answered, holding out the crystal key. "I know it's yours by rights, but I don't want Mandelbrot taking it away again. He still thinks I have it, and if he gets it in his mind to- well... let's just say I don't want to be anyone's puppet anymore. You heard what he said about choices. If we do this thing, I want it to be our choice."

"Aren't you afraid I'll just go home? After all, I know how to use it," Lureli said defiantly.

Eleanor grabbed her by the shoulders and pinned her to the door. Nose to nose, her eyes bored into Lureli's with a stare so intense that she felt her soul begin to shrivel. Then Eleanor released her and leaned back, crossing her arms.

"You might, but I don't think you will. I think you'll stay right here while we train these fairies to fight, and then go wherever the next wave takes us, like the flotsam that you are. You'll stick around because you like the idea of being Chosen, don't you? It makes you feel important."

Though her eyes stung, Lureli held back her tears. *I will not give her the satisfaction - I will not!* She clenched her teeth to steady her trembling chin."What did I ever do to you?" she finally managed, working hard to keep the quiver out of her voice. "I know you don't like me, but what did I ever do to deserve such hatred?"

"You just are; that's all."

"No! That's not good enough!" Lureli shouted, pushing off from the door and taking a step toward her. Eleanor actually backed up a pace. "You can't treat me like I'm nothing; I'm a person, with hopes and feelings! You can't just say things like that without hurting people."

"I don't care if I hurt you."

"But, *why?*"

"Because...because it's always about you, even when it's not. I saw you pouting because no one was paying any attention to you. Oh, poor you! Someone does, and you throw them away - yeah, I'm talking about that Anuran. You didn't even deserve him! You'll find someone else to love and you know it, so you tossed him aside as easily as...as..." stammering, Eleanor ran out of words. Her face grew blotchy red, and she bit her lips together hard.

If she didn't know better, Lureli would have guessed Eleanor was trying to keep from crying.

With an undignified snuffle, Eleanor slapped the crystal into Lureli's hand. Then, wrenching the door open, she stormed out leaving Lureli to stare after her.

## *Chapter 39 – Redeemed*

It was a mild winter in Ka'Andharra. Having learned their arrival came later in the season than they first thought, once Elazaryn agreed to help, they wasted no time. Eleanor had her hands full though, as it turned out, Aryelle's newly acquired skills were what the luminaries would be bringing to battle. While she spent her days tutoring her fellow Kandharra in how to strengthen their healing abilities and channel their light into protective shields, Eleanor found herself schooling them about the other races' and Aurrac ways. In doing so, she found out they held much in common, and even began to soften a bit toward them.

The other newcomers, Jonquin and Quinna, were kept busy teaching the city dwellers how to live off the land, and how to rightly use the labyrinth. Kayanna worked tirelessly alongside them. Their new, close friendship took the edge off of learning about Jonazat's fate. Elazaryn, touched by the Naturras' sacrifice for Aryelle's sake, swore to do everything in his power to try and reunite the two factions of the Empaya into one. Word spread among the few Naturra already in the city, and soon more could be seen coming and going. A few were even invited into Elazaryn's private council. Before the winter was out, emissaries from the Mer were also welcomed in Ka'Andharra.

Mandelbrot was delighted by the luminaries' willingness to reconnect with the rest of Emrysia. After the initial curiosity stirred by the new arrivals, there were, of course, some who would rather the Kandharra remain set apart, but they were few, and mostly kept their opinions to themselves. The remainder joined in wholeheartedly with Elazaryn's call to action. While their parents were busy with training, Mandelbrot spent most of his time visiting with the children of the city, telling stories and filling their heads with wonder as he shifted from shape to shape. His lessons were about their world and others, and they were quick to learn. Soon, it was as if the Seal of Silence had never been.

Spring approached, and Lureli remained at a loss. To her alone the luminaries remained polite, but aloof. Consumed with new purpose, they seemed unaware of her sorry inner state, a fact she found very hard to understand. After all, they were empaths, weren't they? Couldn't they see that she didn't really want to be left alone? But, most of the time she found herself just that; restlessly wandering the corridors with only her memories for company.

One morning, long before daybreak, a preliminary delegation made up of both Kandharra and Naturra was dispatched to fetch Karril home. Waking from a restless dream, Lureli looked out her window to see them leaving. She watched as the telltale aura of a dozen slender figures disappeared into the forest. Soon the rest of the Kandharran troops would march, and then, they must go as well. She was anxious to leave this place, but was she ready for what was to come? While the rest of the house slept on, she left her bed to wander - alone yet again - in the uppermost branches of the royal dwelling.

Though each carved door she came upon was different, she thought she recognized a familiar facade as she strolled along a brightly lit, unfamiliar corridor. Curious, she opened it and peeked in. Ah, yes - it was the grand audience chamber of the El'Kandhar, which she had visited just the once, on the day of their arrival. This time it was empty. She stepped inside to look around. Here the simplicity of Kandharran design seemed grand due solely to scale. Tip-toeing across the vast hall, she approached the marble dais, and settled on the steps to the vacant throne about halfway up. Looking out over the lonely hall she sighed, and imagined it filled with crowds of admirers, all clamoring for her attention. Then Eleanor's painful words came back to haunt her. She's right about me, she thought, hanging her head in shame.

She understood her a bit better now. Aryelle had spent some time with both of them separately, and had shared a bit of Eleanor's sad story with her. Though they hadn't spoken to one another since, Lureli had caught Eleanor looking at her with a little less hostility, too.

Without thinking, she began tracing the blue veins across the cold marble with her fingertip, humming tunelessly as a comfort to herself. Eventually her humming became a song. The melody she sang was hauntingly sweet, and though she sang softly, for her ears alone, it carried throughout the chamber. As the final echo melted away, Lureli heard a small noise and looked up. Elazaryn sat above her listening. How long he had been there she did not know. Embarrassed, she leapt to her feet, backing quickly down the stairs. It was clear by the peaceful countenance of his face that he had been captivated by her song, though not spellbound. For that she was truly thankful.

"I'm s-sooo sorry," she stammered. "I didn't mean to- I.. I wouldn't have if I'd known anyone was listening."

"It was lovely, child; no need to apologize. You have a gift. You should use it more often."

"I would if it helped, but it doesn't."

"I would say the opposite is true. It helped me just now. I know this city like my own hand, but often of late, I get turned around, and forget where it is I am going. Your beautiful voice led me exactly where I was meant to be."

"You are kind, your Majesty, but-"

"What is more, I am right," said Elazaryn smiling down at her, and she could tell by his tone that he meant it. "Those who know themselves will not be led where they do not wish to travel. Hiding your light only deprives those who need it most."

His words were simple and healing. And suddenly, she realized her purpose.

\*\*\*\*\*\*

The crystal key was right where she had hidden it, inside a largish knothole in the valleo branch that wended its way around the walls of her room. She took it out and looked at it. How far she had come since learning how to use this! It was so much more than a vial, now empty, but formerly holding nothing but useless potion. With this key she had traveled the Connectedness Locus, spiraling through time and space – once even all by herself. She had threatened to use it to go home before, though Eleanor was right; she hadn't had the nerve. If Orpheas was dead, she knew she could not face that alone. If he was alive, well, once there she knew she would never be able to leave his side again. At least she had gotten to see him again, and to know that he still loved her. But there was somewhere she would go, somewhere Eleanor would never suspect. And she would never tell.

\*\*\*\*\*\*

"Did you have a nice trip?"

Lureli nearly jumped out of her skin. In the blink of an eye that she had been absent from Ka'Andharra, Mandelbrot - back in Anuran form for her sake - had come into her room, and was now sitting on her bed waiting for her. Flushing guiltily, she hid the key behind her back.

"I, um…" she stammered, attempting to fabricate a lie.

"No need to pretend," he chuckled. "I know where you've been. Did you get him off that mountain in time?"

Her eyes grew wide. Of course he would know; how could she have imagined he would not? She swallowed hard, deciding what to say. Finally, she settled on the truth. "He's safe for now. I sang for him, and he followed my voice, like I knew he would. Just a short distance, but far enough. He was clear when it happened."

"I imagine he took it hard."

Lureli's heart lurched recalling it; the rumbling of the snowy mountain, the strapping Aurrac bighorn, physically unharmed, yet crumbling to pieces before her eyes. Out of sight behind a snow-capped boulder, she waited as he tore back, desperately searching the buried slope for signs of where the cave - *Eleanor's frozen tomb!* - might be. Screaming her name over and over, he dug in vain nowhere near the site until, collapsing in an exhausted, blubbering heap, he finally gave up. From her hiding place she mourned along with him, wishing she could go to him and offer some comfort, some consolation, but knowing he must not see her lest he be spellbound. His pain almost destroyed her, especially when, eventually, he realized that it was hopeless. She saw his resolve harden then, and wiped her own eyes, edging around the boulder as he marched resolutely past, and headed down off the mountain.

"He made it home, you know," said Mandelbrot, patting her shoulder and bringing her back to the present. "My guess is that he will be instrumental in bringing Borrac down."

"Will she ever see him again?" asked Lureli, sniffling.

"Ah, that I can't tell you. You took a chance, and you did what you could. The rest will play out as it will."

"I could go back-" she offered, but Mandelbrot was shaking his head.

"No - you've done your part. You did well, but you can't say a word about it either, or she will want to go back herself, and that would not be possible. It's time for us to go."

Lureli gulped. "Go? Where?"

Mandelbrot answered gently. "On your final adventure here, my dear. It's finally time for the Chosen to step forward."

C. A. Morgan

## *Chapter 40 – Going Home*

Above the stillness of the slow-waking garden, leaden skies made it impossible to tell if it was early or late in the day. Aryelle and Eleanor paced near the entrance of the labyrinth, where Mandelbrot had bid them wait while he fetched Lureli. They turned as one at the sound of their approach. Now that the time had finally arrived, both looked impatient to be on their way. Mandelbrot acknowledged them with a nod and continued walking. Falling into line behind Lureli they were solemn, each one sorting her own jumbled emotions. The immense grove and the treeborn city seemed to shrink with every step they took into the shrub-lined maze.

Lureli's heart was beating out of her chest, she was so terrified, but at least now she was also ready. To tell the truth, she was weary of the struggle, of trying to do the right thing and always falling short. Life had been so much easier when the only one she cared about was herself. Easier didn't mean better though, and she understood that now. This was a chance to redeem herself further.

For Aryelle, just as it had always been, the peace that came from serving a higher purpose prevailed, wiping away all doubt. She walked with eyes forward, not once looking back at the city she loved, savoring instead the knowledge that she was helping, among others, those who loved her most, and whom she loved. Her father's blessing went with her this time, and she almost faltered a step when she considered the possibly never seeing him again this side of the Gate. At least Karril would soon be back to take her place, if need be; she had Mandelbrot's assurance of that. He would be the next El'Kandhar, serving their people with wisdom and compassion. Hopefully, he would also be the one to fully reunite the Empaya, and to reopen the city to the rest of Emrysia. Aryelle was relieved.

Eleanor alone looked back in dismay wondering how long this would take. Ka'Andharra was a strange place, with even stranger people, and yet, in leaving now she was putting the Aurrac's fate in their hands. Would it be enough? She thought of Nodd. Was he Borrac's prisoner? Was he even still alive? And what of her mother and aunt and the rest of the lower villagers; what would they think when she didn't return? They would know soon enough that she had done all she could, once the luminarie delegation arrived. Her clanherd would go on without her, she supposed, provided they survived what was coming. That she would not be there to fight alongside them was something she could hardly bear. It was not her only regret. But... she would not think of Gord! In her mind's eye, that door slammed shut as soon as soon as it cracked open. She ignored the dim light of hope peeking in around its edges, the hope that he might still be alive. She turned away, glad that they were finally leaving this too-brilliant city behind.

They rounded a bend and Mandelbrot stopped short. Directly in front of him was a wide archway woven of barren branches, though all around it was bursting green. He held up a hand in caution, and while they waited, he went to inspect it. After a few moments of muttering to himself, he came back to them wringing his hands. There was something off about his smile.

"A twig or two broken, snapped off - probably just an animal. No worries! It's supposed to look like this," he assured them. "Now, just a few instructions; you remember the gist of the prophesy, I suppose?"

"When the blood of all Emrysia cries out-" intoned Eleanor.

"No, no, no – not that one!" Mandelbrot waved his webbed hands, shooing the conjured unpleasantness away. "The other one, please! Aryelle?"

Though it seemed ages had gone by - *and they had!* - since hearing it, Aryelle recited the Omniscients' rhyme from memory:

"Scales tip unbalanced
Hatred and fear
Evil is winning
End Times are near.

Three royal children
Siblings fair
Serving one master
Land, sea, and air

Sing now, ye sisters
Color, form, light
Gifts freely given
Conquer the night."


"Are you gonna tell us what it means now, or can we just get it over with?" asked Eleanor.

"Patience," he warned. "Great moments should not be rushed. Besides, there are three verses. Why don't each of you take one, and you tell me? Let's start with you, the eldest."

Eleanor scowled. "Alright," she said, clenching her teeth so hard that the muscle in her jaw twitched. "I'll play along, if that's what it takes." She heaved a sigh, feeling sick to her stomach. "It's pretty obvious that evil is winning. I suppose we're the ones tipping the scales somehow, and now we've gotta die or something."

"Dying is just another doorway," said Mandelbrot. "To open it prematurely is foolhardy, but to fear it is unnecessary. Besides, you are all meant to die someday, you know. You already have more than once, my fierce girl. You too, Aryelle."

"What about me?" asked Lureli, feeling strange about still feeling left out.

"Yes, you too, my dear, though when Viviannne bargained for your life long ago - when you were but a wee minnow - it was totally unnecessary. She traded her life for yours, as any mother would, and counted herself fortunate enough to negotiate extra years to spend with you before payment came due. But that is another story. Suffice it to say, you are here now, right where you need to be at this moment in time."

This news was more than she could absorb. "So, my mother didn't have to die after all.." she whispered, horrified and confused. "She saved my life, and now I have to give it up?"

"Oh, gracious no! But you do have to leave Emrysia - all of you do. It's time for you to go home."

"What do you mean?" asked all three at once.

Aryelle, as could be expected, was especially bewildered. "I am home!" she added.

"Are you? Then why don't you take the next verse, dear?" he asked.

She stared at the other two for a moment, and then something clicked. "Siblings fair…" she murmured. "We really *are* sisters, I suppose, serving Emrysia, but…we are not from here, are we?" As soon as she said it, she knew it was so.

"Your insight amazes me!" he said proudly. "Correct on all counts. You were sent here by your parents -

your *true* parents. They were royal, too - yes, but also powerless to save you in your world. And so, they enlisted the help of someone who could. Oh, no - not me!" he admitted quickly, "but someone very like me. His name is unimportant. He is half Lydian, and therefore still powerful. Good at heart, though a tad limited. He was able to send you into this world at the exact instant those souls whose bodies you possess shed them. Can anyone tell me when that would have been?"

Aryelle didn't wait for the others to guess. "The day I was born," she said.

"Correct again! And, when Borrac struck the first time" he nodded at Eleanor, "and when Vivianne pulled your limp body from the wreckage," he added toward Lureli. Lureli's eyes grew huge as she caught on. "Yes, I see you understand now. Mirros hinted that you were adopted, you'll remember. All of these events happened at the same time. The Shadow cast by your coming has thrown this world into a tailspin that only you can correct. And now, it's your turn, dear. The third verse, please," he prompted.

Lureli let out a breath she hadn't realized she was holding, and took in another. Like a bubble bursting, an image popped into her mind. In it she saw three tiny girls, holding hands and standing on the bow of a ship. She was one of them, and the others - her sisters – stood next to her.

"We have to give up these bodies now and go back to where we came from, don't we? We don't really belong here, and leaving is the only way to restore balance to Emrysia, isn't it?"

"No, and yes," he said kindly, a sad sweetness wetting his eyes. "You are right, you don't belong here. You never have. But when I say you must correct it, that is not entirely true. You are upsetting a delicate balance that those who do belong must figure out how to restore once you are gone. This world has its atrocities, certainly. The world you are returning to has some of its own. But, it is not your job to interfere where you do not belong, rather to find your place and grow there. If you truly want to help overcome the present darkness in Emrysia, you will return now to your own world, which needs your giftedness even more. Eventually, and only after you have fulfilled your purpose there, you will return to your *true* home - a place altogether separate, where all worlds begin and end. And there, finally, there will be no more darkness, only light."

He gave them time to absorb what he was telling them. They understood, mostly. Each in her own way, and for her own reasons, had finally come to the point where she could accept the truth; that they were only the smallest part of an incomprehensible picture. Maybe someday they would be big enough to see the whole of it.

"I know you are ready for whatever your new life in your old world will bring. And now, my dears, it is time."

He stepped aside, gesturing toward the archway with a broad sweep of his arm. The three Chosen looked at one another, no one of them wanting to go first. Then, smiling bravely, Aryelle offered a hand to each of her sisters. Lureli gulped and took her hand and, more slowly, so did Eleanor. Together they stepped forward and through to the other side.

In an instant they vanished.

Mandelbrot stared at the space they left behind, then shuddered, muttering to himself. "Whoever passed through before them, well…I only hope they knew what they were doing. It's out of my hands now." Turning, he dissolved into a billowing, purple cloud, his rumbling, disembodied voice swirling throughout it.

"Myrddin, get ready for them…"

*Emrysia: Endurance*

C. A. Morgan

# *Acknowledgments*

Woman is no more an island than man, so although I am extremely proud of this self-published work, I have many people to thank. First and foremost is my husband, Roger for his patience and constancy in putting up with my fluctuating hormones and unappeasable need to create over the years - you are my anchor, and still the man of my dreams. I could never do this without your support. To my sister-in-law, Terri I owe a debt of gratitude for the timely gift of her laptop, which made portability possible - a real godsend! To Joyce Spallone-Medovich and the Benedictine Brothers at Mt. Savior Monastery (who shared their peaceful setting with me while I penned several chapters on said laptop), God bless you for supplying me with the retreat I needed instead of the one I expected. Since the hardest work comes after writing, a huge thank you to Neil Raphel & Janis Raye for generously sharing their time and knowledge about publishing & marketing, and for rooting for me to succeed. Thanks to Roger DeKett and Barb Armstrong for your sharp eyes and gentle criticisms, and for making this a better read. Thank you, Jacob Grant, for your last minute cover design assist; if only it were as easy as you make it seem. To Janet Givens for sharing her writing journey; Ela Golden, whose healing gift and selflessness are beyond inspirational; Chuck (& Nancy) Brown for introducing me to the Alexander Technique; and to the rest of my Continua friends, whose musical and diverse voices bring ever

C. A. Morgan

more beauty into my life, and the lives of many others - thank you. Heartfelt appreciation and good wishes (in lieu of chocolate) go out to the numerous writers I've connected with in person and online for the wealth of support and information they share. I realize with gratitude how little I could accomplish without building upon what others have taught me. Thanks to the various local bookstores, libraries and schools that have invited me to meet with readers, a part of this job that I love. To friends, family, and those who discover Emrysia for themselves for not only reading my work, but sharing it with others – thanks for getting the word out, and for encouraging me whenever doubt sets in. Your belief in Emrysia makes a world of difference, pun intended. And lastly, a special thank you to all who leave reviews; you are a writer's best friend when you help to spread the word. After all, what good is a storyteller without people to enjoy the story?

# More About Emrysians

## ~ *The Aurrac* ~

Eleanor of the Aurrac clanherds is not your typical female mountain fauen. Though member of a fierce race, it is usually the dominate male Aurrac - or rams - that do all of the fighting. But are these partial ungulates half-goat, or half-sheep? That's the big question, and one you're not likely to have answered by the Aurrac themselves. They are a proud, though not spectacularly brilliant race, and most likely cousin to both. They are also (ironically) shepherds whose favorite meals include the meat and milk products of their domesticated relatives. *Hmmm...*

Few Aurrac can read or write, and those who do, do it in Common only, as they have no other language of their own. Histories are kept and passed on orally, and story-telling is considered a highly-prized skill. Those who are able to read ascend to high-ranking positions in whatever occupations they pursue, since other Aurrac automatically turn to them for leadership.

The herd mentality runs thick through Aurrac veins, and it is a rare mountain fauen who prefers solitude. Perhaps due to the human half of their nature, they tend to prefer town and city living for ease of access to services and entertainment. Outcasts are apt to seek out others, creating smaller unofficial clanherds. Lusty and impulsive, it is equally rare to find celibate or monogamous Aurrac couples, though some mated pairs do marry for life. Nodd and Althea have found that their compatibility more than compensates for lack of physical pleasures. Superstitious and naturally territorial, Aurrac interaction with the other races is limited to trade and their yearly Blood Moon Festival, though such was not always the case. Much depends on the leadership, and a more gregarious ruler will often lead to a more gregarious generation. Aurrac do, however, stick to reverencing their own numerous gods rather than adopting those of other races. It does not follow that they don't believe in them, they just can't relate. Stubbornness and resistance to change   (along with a fiery temper!) are characteristic traits, hence the Common-speak quip familiar to other Emrysians - "ornery as an Aurrac".

## ~ *The Glisseon* ~

Lureli is princess of the people known as Glisseon in their own undersea language. Their home in the Chimera Sea lies mainly off the southern coast of Emrysia, although they have been known occasionally to travel inland along the connected waterways of the continent. Characteristic fishlike tails enable them to glide through the water as smoothly as any other sea creature. Human from the torso up, their skin has a silvery sheen which acts as a camouflaging aid as they dart through the shimmering waves alongside ships, and distinguishes them on land once their tails have morphed into limbs. They are equally capable of surviving out of water provided they keep themselves adequately hydrated - however, getting around is another story. Long ago, Glisseon were able to transform at will and, in their bipedal form, they frequently traded with the land races. Gradually, preferring the comforts of the sea to roaming inland, they lost the ability to shape-shift. Now only the Sea God, Orpheas and Japhra the Sea Witch can transform tailfins into legs (or vice-versa), though as part of her banishment, Japhra was forbidden to use this power on others. The privilege of limbs for going ashore is doled out sparingly, mostly to those who hunt out exhibits for the Asylum.

The Glisseon are a sensuous people, highly creative and musical, vanity and jealousy being their main flaws. They are also extremely moody. Frequently bored by the ease of their dream-like existence, entertainment is highly prized. They play a variety of games, and there are always sporting events or other diversions to be enjoyed. Filling every possible moment with activity - *as long as it doesn't interfere with their beauty rest!* - they don't have time for deep reflection. Their favorite pastime is luring ships ashore.

Because they are so captivating, men who see them or hear them sing often become entranced. Colonies of shipwrecked sailors dot the shorelines of Emrysia, their sunken vessels becoming a Glisseon playground of sorts. These mysteriously silent men are known throughout the rest of the continent only as Mer, though their origins are as varied as the winds which bring them. Castaway, they live hoping for glimpses of the sultry sirens of the sea, whose mesmerizing beauty steals not only the men's hearts, but their voices and all memory of their former lives as well.

Glisseon are always born female. Naturally inquisitive, they like to observe the Mer, though usually from a safe distance; they are shy about making actual contact. Occasionally however, males are adopted into the Glisseon from the ranks of these sailors who follow them into the sea. Rescued and shape-changed, they dote on their "mermaids". Lureli is the only known adopted female.

The underwater world of the Glisseon is gloriously beautiful. Its undulating forests of anemones and corals provide a spectacular backdrop when they go on hunts (like foxing) riding giant manta rays in search of camouflaged squid. The Glisseon eat crustaceans, jellies and other fish, foraging and farming the bounty of the sea. Feasting is another favorite pastime. They consider dolphins and whale their friends, and have domesticated several species of fish and sea horse. They avoid sharks, poisonous corals and jellies, and other dangers, yet possess medicines and fairly advanced technologies which make death by disease practically unheard of. They come in all shapes and sizes, though Lureli, youngest daughter of the Sea God, Orpheas is by far their crowning jewel.

## ~ *The Empa'aya* ~
## *(Kandharra & Naturra)*

All luminaries are healers and empaths, but none so skilled as the ruling class of Kandharra, perhaps owing to time invested in developing their talents. The Kandharril - a circle of elite healers - devote their lives to study and contemplation, further increasing their healing capacities. While this is effective, something of their natural empathy is lost through seclusion.

The reigning monarch is as you would expect part of this circle. As the current El'Kandhar's firstborn child, Aryelle has been groomed to be the next El'Kandharra, or Brightest Candle - not that she will get the chance now! Luckily, Karril, next in the royal line of succession, is equally well-equipped; otherwise rule would fall to Elazaryn's nearest in age blood relative, male or female - in this case Rachaan, despite his recent removal from court. Talk about a Reign of Shadow!

The schism between the Kandharra and Naturra occurred over growing disharmony between the erudite and working classes of luminaries. Normally pacifists, even luminaries can be dangerous when riled, and the factions became bitter enemies when disease and famine decimated the ranks of the Naturra, and no help was forthcoming. They began raiding the city, eventually withdrawing into the deepest part of Wellwood Forest, leaving the city in ruin. Over the last five generations, progress has been made in reuniting the Empa'aya into one unified race. Were Rachaan to ever rule, that tenuous unity would likely be shattered.

Luminaries, while possessing natural good taste, do not dwell overmuch on appearances and creature comforts, and tend to think little of those who do. The Kandharra, however, take certain luxuries for granted: the beauty of their city, an abundance of material goods, and the leisure to do as they please. The hardworking Naturra live under no illusions of what that lifestyle requires, though they themselves care little for a life of ease. In their own way, they feel superior to the Kandharra, who are dependent upon them for almost everything. It is the lack of mutual respect and having no choice that rankles most. Were the Naturra considered equals by the Kandharra, most would still opt to live as they do, outside the city in communion with nature.

Luminaries worship no deities, considering themselves to be the epitome of spiritual, physical and mental perfection. (They do however, hold Lydians in high esteem.) By recognizing that they are indeed a flawed race, Aryelle has become open to the possibility that there is some greater aim than self-interest. Luminarie life spans are short compared to some of the other races in Emrysia, but they generally enjoy full health up until their passing. Even the eldest among them have youthful features without wrinkle, and their hair never grays nor whitens.

## *A Word About Outdoor Winter Survival*

Eleanor endured her wintry ordeal, though just barely. Understanding your physiological needs is key for survival, especially in harsh conditions. The four basic needs are: oxygen, food, water, and shelter/warmth. Circumstances will dictate how to prioritize the last three, but unless you are part tree and can make your own oxygen, breathable air is always first on the list; usually, thank goodness, that is a given. Humans can only survive an average of three minutes without air. Knowing you can breathe, how do you determine what to consider next? Continue to apply The Rule of Three. You can survive for:

- **3 Minutes without air** (oxygen) or in icy water

- **3 Hours without shelter** in a harsh environment (unless in icy water, then less)

- **3 Days without water** (if sheltered from a harsh environment)

- **3 Weeks without food** (if you have water and shelter)

The point of The Rule of Three is to concentrate on the most immediate problem first. There is no need to worry about food if you are cold and wet and the main threat to your survival is hypothermia. If you are unable to warm up and get dry, you may not able to function after three hours. Alone, you may have only about three hours to live.

*For more, research safety and survival, online or in survival manuals. Save a life - yours or someone else - in the future.*

*Not ready to leave Emrysia yet?*
*Then enjoy this snippet from my upcoming pre-quel...*

## The Daughters of Ka'Dharron

"Her ladyship is indeed with child again, my lord," said Allora upon entering the antechamber between Leandhra's and Elazaryn's private suite of rooms. A satisfied smile lit her face. This time around, she knew the El'Kandhar would trust no other with the care of his beloved spouse. As current head of the Kandharril, there was none whose healing powers exceeded her own, except perhaps the El'Kandhar himself.

Elazaryn leapt to his feet. "Are you sure?" he asked, hope and fear in equal measure reflected in his eyes.

"Nearly a quarter revolution" she confirmed with a nod. "She is sleeping now, but aside from the normal discomforts of carrying a child, she is in perfect health. Obviously though, she has been under some strain of late..." She allowed her words to trail off meaningfully, rather than question him directly.

"Yes, I am afraid she has. My father's death. And, of course, my own return. The former miscarriages still weigh heavily on her, and now this..." he hesitated before continuing with eyes averted. "She thought she was past her time, you know. That is the only reason we agreed that I should take Ladhonna as a second wife. I must, as you know, produce an heir." It was almost an apology. "I regret to have been so distracted by the preparations that I did not notice her condition."

"Our bodies are mysterious things, to be sure" Allora murmured noncommittally. Never would she make the mistake of criticizing his recent actions. Fortunately, her thought-shields were firmly in place.

"And the child?" he asked, belatedly.

"I sense nothing amiss, though I understand your concerns. She has not before carried to term?"

"No. Each time everything appeared well until the six candles mark, and then... she would lose them."

So, he too was still in mourning. "Leave her care to me exclusively, my lord" said Allora firmly, "and I will see that this child comes to light."

Elazaryn searched her eyes, willing it to be true. "Danka'zu, Allora. I am grateful. She has normally had her sister to look after her in this condition, but somehow I think Ladhonna will be less than pleased with the situation..."

Ladhonna lay in her darkened bedchamber, fuming. Embarrassing as Elazaryn's first rejection of her had been (after the fiasco of their original wedding feast, so many revolutions ago), now that history was repeating itself, she was positively mortified! How could she ever show her face again? Granted, it was her sister who made a public spectacle of herself this time, throwing up beside the table before fleeing. But somehow, it was she, Ladhonna, who looked the worse for it. Elazaryn had immediately gone to his wife's aid, grabbing the linen napkin from her very hand to wipe the drool from her sister's disgusting chin. He had not even looked back at her as he led Leandhra away. Humiliation flooded over her again. *Twice scorned, but never again,* she vowed. He would pay for this, and so would her sister.

A knock came on the chamber's outer door.

"Go away!" she spat.

The door opened nonetheless, and a young female page entered hesitantly. Curtsying, she approached the side of Ladhonna's bed, and whispered her report.

When she went to the healers later that evening, the page refused to explain how the jagged scratches came to be on her face.

******

It was early spring, and her tenth moon had come and gone with the rains. In just under one full candle's time her child would be born, its first revolution of life complete. Leandhra could barely contain her excitement. She loved feeling the babe move within her, but longed as well to meet it face to face. Though her confinement had passed thus far without incident, she would never feel completely at rest until a living, breathing baby was placed safely into her arms.

Allora had cared for her well, but was, in her mind, overly strict. Leandhra was supposed to be napping right now, but was too restless for that today. She missed her sister's visits. True, Kayanna still came regularly, but because she herself had recently experienced a difficult pregnancy and loss, it was often awkward. Odd that her younger sister was so like her, even in that regard. Perhaps if they had been closer in age than she and Ladhonna they would have been better friends. Ladhonna, though, had made herself scarce since her first visit after learning of Leandhra's condition. Then, she had brought a servant with her bearing a polished silver tea tray, but Allora had insisted her patient was to have nothing that she herself had not prepared. While proficient on every other count, Allora certainly had not Ladhonna's touch with spices and herbs. Leandhra's mouth had watered at the aroma coming from the carafe of tea and platter of delicacies, but her watchdog held her ground. Insulted, Ladhonna had turned on her heel, taking her servant and her treats with her.

Deprived of both her favorite morsels *and* her favorite sister, Her Ladyship had kept herself busy preparing a layette of gossamer buntings and wing bindings fit for the royal heir. Since the child's eyes would need to be shielded for its first revolution in the light, she had also woven several of the special low hanging bonnets - *jaboqua* - lining them with thistledown, and dying them a luscious deep violet, her favorite color. Only recently, with the passing of her tenth moon, had ladies of all the noble houses come bearing gifts for the child; beautiful silken robes, blankets of down, and the softest sleeping nets re-spun from spider's silk. Though no one said as much, it was understood that they had thought her incapable of bringing a child to term, and thus had waited. Gushing over each gift, Leandhra attempted to appear oblivious. She was optomistic by nature and never one to hold a grudge, and so accepted their visits graciously, tacitly ignoring any comments or ill-concealed thoughts that might dampen anyone's spirits. Elazaryn was the only one with whom she let down her guard, now that Ladhonna would not come to her. And while she loved her husband with all of her heart (and was so thankful that she could truly call him all her own!) she ached for the sister of her youth, her best friend and confidant. She was not unaware of Ladhonna's embarrassment over the turn of events, and had, in fact, convinced Elazaryn that he should still take her as second wife - though in name only now - as a peace offering. Still, Ladhonna refused to enter the royal compound as long as Allora remained in charge of Leandhra's care. After all they had been through together, Leandhra felt as if she were missing a wing. She longed to go to her, but Ladhonna had recently taken a retinue from her own household with her to visit Wellwood and Lac Ril. Hopefully, her sister would at least return for the birth of the child.

Her murmuring thoughts were giving her a headache. Perhaps a walk in the gardens would brighten her mood. Allora, while vigilant about her patient's diet, was not always quick to recognize her need for fresh air and exercise. Quietly, so as not to alert her, Leandhra grabbed a sheer cloak off a hook and used its hammered silver ornaments to clasp it around her neck. The day was still warm, but perhaps she would venture toward the river, where the damp and chill shade could make one shiver on even the hottest of days.

Strolling over grassy, garden pathways toward her destination, she breathed in the heady fragrance of the many flowers and herbs that grew there. *Quite cheering,* she decided, *and exactly what I needed.* Her thoughts again strayed to the delicate person who had conceived this marvelous space. While most high born luminaries engaged in learning to channel their empathetic healing energies, Ladhonna had created a pharmacopoeia as soothing to the soul as to the senses. She had not done the actual digging, of course; there were Naturra servants for that. But the amount of time and thought that had gone into its design was staggering. Leandhra knew that she could never have created such beauty. Ahead and to her left, the ground was even now being turned by workers planting the last of the flowering shrubs that would soon grow to form an immense labyrinth. Her sister had completed its design before taking her leave, at the request of the Council of Elders. Leandhra had heard rumors that they foresaw a time when the labyrinth would be used to replace questanna, the traditional pilgrimage of discernment that all luminaries - young and old - undertook when facing an important life-changing decision.

Hearing laughter from an approaching group, Leandhra turned to her right, taking the first path that led down to the river. Soon she could hear it babbling and gurgling as it coursed its way along the rocky streambed. The cool shade of overhanging tree branches enveloped her, and she sighed. But the laughing group seemed to be following her. Realizing that her loneliness had been replaced by a need for solitude, she lifted aside a drooping bough and ducked beneath it, careful of her footing on the moss-covered stones. Ahead, she knew, was an enormous granite boulder, seemingly dropped from nowhere into the middle of the stream. It had been a favorite pondering spot of hers as a child, and she and her sisters had spent many carefree hours playing in the shallow water surrounding it, or sitting quietly, transfixed by the play of light off the glistening ripples. Indeed, it seemed that others had since discovered its charm, for, stepping silently onto the pebbly shore Leandhra saw two small urchins, their wings toward her, sitting still as statues and staring into the water. She watched them with longing for a moment, then ducked back into the lush foliage. Recognizing the distinctive fragrance and celery-like leaves of angelica, she remembered a much younger Ladhonna lecturing her that this was actually water hemlock, and that she should never touch it, since it could take you to the great unknown before you could count to quo'de quo! She hoped that these children had received a similar warning. Further upstream she found a place to cross into the forest.

Lost in thought, after some time casually strolling through New Forest, Leandhra began to tire. She left the chill of the river behind moving steadily uphill, pausing only occasionally to catch her breath. The babe was quiet within her now, snuggled as it was under her ribcage and lulled to sleep by the rocking motion of her exertion. She was thankful that she had always been so strong: Allora said it would make for an easier delivery. But for a slight thickening of her waistline, anyone seeing her now would have had difficulty telling she was expecting at all.

Just ahead the trees began to thin. Leandhra made for this clearing, unconcerned about finding her way back. Though she had avoided them on her way out, the forest was riddled with paths, all leading back to Ka'Andharra. After a brief rest in this glade, she would return by one of these, having experienced enough bushwhacking for the day.

She stepped out into the brilliant sunshine. The clearing was covered in wildflowers, several of which Leandhra recognized as herbs that Ladhonna now culti- vated. She ran her clasped hand over a leafy stem, col- lecting several small leaves in her palm. Sniffing, then tasting one she grimaced at its bitterness. Yet... it was a familiar flavor, one she had tasted several times before, though she could not pinpoint just when. She squatted next, finding it easier than bending, and popped the head off a nearby red clover, and put it into her mouth. Its sweetness balanced the bitter aftertaste - *of rue*, as she now recognized the first plant to be. Ladhonna made tea and those delicious little cookies with just this combination, sprinkled with anise, which she also found growing close at hand. A feeling of nostalgia, coupled with the appetite she had just worked up, com- pletely drove all of Allora's warnings from her head. Gathering handfuls of first this, then that, Leandhra feasted...

******

## *About The Author*

**C. A. Morgan** is an artist, writer, singer/performer, blogger, teacher, wife, mother of five children, and now a publisher --- in other words, a very busy woman! She is an autodidact who also holds a degree in Commercial Art from Michigan's Ferris State University, and for the last twenty-five years has called Vermont's rural Northeast Kingdom home. This is the third novel of her premiere fantasy series.

**Contact Info:**
www.camorganwrites.com
www.facebook.com/reademerysia?skip_nax_wizard=true